The Briss

THE BRISS

A Novel

Michael Tregebov

VANCOUVER
NEW STAR BOOKS
2009

NEW STAR BOOKS LTD.
107 — 3477 Commercial Street
Vancouver, BC V5N 4E8   CANADA

1574 Gulf Road, #1517
Point Roberts, WA 98281   USA

www.NewStarBooks.com
info@NewStarBooks.com

The Briss is a work of fiction, a product of the writer's imagination. Any resemblance by any character to any person, living or dead, is entirely coincidental.

We acknowledge the financial support of the Canada Council, the Government of Canada through the Book Publishing Industry Development Program, the British Columbia Arts Council, and the Government of British Columbia through the Book Publishing Tax Credit.

Cover by Mutasis.com
Printed and bound in Canada by Imprimerie Gauvin, Gatineau, QC
First printing, June 2009.

LIBRARY AND ARCHIVES CANADA CATALOGUING IN PUBLICATION

Tregebov, Michael, 1954–
   The briss / Michael Tregebov.

ISBN 978-1-55420-043-6
   I. Title.
PS8589.R34   B75 2009   C813'.54   C2009–900721–5

To Virginia

In a revolution, people are stupider than ever.

V.I. LENIN

Grandchildren are your reward from God for not having murdered your children.

JEWISH PROVERB

I

"Aw, Christ!" Sammy was so irritated it looked as if he had been electrocuted.

"Dad."

"Aw, Christ."

"Dad?"

"Tell it again. You're a what?"

Teddy told him again. Sammy's heart plopped.

"Aw, Christ. Say it ain't so."

"Can't," Teddy said.

Only seconds before, Sammy's wife, Anna, unnerved, had given such a *geshray* that she had jolted him off his recliner, and out of his Sunday dereliction. When he had made it to the kitchen she mashed the cordless phone against his breastplate.

"You talk to him," she had said.

And then she had shut herself in the bedroom and now he knew why. He had been watching a ballgame. The Blue Jays were muddled once again.

"Shut the ballgame off," she had shouted, "and get in here, Sammy." He did as he was told. He went to the kitchen and she had mashed the phone into his breastplate and now he was suddenly in *galus*.

"Chrissakes, Teddy."

That's how it had started. In the middle of the ballgame. In just a flicker, and now he was in *galus*.

"Well, what's it going to be," Sammy had said, when he had taken the phone. This was his usual greeting, his private "wassup."

But then Teddy filled him in on a few things.

"A human shield?"

"A human shield."

"A human shield."

"A human shield."

"Who for?"

"Which side do you think needs human shields?"

"Chrissakes. There's something wrong with you."

Teddy had always had the feeling that there was something wrong with him, while family and family friends always had the certainty, offering audibly behind his back, "That kid, there's something wrong with that kid."

That sort of thing, once it gets rolling, never stops. So, when he announced he was a human shield, and had been issued a residency document by the Palestinian Authority in Ramallah, the people back home would comment, "there was always something wrong with that kid." Even the watchless official, Yussuf, at the ransacked PA office in Ramallah, to whom Teddy had expressed his wish, looked at him with concern and asked if there was something wrong with him.

"No, there's nothing wrong with me. I want to be a human shield."

The next moment the PA man cupped his mouth as if he was trying to avoid water gushing out.

"Are you certain in your action? We all have our foibles."

It was a liminal moment. But Teddy had already stepped up to the plate. "Yes. I am certain in my action," he said, in the diction that was rubbing off on him.

"Are you pressed for time?"

"Not really."

"What time have you?"

"I don't know."

Teddy didn't have a watch either. It was a time in Ramallah when no one had a watch. Or, to be exact, no one had a watch left.

The PA man and his staff had been visited just a few days earlier by an incursion of a helpful unit of the Israeli Defence Force, made up of watch repairmen it would seem, because, during their search, as was the case in their search of the house that he was living in, they interrogated the terrified PA civil servants with a professionally relentless single line of intelligence questioning, pointing at each person's wrist asking:

"Watches?"

"You? Watches?"

"You there? Watches?"

That's how Teddy lost his watch — the Dynamite Watch, as Baba X called it.

■ ■ ■

"There must be something wrong with you," said the PA man, Yussuf. "Everything's going to shit here. There's no future here. In two years' time, half of Ramallah will be in Los Angeles running liquor outlets. No one will defend us. It's all over. Like no one defended you Jews against the brownshirts. We can't keep on living like this. There comes a point when enough is too much."

The PA man's confused locution made Teddy smile.

"Why are you doing this? May I ask, for I am gobsmacked."

"What?"

"Astonished."

"Oh. Out of shame, I guess."

"Don't be a silly oaf. This is none of your business. You're not Israeli. You'll give your mother a heart attack."

"It won't be the first time."

He looked at Teddy. Teddy looked at him and smiled.

Yes, it was true. He actually had given his mother angina once.

The PA man saw what was wrong with him. He lacked limits, this boy. Family and family friends always said something was wrong with him, but none of them could put their finger on exactly what it was. But the PA man saw it, the way someone sees it's raining.

Teddy had followed the PA man through a warren of rooms, then farther back into an office that looked as if it had been totally unhinged from the building itself and was swinging above the ground, held shakily in place by an invisible membrane. The PA man started searching his desk for paper and his rubber stamp.

The creak and flop of a shutter thrilled Teddy, making him feel exposed. For a moment he thought he saw a sunbird hovering, glittering with green and purple iridescence.

The computer monitors were smashed in and Teddy suspected that the printers had gone the way of the watches. All the filing cabinets had been flung open, some shat in. The PA man had to take a copy of *Ha'aretz* which Teddy was carrying, cut out the blank paper from a minimalist Lexus ad, and write out a declaration in Arabic and stamp it with one of the few stamps left on his desk, and then sign it. The historical piquancy of a Palestinian helping a Jew didn't escape him either.

"You'll see this is quite the white elephant."

"A what?"

"A possession entailing great expense beyond its usefulness."

While Teddy smiled the man folded his new pass into an envelope, tucked in the flap, and handed it to him.

"This is great."

The PA man smiled and said, "God is Great. You've just made *aliyah*."

Teddy felt the hot dry print of Yussuf's palm on his nape, its fatherly intent.

"I am gobsmacked," said Teddy, feeling tremors of emotion.

In any case, when he walked out of the office he held a piece of paper in his hand that made him a resident of a state that didn't exist whose entire infrastructure had been demolished and shat in. He felt a tremendous sense of relief as he walked back to the house near the Amari refugee camp where he was staying in Ramallah. The first thing he did when he got there was phone his parents and tell them the news.

"Ma?"

"Yes. Hello. Who's this?"

"It's me."

"Teddy?"

"Hi!"

"You're there?"

"I'm here."

"Where are you?"

"In a camp near Ramallah."

The word Ramallah was so foreign to her, he could have just as well named a crater on the moon.

"In a Palestinian refugee camp near Ramallah," he said.

"It must be crawling."

"It's not crawling."

"Who goes off to live in a camp?"

"Jean Genet did."

"Who?"

"Jean Genet, the French playwright."

"Ah, the lunatic French."

"That's fringe, Ma."

"What are you doing there?"

"I made *aliyah*, sort of. I'm a human shield."

"A what?"

"A human shield."

His mother was quiet. He absolutely knew what she was thinking and what she would say next. He knew it. He knew it. Here it comes.

"Do you know what a *neshome* is?"

He was right. "Of course, I do."

"If you knew, you wouldn't have told me what you just told me. I can only presume you don't know what it is."

"I know what it is."

"A *neshome*?"

"I know the word."

"You've just taken my *neshome* out."

"Ma."

"You've taken my *neshome* out. I have no more *neshome*."

"Ma."

"Sammy!" she yelled. "He's watching the game, your father. Sammy!"

When Sammy came to the kitchen phone Anna, unnerved, mashed the phone against his chest and fled to the bedroom.

"You talk to him! The little shit."

She was "afflicted," she said. Once inside her bedroom, she banged the door shut and started to cry; she couldn't resist looking in the mirror to watch herself cry, commiserate with herself a little, until she saw a loose thread hanging from the bedskirt, and then went after it with a little scissors.

"Where's the big parade?" inquired Baba X, Anna's mother, who had been sitting at the dining table, eating coffee cake with

her and drinking tea when Teddy had phoned long distance.
Sammy ignored her.

"Where's the big parade?"

■ ■ ■

Ancient Baba X — the kids, Marilyn and Teddy, but mainly
Marilyn, had named her Baba X — wearing her usual bright
African shift with multi-coloured chevrons, her permed white
hair, the wickerwork wrinkles on her cheeks and eyes, her huge
post-cataract Ray Charles sunglasses, was startled by all the
action.

"Why the big parade?" she asked Sammy again, changing the
interrogative, looking about the room for Anna. "Where's
Anna?" She didn't like being ignored.

Her bosom was full of crumbs and she was brushing them off
onto the table, then forming them into lines with the heel of her
cracked palms.

"Who phoned?"

Sammy ignored her again.

"Who phoned?"

"It's Teddy."

"It's Teddy," she said, to no one in particular. "Teddy," she
said again, " a *shtick* gold."

"He's no *shtick* gold," Sammy said under his breath.

"He's a *shtick* gold."

"He's a *shtick drek*," Sammy said.

"What's he saying? Where's Anna."

Sammy ignored her again and took the conversation into the
hallway, walking in Anna's footsteps to the bedroom, holding
the cordless phone outside the door, maintaining two conversa-
tions at the same time, one with Teddy, at a distance of thousands of miles, in which he spoke softly, as always, and one with
his wife, at a distance of one yard, in which he had to shout.

Sammy was someone everyone liked, full of jokes and charm,
but low on responsibility. But now he was serious, being stuck
with the parenting for the first time in his life.

He put his eye to the crack in the door, but he couldn't see a
thing.

"Your mother's crying in the bedroom, she won't let me in," he said evenly.

To Anna: "Anna, come out of there."

To Teddy: "We were going to the Sophisticates. We were almost ready. I was going to play Omaha."

"High–low?"

"High–low. Twenty–five–fifty."

"Dollars?"

"Cents."

Behind the door Anna was still feeling sorry for herself, still looking in the mirror.

"Dad, there's no lock on the bedroom door, just go in."

"Does anyone else know about this?" Anna shouted at Sammy through the door. "Ask him that!"

Sammy to Teddy: "Who else knows about this?"

"You mean besides the PA?"

"What's the PA?"

"The Palestinian Authority."

"Don't mention that word. For us, there is no such thing as Palestinian." Sammy could hear his own heart thump that thump as he raised his voice.

"The adjective?"

"They don't exist. They're mosquitoes."

"Actually, I might come out on CNN in a story they did on Jewish human shields in the occupied territories, but I doubt they'll air it."

"They'd better not. For your sake."

To Anna: "He's a human shield."

"I know," she said, "he told me."

To Anna again: "He's a human shield."

"I know. It's not normal," his mother squealed through the door.

"What?"

"'I know. It's not normal,' I said."

"Would you come out. Chrissakes, Anna."

To Teddy: "What do you mean a human shield?"

"You know what it means."

"She wants to know if people here will find out?" he asked.

"Sooner or later. I told you it might be on CNN."

"On CNN? Everybody will see you."

"No they won't."

"Everybody follows the news here. Wait, your mother's coming out."

"Give me the phone," she snuffled. "Let me talk to that little shit." Shit, the magic word, dried her tears.

"Just wait a while," Sammy told her.

"Give me the phone."

"No."

"Why not?"

"You can't hear him and it's costing him money."

"I'll put my hearing aid on."

"I thought you said the batteries were shot."

"They're only worn down."

"What's the difference? You said they were shot."

"So what? You say a lot of things, too."

"What do you want to tell him? It's long distance. It's costing him money."

"Tell him I don't want him getting hurt or injured. The little shit."

"Dad?"

"She doesn't want you to be a human shield if it means you're going to be hurt or injured."

"Dad, hurt is the same as injured."

"I don't want him being a human shield period, the little shit."

"She's worried. She's a worrier."

Anna gave him a vinegary look.

"Tell her not to worry. I've been assigned to what's left of the Department of Education building. Right now the most dangerous place is the Mukata, protecting Arafat. I may get assigned there next week though. I'm on the list."

"I'll put you on a list. Schindler's list."

"What's he saying? What Schindler?"

Sammy repeated what Teddy told him, that he was on a list to protect Arafat's Mukata.

"Let me talk to that little shit. I'll give him a Mokata. I'll give him a Mokata up his ass."

"Wait a while."

She grabbed. Sammy spun, holding on to the phone as if it were the Torah being snatched at by skinheads.

"I don't want to hear the name Arafat in my house," she said, pulling on the phone. "It's killing me. He's sucking my *neshome* out. He's grinding it down. Tell him that."

Anna barged off to the bathroom.

"She can't stand to hear his name. You're killing her. Again."

"Don't mention it then."

"It's too late."

"Let me talk to her."

"She's gone into the bathroom."

"What's she doing in there?"

"She's doing a lot of flushing."

"What's she flushing?"

"Controlled substances — how should I know? This is killing her, you know. She doesn't want you to be a human shield. Here she comes. She's back."

To Anna: "What were you doing in there?"

Anna: "I was looking for my hearing aid."

"Dad, nobody wants to be a human shield. An American girl got killed by an Israeli bulldozer while trying to protect someone's house. They scooped her up, dropped her and smashed her with the blade."

"You believe that?"

"I was there."

"What do you mean you were there? What's it your business?"

"Well, it's your fault. You're the ones who sent me here. She sent me here. What was she thinking of?"

"Not to consort with terrorists."

"They're not terrorists."

"What are they?"

"Resistance fighters. Insurgents."

"You say insurgents, I say detergents."

"Anyway, I'm a human shield, not a terrorist."

"She didn't send you there to be a human shield. And she didn't send you to Ramallah. She sent you to Jerusalem."

Anna spoke into the receiver: "She, she, she. Why she? He's not going to make me feel guilty. You neither. The two of you. You're not going to make me feel guilty."

"You told him to go."

"You wanted to have children."

"Now that was uncalled for."

"You wanted them."

"I wanted to make sure somebody would be at my funeral."

"What makes you think I'd spend money on your funeral?"

"They won't let me rot. Somebody will organize something, sooner or later."

"Give me that phone, or it'll be sooner than you think."

"Just wait a while! You're not having the phone!"

Sammy gently pushed her away and walked back into the kitchen-living-dining area, and then around his recliner, Baba X watching him from the dining room table. Sammy looked at the television set, the screen greenish black. Anna followed him, uncapping the hearing aid case and shaking the device.

"What are you shaking it for?"

Anna: "He's not going to make me feel guilty."

"Who are you talking to?"

"You."

"Why in the third person?"

"Dad?"

"Hold the line."

"Dad, what's she saying?"

"Her usual. Nothing. She knows from nothing. She hears nothing, and she knows from nothing. Like her mother. They're both stone deaf."

"I'm not tone deaf; I have a deficit."

"I said stone deaf."

"What?"

"Dad, how's Baba?"

"She's out of it, too. They're both out of it."

"It's shocking the things going on here, Dad."

"We didn't send you there to be a human shield. We thought it would straighten you out. She's begging you not to be a human shield. You're taking her *neshome* out."

"I'll pay him," Anna threatened.

"She says she'll pay you."

"I don't want her money."

"He doesn't want your money."

"Dad, it's a war zone. We're committing politicide against innocent people."

"What's politicide? Genocide we know."

"Why did you send me here?"

"Shock therapy. God knows you needed it. After what you did. Personally, I would have sent you down into the mines, but she thought you'd be better off there, for what you did."

Then there was a silence. "What he did" was always met with silence.

"Dad?"

"Just a second."

"Dad?"

"Wait. There's something wrong with your mother."

Anna had sat down at the dining room table next to Baba X to load the batteries into her hearing aid. But now she was perfectly still, staring at the device, so still that Sammy thought she was having angina.

"Are you having angina?"

Baba X stopped forming rows of crumbs.

"Anna, are you having angina?"

"Dad?"

"Shhh."

"Dad?"

"Hold on a second. There's something wrong with your mother."

"Are you having angina?"

Sammy thought Anna might be faking it, just to get attention. But then again, he had thought that the last time and she actually did have angina.

Teddy listened to a galactic silence that was glancing off a satellite.

"Dad?"

"Shhh!"

Anna was practically catatonic.

"Is ma okay?"

"*Shhh*, I said."

Anna finally looked up and made a wave with her hand, picked up a new battery with the tweezers and refitted it. She was handy with gadgets, she always said.

Sammy drew a breath, relieved.

"Dad? Is ma okay?"

"She was overacting. It was just her hiatus hernia."

"It wasn't my hiatus hernia."

"Maybe it's her heart condition?"

"She thinks it's a heart condition."

"Dad, innocent people are being killed here. The money you send through the synagogue, it goes for settlements, and then there's the helicopters, the curfews, and worse, the collective punishments."

"Good."

"Do you know they have something here called Minhal Harisot, a Demolitions Administration, to organize the destruction of Arab homes? Dad, I'm ashamed."

"Of that. But what you did? That didn't shame you?"

"What I did? What did I do?"

"You know what you did."

He certainly did.

"Hey, she knew what she was doing."

"A married woman. Why a married woman? Why did you have to be a sneak?"

Unusual to hear his father mention "what he did," because at the time he did the thing he did, his father didn't say a word. He never did. When he dropped out of medical school: nothing. Or when Marilyn dumped her husband, Jack, the nebbish, he didn't say anything then either. Sammy the Ostrich, Anna called him, a play on his name, Ostrove. He should be on Sesame Street, she'd say, with Big Bird. Sammy the Ostrich. She could really repeat herself.

"And a rabbi's wife."

"Wasn't a real rabbi, dad. It was someone who marries lesbians."

"He's got more than one wife?"

"No. And the rabbi wasn't a he."

"All the worse."

"They were a lesbian couple. They were supposed to be cool about it."

"That's not how it plays here, in the community."

"What's done is done."

"What's done is never done. And then the running away."

"I didn't run away. You sent me here."

"She sent you there. She did it."

"You're not going to make me feel guilty," Anna piped in. "And that goes for him, too."

"Yes, I am."

"This is such a *shande*. Such a *shande*. He wants to kill me, the little shit." Anna stuck the hearing aid into her ear and with her pinkie adjusted the volume, loud enough to make it whine with feedback. Baba X shivered. "Give me the phone, let me talk to him, the little shit."

"You had the phone; you handed it off to me."

"You don't know how to talk to him."

"And you do?"

"Dad, we have to protect the innocent. It's part of our Jewish humanist heritage."

Sammy to his mother: "He says he has to protect the innocent. It's part of our human Jewish heritage."

"Tell him to come home, the little shit. I'll protect his heritage alright. I'll cut off his heritage."

"You tell him!"

"No, you, he's your son."

"I thought you were so hot to talk on the phone."

"I changed my mind. You tell him to come home. For once in your life, you tell him something."

"*Kackerveisscourage*," muttered Sammy.

"That was uncalled for."

This part Teddy heard, and the *kackerveisscourage* crack made him smile.

"Ask him why he's not a human shield against terrorist suicide bombers, the little shit," Anna urged, snapping the hearing aid case shut.

"She wants to know why you're not a human shield against terrorist suicide bombers."

"Killing Jews," she added.

"I thought she said she didn't want me to get hurt or injured."

"She's upset. She didn't mean it."

"I'm a shield against helicopter bombing, tank bombing, F-18 bombing. Is there any difference between suicide bombing and helicopter bombing?"

"Of course there is," said Sammy.

"What's the difference?"

"A big difference. Suicide bombing is cowardly. And they do it for the money that Saddam Hussein sends the families."

"And bombing from a helicopter is brave?"

"It has more dignity."

"Dad!"

"People are going to call you a self-hater, *ocher Yisroel*."

"I'm not the only Jew who criticizes Israel."

"The only Jew I know."

"What about Chomsky?"

"Who's Chomsky?"

"Never mind."

"Look, I'm not going to debate you long distance on this," Sammy said.

His father wanted to wallop him, but he was far away, and besides, he had never laid a hand on the kid in his life. Never even raised his voice.

"There is a difference between suicide bombing and helicopter bombing," said Anna, having come up with something. "Suicide is against the Torah."

"Suicide is against the Torah she's telling me."

"What about Massada?"

"In Massada they were fighting the Roman legions, there aren't any of those on those buses in Tel Aviv."

"So suicide can be justified."

"No, it can't."

"You just said it could."

"If you're fighting Roman legionnaires, but not kids on buses."

"What about Arie Itzhaki?"

"Who's Arie Itzhaki?"

"A Jewish bombmaker fighting the British. He blew himself up shouting 'Death to the British.'"

"I don't know from any Arie Itzhaki."

"Or Shlomo Ben Yosef?"

"Who's he?"

"They have songs for him in Israel. He threw a grenade into an Arab bus."

"I don't know from these people."

"And you know, there's a Jewish school in Australia called Massada College. Isn't that glorifying suicide too?"

"I don't know from Arie Itzhaki or Shlomo Ben Yosef or Massada College in Australia. And you're probably making it up. All I know is that suicide is against the Torah."

"So is all killing."

"No it's not."

"Thou shalt not kill."

"You're making a literal interpretation. In the Torah it says you can break the laws if it's to save a life. And the Jews hold life sacred."

"Not like people we know," piped in Anna. "Ask him how many Jews have to die for us to have a little homeland?"

Sammy did this.

"Well you ask her how many Palestinians have to die before they can have a homeland, too."

"I can answer that myself: Six million."

That seemed to be the end of the argument. The ultimate ratiocination.

"Dad, the Palestinians didn't exterminate European Jewry."

To Anna: "He says the Palestinians didn't exterminate European Jewry."

"The Mufti of Jerusalem was an ally of Hitler, tell him that," said Anna.

He told him that. Teddy sighed.

"Well, tell her that in the archives in Jerusalem they've found letters from Shamir to the Nazis during WWII offering to help them fight the British in mandate Palestine."

Sammy didn't even bother relaying this to Anna because it was so absurd to him.

"Did you tell her that?"

"Don't talk nonsense."

"Ask her about Feivel Polkes."

"Who's Feivel Polkes? She doesn't know any Feivel Polkes."

"Adolf Eichmann's contact in Palestine. Hagannah. Eichmann

deported 100,000 Jews in 1935, when he was in charge of Jewish transfer. That's why Eichmann had been in Palestine."

"None of this is true."

"It's true."

"It's not true."

"It is true, I can show you the documents."

"Why would they give those documents to you?"

"I mean photocopies, from books."

"I want to see the real documents."

Teddy sighed and gave up.

"This is costing you too much money," Sammy said. "I'm hanging up."

"Don't hang up yet, Dad, I have something to tell you."

"Have you got enough money?"

"Ask him if he has money," said Anna.

"I just asked him that."

"Ask him again." Anna got up, taking out her hearing aid and leaving it on the table. She checked the note pad on the kitchen counter for the account number to which they would wire funds if he ran short. "Check the number with him."

"I'm not checking no number."

Baba X slid the hearing aid her way, not knowing exactly what it was.

"Ma, leave it alone."

"Don't get on your high horse," said Baba X, pushing the hearing aid back to where it had been.

"You're always fiddling."

"I'm bored. I need something to do with my hands."

"She's out of it."

Anna brought the bank account number to Sammy.

"Check it with him."

"I'm not checking it."

"Just check it."

They both repeated the number into the phone in unison, like a countdown at Cape Canaveral.

"We're sending you $500 for your birthday."

"It's okay. I've got money." Teddy felt an ache in his throat that anticipated tears.

"Rich or poor, it's good to have money."

"I said I'm okay for money."

"We're sending it anyway."

"Tell him we've got the Dickie's. But they didn't have a 31 leg. Ask him if a 32 leg is alright. You can't get a 31 leg. I'm sending him the 32 leg."

"Ask him if he still has the Dynamite Watch," said Baba X more importantly.

Dickie's, watches? Sammy wanted to ignore her but he thought it was a valid question: "Do you still have the Dynamite Watch?" Watches? Teddy remembered. How could he tell them that Israeli soldiers stole his watch, had stolen everyone's watch. Either they wouldn't believe it, or they wouldn't like it. So, at this point he almost hung up, but he had to go through with it. The big news was still to come.

"I've still got the watch."

"He's still got the watch."

"He's lost the watch?"

"He hasn't lost the watch. He's got the watch."

"Dad, I still haven't told you why I phoned."

"There's more?"

"Dad, something amazing has happened. I've met someone."

"He's met someone."

"You've met someone? Where?"

"In Jerusalem. Someone amazing."

"When did this happen?"

"Three months ago. Right when I arrived."

"You work fast."

Sammy to Anna: "He's got a girlfriend."

Anna, sarcastically: "Good for him. We're suffering and he's getting laid, the little shit."

"We're going to have a baby, Dad."

Sammy said, "Real fast."

"What did he say? What's real fast? What's he saying? Sammy? Sammy!"

Sammy to Anna: "He's expecting."

Anna stuck her hearing aid back in and rushed up to Sammy and tried to put her hearing aid ear close to the phone.

Baba X: "Who's expecting?"

"Dad?"

"You're positive?"

"We did the tests! You're going to be grandparents."

"He did the tests."

"When are you expecting?"

"Late summer. Maybe September."

"What's her name?"

"We haven't named it. We don't know if it's a boy or a girl."

"No, the name of the girl?"

"Aïda."

"Ida. Nice name."

"What's he saying?" asked Anna. "You're not letting me listen."

"You can't hear anyway."

"He's expecting, he says."

Sammy sat down at the dining table, to dramatize the news. Anna sat down next to him. Baba X, now straining to listen, swept all the coffee cake crumbs into one pile.

"Who's expecting?" Baba X asked again.

"What did he say?" asked Anna.

"He's met a girl. She's expecting."

"I know that."

"They're going to have a baby in September. Her name's Ida."

"Ida?"

"Dad, her name's Aïda."

"What?"

"Ida who?" his mother interjected. "Ask him: Ida who?"

"Who's Ida?" inquired Baba X.

He could hear his mother's excitement in the background and his grandmother's bronchial rasp. "Who's Ida?" The fact that her son had gone to Israel and had met a girl there, and was going to settle down, have a baby, all blended together, consuming on its pyre the shameful business about the human shield.

"I knew it," he heard his mother say. "I had the feeling there was good news. I'm psychic. I'm really psychic."

"You're not psychic," Sammy said.

"Who's expecting?" Baba X asked again.

"Teddy's expecting," Sammy told her, the way he would swat at a mosquito, almost shouting. Then he beamed. At last a grandchild. Marilyn would probably never have one.

Anna smiled at him.

"Ma," she said to Baba X, "Teddy's expecting."

"He's expecting? He's not married."

"Don't mix in."

"Do you want my say-so?"

"No."

"That's uncalled for."

The two parents grinned at each other stupidly, relieved that someone else would take charge of their son from now on. The burden, like storm clouds, seemed to have parted and decamped, forever.

"Who's Ida?" the grandmother insisted, completely left out.

"Shhh."

Baba X shut up, feeling sorry for herself, vowing never to talk to them again for the rest of her life. She started working on the crumb pile again.

Suddenly Sammy's face went yellower than hen's feet, and he put the phone down on the table by the pile of crumbs Baba X had heaped together.

"Sammy! What's the matter?"

Anna grabbed the phone, eyeing Sammy, who was now turning white.

"Teddy? It's me."

"Ma."

"Who's this Ida? Have you met the parents?"

"Not yet. I've only met her great-aunt, when I was sick."

"You were sick?"

"Just a bad flu."

"You should go to the hospital."

"I'm over it."

"Just a second, your father doesn't look so good. Sammy, what's the matter?"

"Ma?"

"Your father doesn't look so good all of a sudden. Hold the line."

"Ma."

"Can't you hold the line? He's pale."

"Sammy?"

"Something's occurred to me," Sammy said.

A terrible thought had occurred to Sammy, and he was digesting it first because he knew Anna wouldn't be able to take it.

"Sammy?"

"Give me the phone," he said, with mosaic authority.

She handed him the phone. He fumbled it, and it dropped on his big toe.

"Fuck!"

"You dropped the phone."

"I know I dropped the phone! Fuck, fuck, fuck!"

No one had ever heard Sammy say this word before.

"Sammy?"

Sammy picked up the phone from the floor. His heart had split in two. And his toe was throbbing with pain.

"Teddy?"

"Dad?"

"What name did you say this girl Ida was called?"

"Aïda. With a dieresis."

"What's a dieresis?"

"It's those two little dots above a vowel."

What Sammy had to ask was difficult to get out because his saliva was frozen: "So, this Aïda person, she isn't an Arab, is she?"

This was the closest word to Palestinian he could utter.

"Sammy!" Anna gasped, grasping for breath with both hands. "Who's an Arab?"

"Who's an Arab?" Baba X parroted, breaking her pact with herself not to speak to them for the rest of her life. "Anna, who's an Arab?"

"Ma, don't mix in," Anna said to her mother. "And leave the crumbs alone!"

"What crumbs?"

"Those crumbs."

"They're not crumbs."

"Yes, they are."

"Who's an Arab?" Baba X insisted.

"Shhh."

"Don't you Shhh me. Who's an Arab?"

"Ma, you're out of your element."

"What element?"

Sammy made a gesture with his hand to shut them up, spreading out his five fingers with such severity that you could see webbing between them.

"Teddy, is she? Is she an Arab?" His saliva had frozen. "I'm not going to ask you again?"

"Dad!"

"Teddy!" he began again, "what kind of 'Ida' are we talking about here? Ida like in Ida Lupino? or 'Aïda' like in the opera?"

"Aïda, Aïda, her name's Aïda, like in Aïda, the opera, with a dieresis."

"Again with the dieresis."

"Her name's Aïda Shawari al-Husseini. But a lot of people call her Ida, too. Not everybody pronounces the dieresis."

"Stop with the dieresis."

"Tell me plain and simple, is she an Arab?"

"Yes."

Anna only needed one look at Sammy's face.

"She's an Arab," Anna said to her mother, "look at Sammy's expression."

Sammy's lower lip hung down, almost to his throbbing toe.

"We are fucked," he announced.

"Who's fucked?" asked Baba X.

"She's an Arab, " Anna said, again. "I knew it. I'm psychic. I told you I'm psychic. I'm dying. Tell him I'm dying, the little shit."

"Teddy, are you sure?" asked Sammy, his heart in his pants.

"Of course he's sure, the little shit," his mother blurted. "Give me the phone!"

"Are you sure she's an Arab?" said Sammy, pre-empting her. "Maybe she's just part Arab."

"Part Arab — give me the phone!"

Anna to Teddy, after grabbing the phone: "Are you sure she's an Arab?"

"Of course I'm sure." Teddy said. "Her name's Aïda, like the opera, some people call her Aïda and some call her Ida. She grew up in Europe."

"So is it Ida or Aïda?"

"Who's Ida?" asked Baba X.

Anna to Baba X, as if it were her fault: "It's not Ida, it's Aïda, like the opera."

"Aïda? Like Verdi's opera?" Baba X knew some opera. Before television she had twenty Mario Lanza records that Teddy had scratched up with her knitting needles when he used them for drumskins. She hummed a phrase from the overture of *Aïda*.

"Ma, you're out of it."

"What?"

"You're out of it."

"You always say that. I'm out. I'm in. I'm out. It's like poker with you."

"Shhh. I'm on the phone."

"I can see that."

"Teddy, is she a real Arab?"

"Ma, she's Palestinian."

Anna's lips tightened. She put the phone down in the pile of crumbs.

Sammy took up the phone and said, "Teddy, are you sure?" His toe was really killing him now. "She's really an Arab?"

"I told you. She's Palestinian."

"A Palestinian."

"Sorry."

"To hell with sorry!"

"Now he's sorry," said Anna.

"Dad, she's carrying your grandchild."

"Who's an Arab?" Baba X asked.

"Ma! You're out of your element," Anna shouted, "you're out of your element. We'll tell you what's going on in a minute."

"I want to know what's going on now."

"In a minute."

"Why not now?"

"Just a second."

"Tell me now," Baba X insisted.

"You're so stubborn."

"I'm stubborn?"

"Teddy's going to have a baby."

"I know that. That's wonderful. A *mazel tov* is due."

"With an Arab girl!"

"A *shikse*?"

"She's a fucking Arab!" Sammy shouted at her.

"So she's not a Jewish girl."

"She's a Palestinian, for Chrissakes."

"A *yasel*," Baba X said. "If she's not Jewish, the baby will be a *yasel*."

"A *yasel*."

"A *yasel*," smiled Baba X with some concern.

A *yasel* was on the way.

Teddy's parents sat mutely, awed by Baba X's remark.

Baba X, whose natural impulse it was to give Teddy everything he asked for, even the knitting needles that put paid to her vintage Mario Lanza records, said: "Teddy's *yasel*." She had sized up the situation and it was all right with her. She had wanted to see a baby from him before she died. "Do you want my say-so?"

"No, we don't."

"Do you want my say-so?"

"We just said no."

"Dad? Are you there?"

"Where am I going to be? You're going to have a *yasel*, you know that."

"A *yasel*? Dad, what's a *yasel*?"

"It's Yiddish."

"I know it's Yiddish. What does it mean?"

"It means, what, I don't know, it's hard to translate a word like that, something like 'false messiah'."

"The Christ?" asked Teddy.

"That's right. The Christ. The Christchild, something like that. That's all the world needs. Another crucified Jew."

"Dad, don't worry."

"Why shouldn't I worry?"

"It's only the size of a macaroni."

2

Driving overcautiously to the Sophisticates card party they were fearful that someone was going to say something.

They had debated going, not going, going, not going, and in the end habit won out. They were supposed to go last night, were just about to go when Teddy called, but they were too upset and postponed it. They weren't going to just sit at home — it was Monday, Monday night, and it was poker night, too.

Anna put on her peach-coloured makeup and out they went.

On Mondays, their usual was going to the Sophisticates. It was part of their ironclad routine since his retirement years ago. Monday was poker night at the Sophisticates, Tuesday, curling (winters only), Wednesday, free movies for seniors, Thursday, mahjongg, Friday, crossing the line to go to the casino, Saturday, *shul* — for *Yortzeit*, Sunday, their daughter Marilyn's faultless apartment. And each day was accompanied by a specific restaurant for lunch, brunch or supper. Mondays, Rikki's (truck-stop fare), Tuesdays, Abosh's (corned beef and Boston cream pie), Wednesdays, The Good Earth (Chinese food), Thursdays, the food court at the mall, where a squad of *grine* always hung out, and which they called the Botanical Garden because of the "greenery," Fridays, Rikki's, Saturdays, Dem Bones (ribs and cole slaw), and Sundays, Rikki's for brunch, and supper at Marilyn's.

It was the sheer force of routine that drove them to the Sophisticates poker night, in spite of the fear that people would say something about Teddy. How much shame can a child bring upon his parents? They totted it all up. A lot, they concluded. They were still afraid of what people would say about their son, and dreadfully depressed. Although not despondent, which was the word Anna came up with in the car.

"I'm despondent."

"No, you're not."

"I'm despondent."

The question was, would news from the outside reach the Sophisticates? Did anyone watch CNN or did they all watch Fox?

But just how much would people know? That Teddy was a human shield? That he had a girlfriend named Aïda, not Ida? That she was pregnant? That their *yasel* was on its way?

It's only the size of a worm, Sammy thought, to console himself. But that was no consolation.

You don't do these things to your parents, he had wanted to tell him on the phone, it's in the Torah.

Last night Sammy had lain in bed unable to sleep, fretting over his son. Normally, of all places, he liked his bed best of all, always had, it being the most conducive to daydreaming: camel trains in the desert, dogsleds in the Arctic, submarine trips under the North Pole.

He had tried to read a trashy novel with the glossy covers and embossed print, but he soon lost the thread of the storyline. He tried another one, trashier still, with print any bigger the blind could read it, but it didn't work either.

He closed the book and lay on his bed and felt that he was falling down an elevator shaft. That was nice, almost like sleep, but then the falling sensation ceased, and he thought about death: his own extinction, Anna's, Teddy's, Marilyn's.

A *yasel*. The *yasel*. It would be a *yasel*. He could hear Baba's loving rasp: a *yasel*.

That's all we needed. Another crucified Jew.

And he was the crucified Jew here already; and with that thought the precision of the dream he had of himself was blighted.

Which made him think about death again. A fine line of sweat circled his neck and slid into the dip between his collar bones.

I'm sweating. He should wake Anna up to show her.

But he thought about death again. The world is up to its eyeballs in death. Just watch the news. The whole world was chock-full of death.

He had wanted to wake up Anna and ask her to make him a cup of tea. This he could have done himself, but it was not the same.

And his toe was still throbbing from when he dropped the phone.

"I'm going to lose the nail," he had said to Anna, both palms open towards his foot.

"No, you're not."

"It's blue."

"It's nothing."

Where did they go wrong? Who must Teddy have met in Israel that made him into a human shield, that made him ocher-Yisrael, that turned him against his people? Who was this Ida person — Aïda person?

He thought when people found out about Teddy he would die of shame. What kind of parents were they? This is what people would go around saying:

"I fault the parents."

Other people's children seemed to be doing well. But them: it was as if their fortunes had shrunk, as if they were losing on their investments even though the stock market was booming and everyone else was cashing in. Life had cheated them. Teddy was an Arab-marrying, *yasel*-bearing human shield, and his older sister, Marilyn, was childless, and in the midst of a divorce, which was her fault; she had gone outside the marriage. And instead of grandchildren running around the house, there were rumours that Marilyn was running around the city. And to top it off, they still had Anna's mother living with them. Even he was calling her Baba X.

He had tried to think nice thoughts in bed. He remembered the time just after meeting Anna. Their walks in the snow at night in Assiniboine Park. Ah, the snow, crisp and even, like the song. The snowflake jewellery twinkling on the crown of her wool tam, on his Leafs toque. Side by side they pressed on along the deserted park avenues under bare trees, like Hansel and Gretel, snowbanks on either side, and then trawling through drifts, on and on, until he finally fell asleep thinking of their unstinting love.

In the morning when he woke the first thing that came into his consciousness was that something terrible had happened, and that if he could, he would rather not have woken up, ever.

This can't be happening, he thought.

"Anna?" Sammy said, his voice foggy, toe in pain, puffy dark circles under his eyes.

"Sammy?"

"Lie to me. Tell me it was a dream."

"It wasn't a dream. And you've got circles under your eyes."

"I slept lousy."

"You think you slept lousy. I slept lousy."

Sammy took all day to decide whether to go to the Sophisticates card party. Go, don't go. Go, don't go.

From one angle it looked simple.

Anna said, "You just go, sit down, play cards, have some hot fish, a *knish* or two, then some cheesecake and listen to the minutes of the last meeting. You have some coffee."

"The Sophisticates coffee gives me the jitters."

"So you don't have the coffee. You clear and wash up the dishes and then play a few more hands. If anyone says anything, just tell them to shut up and mind their own business."

But Sammy had never told anyone to shut up in his life. Mahatma Gandhi, his wife called him, amongst other things, or sometimes Ostrich.

Anna really wanted to go because she didn't want to be home when the lady from social services came to bathe her mother. Baba X always put up such a fuss.

"Who's going to know he's a human shield? The little shit."

"Somebody will know," said Sammy.

"Nobody will know."

"They'll know."

"You think?"

"I know they'll know."

When the lady from Social Services came and Baba X started up with her right away, Sammy realized that they had better leave so that Anna wouldn't have to suffer through the ordeal, as Baba X really only wanted Anna to bathe her.

"Ma, what's the difference whether she bathes you or I do?"

"You want my say so?"

"Not really."

"So why ask me?"

The social services lady had savvy and managed to steer Baba X into the bathroom. This was their window of opportunity.

"Where's the car keys?" Sammy asked, making the decision.

"Over where the telephone used to be," Anna answered. The phone had not been in that spot for years, but the spot was still called "where the telephone used to be." It was reassuring and senseless.

"I think we'll go to the Sophisticates."

"You think?" said Anna. She knew he'd give in. "You should take an aspirin for your toe."

She was right. His toe was killing him. But he hated swallowing pills.

"I'll be alright."

"You're sure we should go?" she said, trying to finesse the situation so perfectly that he would think he was getting his way, not she hers.

"Yeah, sure I'm sure."

So he plucked up his courage and they went out.

It was long after Poppy Day. The day was grey and autumnal, with a sharpness in the air. Snow was coming. There were signs.

They got into the clunker, their maroon Olds Cutlass.

After warming up the car they rolled out into the street, heading for the Sophisticates.

"What I can't believe is that she's pregnant," said Sammy, out of the blue, punching the radio off.

"She's only a little bit pregnant," Anna replied.

"You can't be only a little bit pregnant."

"Time-wise," said Anna.

"How pregnant exactly do you think she is?"

"He said around summer she was expecting."

"But how long exactly?" Anna insisted.

"How should I know? Did you ask him?" Sammy said.

"Did you?"

"I was in shock."

"So was I."

"You were in the bathroom; I was in shock."

"I came out of the bathroom."

"I'm still in shock."

"It's yellow. Stop."

"It's still green."

"It's yellow."

"Now it's red."

They stood staring at the frozen pavement ahead, waiting for the light to change.

"Are you thinking what I'm thinking?"

"Why don't you phone him? Make a suggestion."

"An abortion?"

"Do you think they do that sort of thing there?"

"I'm not sure. Those people usually have a dozen kids. I don't think they have a reverse gear."

"Probably not."

"It's green."

"I know it's green."

"So go."

"Just a second."

The car rolled slowly off the line.

"Poor Teddy."

"Poor us."

"What are we going to do?"

"Don't tell anyone. For now."

"They're bound to know about the human shield business."

"Sammy, we don't know that."

"Do you think people will have seen him on TV?"

"Go know."

"Honestly?"

"Did you see him on TV?"

"No."

"So keep your fingers crossed."

"The little shit."

"I'll kill him, the little shit," Anna said. "No, you should kill him."

"Why should I kill him? You spoiled him. You sent him there."

"It's *bashert*," Anna sighed, hard enough to sink a ship.

"It's not *bashert*."

"It's *bashert*, the little shit."

"Stop calling him the little shit."

"It's *bashert*."

Anna, whose grandfather had been a Hasid, had this view

sometimes that everything past, present, and future had been predicted in the Torah. But then at other times she believed in science.

"It's not *bashert*."

"What's *bashert* is *bashert*. Don't tell me what's not *bashert*."

Sammy always denied this view, but believed it some of the time. In his case, he was more inclined to seek an explanation in reincarnation (which he thought meant reprisal), combined only with a pinch of the *bashert*. He had done something terribly bad in an earlier life and his kids, Teddy and Marilyn, were his punishment. But sometimes he believed in science, too, like when getting a CT scan or flying across the country, or removing moles and cataracts with lasers.

It wasn't enough that Teddy broke his heart by dropping out of medical school in first year and becoming a male nurse. No. He had to become a human shield, for Arafat, no less.

But the little silver boots on the turkey was Teddy actually hooking up with an Arab and getting her pregnant. The worst thing by far though was that soon everyone would know. Chrissakes.

They drove up to the outdoor parking lot behind the synagogue and took a long hard look at the vast empty lot. For some reason he drove far to the back, in the bleachers, as his father used to say. And inside the synagogue, too, on the high holidays, they would sit at the back. Sammy often wondered what it would be like to be up at the front, with the hoi polloi, with the Silverbergs and the like, close to the action. He knew the *siddur* better than they did and sang more sweetly, but being so close was purely a question of stocks and bonds, not prayers and melodies. To be honest with himself, it didn't really matter, because he didn't really believe in God.

"Why are you parking so far away?"

"I don't like the way they look at me when I get into the car."

"How do they look at you?"

"Like as if I was a rickshaw driver."

"You're ashamed of the car."

"Of course I'm ashamed of the car. Who wouldn't be?"

"There's nothing to be ashamed of."

"When you have a lousy car, you're supposed to be ashamed. If you don't like being ashamed, you buy a nice car. That's the price you have to pay to avoid humiliation. Come on, the walk will do us good."

Anna shifted in her seat and adjusted the poppy in his coat, pricking him with the pin.

"Chrissakes."

"How long are you going to wear this poppy? It's almost Christmas."

"I always wear it till New Year's."

"We're half a mile from the entrance."

"We'll manage. We do on the high holidays."

"But then the lot is full. There's no choice."

"Imagine it's the high holidays and get out of the car."

"What about your toe?"

"I'll manage."

"Go manage, but me you're driving up to the door, dropping me off. Then you can park where the hell you like and imagine it's the high holidays."

He did as he was told but when he got to the top of the lot he decided to park there anyway, next to all the other cars. He found one that was as busted up as his and parked next to it. It was Nate Kimmelman's.

There was a bitter wind.

In spite of the silly argument they walked to the big doors, her Gretel's hand in his Hansel's, as usual, and thought of Teddy's news again, but out loud.

"The Solomons' daughter married a gentile."

"But he converted."

"Mrs. Adelman married a Greek."

"And he converted, too."

And almost died in the attempt. Her mother, Baba X, and her friend Sadie, had gone back to Sadie's house one day and Bill was sitting holding his bleeding penis over a bucket.

"Those are just examples: those are people who could convert. We're dealing with an Arab here. The girl's an Arab. A Palestinian Arab."

"Don't say Palestinian."

"A Palestinian *pritzteh*."

"Maybe she can convert."

"An Arab can't convert," Sammy said point blank. "It's like a black converting. Can't be done."

"Why not? Sammy Davis converted."

"He was an entertainer, Anna."

This was so, Anna thought.

"Jews and Arabs don't convert. Being an Arab isn't a religion. Even if she converted, she'd still be an Arab. She'd still be a Palestinian."

"Oh."

"Oh."

"What about the Baker boy, a *shtick* gold, who married a Japanese girl. By your own logic . . ."

"But they moved out West."

"Bella Baker is miserable without her Michael. I heard it from Sophie. She regrets all the trouble they gave them."

"Or what about his brother, married that Italian *tsatske*."

"But nobody faulted the parents."

"That's because they own half the land in Garden City, and three hotels downtown."

"What's true is true."

Sammy's left eye started tearing in the wind. It would snow soon, he thought. His toe was throbbing, he realised. He should have taken that aspirin.

There were other cases. The Teski boy became a follower of a Rajneesh Something. Misery loves company, they thought. But misery of the many was the consolation of the fool. Teddy should be castigated. They shouldn't have sent him his birthday money. They should have spent that money on themselves. They even sent him an extra hundred dollars.

"Why did you send him an extra hundred?"

"Go know."

"Maybe they'll abort."

"Is abortion a sin for the Jews?"

They didn't know.

"Maybe she'll have a miscarriage." She was going to add, *if we're lucky*, but thought better of it.

"You're limping."

"I'm not limping. My toe's killing me."

"It might be broken. We should go to Emergency. You might need a cast."

"They can't put a cast on a toe."

"They'll take an x-ray."

"What am I going to do with an x-ray? Wrap it around my toe?"

"They'll put it in a cast."

"They don't put a toe in a cast. They'd have to amputate the others first."

"Maybe they'll put your whole foot in a cast."

"Not for just one broken toe. You have to break your whole foot."

She walked, he hobbled, into the warm vestibule and he put on his *kipe* in front of a bank of tear-shaped yartzeit light bulbs, all of which had been turned on by some brats from the Hebrew School, making it look as if an entire generation had all died on the same day. They stored their coats in the huge empty Meyer Slansky Cloak Room, which people nicknamed The Godfather Cloak Room, and which, on the high holidays smelled to heaven of perfumed furs, wet wool, and rubber galoshes.

"Why don't we hang our coats up at the back, too, away from the action," she said.

"Don't be like that."

There was a long wide staircase down into the basement social rooms. Sammy held onto the banister, gingerly stepping on the plush carpet, careful not to lose his balance or stub his bad toe. Then they followed the long corridor to the Bernie Silverberg Lounge, "donated in life," which was "the bigger mitzvah."

"He didn't trust his kids to give the money to the shul," Sammy always said as they passed the plaque.

"Can you blame him?"

"I don't think the shul should allow donations like this in life."

"It's politics."

"You always say. You and Oz, you always say that."

"Everything's politics."

"You always say that, Anna. You and Oz."

"What's the difference? Isn't it better to be honoured while you're alive?"

"It's phoney. Paying to be honoured. It's all politics."

"If you don't pay, they won't honour you."

"My point."

"Don't be like that."

As they approached the Bernie Silverberg Lounge Sammy suddenly remembered and felt terror.

"You'll see, they'll give us the cold shoulder," Sammy said.

"Maybe nobody knows."

"They'll know."

"Why should they know?"

"We went through this. He was on CNN."

"Nobody watches CNN. They watch Fox."

"They say they do. They say they don't watch CNN, but they do. It only takes one person. News spreads like a wildfire."

"I'm hungry."

"Sally Singer made three cheesecakes. Extra rich."

When they opened the door they smelled egg salad sandwiches.

As soon as they walked into the room they felt like they were intruding. Why did they feel this? They couldn't put their finger on it. But they felt it. No one said hello, it's true, but then everyone was playing cards, which was taken very seriously at the Sophisticates. Normally they would have sat down at one of the card tables right away, but tonight they held back, standing close to the door, forlorn — once again like Hansel and Gretel — with only each other's hand to hold.

Luckily Nathan Uzransky, AKA Oz, with his small head, the wreckage of his bottom teeth, a little dab of Brylcream on his hair, lost gaze and big Windsor knot came up to them and they exchanged some small talk about his heart aneurysm operation scheduled for the coming Thursday. Oz looked poorly, as usual, but he obviously hadn't heard anything about their son being a human shield protecting Arafat. Although even if he had, he wouldn't have given a shit. Oz was a decent human being.

"Hey, Oz, what's it going to be?"

"Hi, Sammy."

Oz didn't mention any human shield business, only remarking about the people in the room: how evenly they were divided between the blow-drieds and the perms.

But other people were thinking it. You could feel it. Usually people invited them to their tables, because Sammy was a charming man and good at games, and more importantly, never lost his temper, a good loser. If Sammy was at your table, it was worth having gotten out of the house, warming up the car, and making the drive.

What they needed was a table. They couldn't stand there all night with Oz; it would have been unfair to him because he was really doing poorly. In fact, they sent him back to the kitchen to sit down by the ovens where he was watching the kitchen help.

But they didn't know who to join.

At all costs they wanted to avoid the Hershberg table, but it was the only one with an empty seat. Anna, who didn't want to be a *kibitzer* (odd how Yiddish is the only language with a word to describe the person who is a spectator at a card game), least of all at that table, went over to sit with her friend Sophie, leaving Sammy alone.

In the end they he went to centre stage, to the worst table, where else? This was the Hershberg table, with the high rollers, with Mannie Hershberg, in his rich suede jacket, who was or had been his brother-in-law Alex's best friend (Uncle Alex, whom Marilyn called "Homuncle Alex," he couldn't stand either). There was Hershberg's wife too, of course, Sally née Pushnik, changed to Pussey, who Anna called the Sourpuss, missing the obvious pun picked up by Oz, who called her Sour Pussy; their friends the Goldmans, who sold rubbing alcohol to the Indians, and the table's doyenne, Jack Ruben's widow, Sophie, the first woman in the Jewish community to wear hot pants, who Anna called Queen Elizabeth, along with her unmarried brother, Bernie, who Oz, for obvious reasons, called The Queen. This was not Sammy's usual table; he called it a cold table, and he normally shied away from it. These were wealthy people who looked down on the less wealthy and up to the wealthier.

When he sat down they nodded to him. A frosty nod. How these people despise the poor, he thought.

"Sammy."

"Hershie. Sally. Sophie. Bernie. What's it going to be?"

"Hi, Sammy," said the Hersh, licking his lips. Sammy thought he noted a trace of contempt.

The card deck clicked against heavy diamonds and thick gold bands pushing up the wrinkles on knuckly fingers. And that was just the men.

Same fashion ring thing going with the women, only they had pointy, ruby fingernails with sprinkles, as if they were ten years old. Sophie Ruben, with her long, blackening teeth, was wearing a T-shirt with her granddaughter's face silk-screened on top, with sequins yet, stretched over her massive bustline that itself hovered over two, three, four bulges. Anna called Sophie Ruben The Woman With Hippopotamus Calves. Hershberg's wife, the Sourpuss, wore a sequined cowboy blouse.

The men were over-groomed, all their ear and nose hair removed, with their heavy chains and their crystal watch faces larger than tea coasters. They intimidated Sammy. They always had.

It was not the kind of action Sammy liked. These were people who took cards too seriously, as if they were sitting an exam, but only to show off because they weren't very hot players. They were poor losers and sadistic winners: relentless when lucky, ill-mannered when unlucky. It was also difficult sitting with Mannie Hershberg, the CA: firstly, because as a kid in high school he always let Mannie copy his maths exam; secondly, because Mannie became a CA and Sammy didn't; and thirdly, because Mannie could never recall that it was thanks to Sammy that he got into university. Although he could recall that Sammy had been just a bookkeeper who never became a CA. Sammy felt his envy gouge his heart. He looked at Mannie and his massive head, his booming voice. He reminded Sammy of the strikebreaker that once beat up his father outside Schatz's candy factory. Sammy had been sent by his mother with a thermos of potato soup while his father walked a picket line, getting there in time to see this strikebreaker kicking his father in the butt. The guy had a big head, like Mannie, and was relentless.

Sitting down with Mannie reminded Sammy of his childhood misfortunes. And the misfortunes of others.

But he had come to play cards. He'd clobber these people.

He sat in the empty seat and took out his winnings from the last card party.

Nobody made an attempt at small talk. A game was in progress.

Mannie had that look like the last forty years had been easy for him. Rumour had it that he had had a tummy tuck and an implant in his penis which was activated by a small pump, where? In his groin? In a testicle?

They were playing Texas Hold'em, which the card party called "bundles," because the flop looked like bundles. Sammy knew the game well. He knew that if everyone plays tight, then no one loses and if everyone plays loose, then no one wins. To win at bundles you had to play tight while a sucker played loose. Luckily they had Sophie Ruben there playing loose, as usual.

The game went on quietly for an hour, the house slowly but surely raking it in. Sammy was playing tight, folding immediately on bad hands, winning moderately the odd game, but Thelma and Mannie, the Hershbergs, were also playing tight, and so were the Goldmans. Only Sophie Ruben was playing loose, as usual, as she liked to see the flop, "out of curiosity"; the river too, also out of curiosity. She was losing. She always had the same philosophy: "I can't get a hand. I can never get a hand. They never deal me a hand. If only they dealt me a hand," and she would rail against the dealer. But when she was dealt a good hand, everyone folded and she won nothing, then railed against the stingy. When she lost, she would ask, what kind of dealer are you. But as time went on, the Goldmans and Hershbergs began to play looser and lose, although after the game Jack Goldman would lie and tell everyone that he broke even. When they broke even they said they won. And when they actually did win, well, nobody believed them.

Sammy thought that there was something wrong with the game. It was cordial but not friendly, almost like playing on the Internet.

He noted that Mannie was pushing him a bit.

Whenever Sammy hesitated about making a bet, Mannie would say, "Come on, what's *shtupping* you?"

Exactly. He didn't ask "what's stopping you" like normal people. He insisted on using that stupid, vulgar Yiddish/English pun: *shtupping*, which also meant, in polite terms, "exploring a bodily orifice with a cylindrical object."

"Sammy, you in?"

"Just a second. I'm not sure."

"What's *shtupping* you?" the Hersh queried, smiling at his own inanity, licking his lips.

But Sammy kept playing tight, hesitating about his bets, mostly folding.

"Sammy, you in?"

"Just a second."

"What's *shtupping* you?"

Mannie would keep coming back with his "What's *shtupping* you?" But then came a hefty flop, three high clubs. Oh, the craving for a hefty flop is like a craving for morning coffee, Sammy used to say — and then came the fourth card, and finally the river card, an exciting river card, bursting the dam, when he pulled an ace-high flush.

He hesitated on all the bets and on the first and second raises, hoping to draw in as many people as possible.

"You in, Sammy?

"I don't know?"

"What's *shtupping* you?" Mannie needled.

He says the word, the *shtup* word so aggressively, thought Sammy.

Sammy bumped the final bets masterfully and caught Mannie Hershberg with a low straight, and taking him for ten bucks, the biggest pot so far. No one said anything. Not a word of congratulations. Mannie was livid for being bested, but kept his mouth shut. His wife sneered. Usually this would have been grounds for comment. Because talking about poker goes with poker.

The Hersh's wife, who long ago had the joy of life squished out of her leaving nothing but her squeaky voice, squeaked, "What did you go in for?"

"I had the nut."

"You though you had the nut. He had the nut. You're the nut."

"I must've miscounted," said Mannie, keeping up this pretence that he counted the cards, that he could remember what cards had been folded, what the odds were of his card coming up and all that.

"You shouldn't bother," said his wife. "It's just a friendly game."

The lying bitch, thought Sammy. For years Mannie kept up

this pretence, basically because no one challenged him on it, and his wife and friends fed the myth. Sammy knew that it was bullshit. People who can count cards usually play bridge. Sammy could never understand why Mannie insisted. Who cared? But he had to say it.

"You're right. I should stop. But I can't help counting cards."

Sammy thought, *But you can't count cards, you shit. You only lie about it, and everybody knows.* Still, it gave him a little satisfaction to have beaten Mannie out of the ten bucks in the pot.

Luckily refreshments were served. Hershberg's wife edged her bulk close to the edge of her seat and levered herself up. The others followed.

But they snubbed him by not bringing their food back with them, which was normally the custom. Instead they sat at another table with the Hellmans and Bermans.

The spread was sumptuous: hard-boiled eggs, sweet and sour meatballs, *kreplach*, hot fish, potato *knishes*, not too oily, and then desserts, the extra-rich cheesecakes.

Sammy sat alone with Anna at the poker table and ate in silence.

"I can't eat anymore," said Anna said, wiping her mouth.

They had reached the kiwi fruit cheesecake. Sammy scraped the kiwi fruit off.

"I don't know why they put this green stuff on perfectly good cheesecake. What is this?"

"Kiwi fruit."

"I know it's kiwi fruit. But what is kiwi fruit?"

"It's a natural laxative. It's a fruit."

"They think everyone's constipated here."

"They don't have a hidden agenda, Sammy."

"I can't eat this."

"Just eat it."

"They ruin perfectly good cheesecake."

"Anyone say anything to you?"

"No, not yet."

"Do you think they know?"

The clatter of cups, saucers and cutlery coming from the galley was unbearably piercing.

"Where's Oz?"

"He's in the kitchen still."

"He doesn't look so good."

"He looks like death warmed over."

Sammy ate, watching Mannie Hershberg's table. The women were gnawing away, but Mannie had chowed down. The food went down his gullet like a parade. Sonny watched him swallow first the hard-boiled eggs, then the meatballs, then the hot fish . . . and then came the cheesecake, kiwi fruit and all. Having lost a big hand didn't make him lose his appetite. Mannie swilled the whole parade down with coffee, smacked his lips and then craned his neck this way and that to find the kitchen help to pour him more coffee.

As usual, while people got to the part when they were scraping the last crumbs from their plates and the kitchen help wandered about topping up the coffees, the Sophisticates nabob, Dr. Hellman, went to the front of the room by the bingo machine and read the agenda for this meeting and the minutes of the last. Then came the treasurer's report and a list of the people with dues in arrears, the Shame Gang, or the PLO — People Likely to Owe. An announcement was made on the coming Hanukkah social. The leader of the drama club announced that this year they would be raffling two tickets to a Red Sea resort at Eilat.

Every year they raffled off two tickets to a Red Sea resort at Eilat, but Sammy and Anna never won, because in order to win you had to sell at least a hundred tickets and they never had that many contacts. The only people who did were the Hershbergs and Silverbergs and the Kaufmans and Penners and so on, but not them. You had to be in business to have that many contacts, so the people who won were usually the ones who could afford to go anyway.

The announcement of the raffle provoked smiles and throaty laughter about how it was always the same people who won and that this was a good reason to get out there and sell tickets, go door-to-door, do something.

There was also an announcement of the hundred-dollar plate dinner with Benjamin Netanyahu, and another dinner for the choir, and a luncheon for someone's granddaughter's engagement, and then two *Yortzeit*s, a bat-mitzvah, and the unveiling

of the headstone of Oz's brother, who passed away six months
ago after losing his nose.

"How's Oz going to go to the unveiling?"

"The operation's after the unveiling."

"Oh."

Mrs. Lakovetsky opened her mouth as if to chew and shushed
them. The nerve. She was always talking and was aggravatingly
deaf anyway. What was it to her? Anna shot her a dirty look.
Mrs. Lakovetsky, Sadie, shot her one back.

"She's got such a big mouth," she heard Mrs. Lakovetsky say
to a crony.

"Imagine her saying I have a big mouth, the DP," she said to
Sammy.

"Shhh."

Dr. Hellman made an announcement of a speaker coming to
talk about Lacan (said in such a way that it rhymed with bacon)
and Jewish Neurosis.

There were a few murmurs. As there was only one intellectual
in the group, Sid Rosenstock, everyone knew that this was his
idea. Sid The Professor, with his trimmed beard and rimless,
glare-free glasses, and invited young women, teaching assistants
from the university, once a month to give a lecture on hot topics
somehow related to Judaism. Although Sid was practically harmless now, his true motive in life had become "tits," as he put it.
The older he got he said, the only thing that interested him was
"tits," and "the bouncier and perter the better." But this had not
always been so. He had been married four times. His first wife
was a genius, sensitive, the poetic type, with a PhD. The second
was a lawyer, the third an air hostess, and the fourth a cocktail
waitress. He always said, "As the brain power diminished, the
boobs grew."

"Yours or theirs?" Anna used to say to him.

"You've got a big mouth, Anna," Sid would say.

One month Sid had brought a young Arabist and a terrorist
expert, once interviewed on CNN — with a D cup to boot, he
bragged, "very fetching" with "nipples like olives."

"Black or green?" asked Oz.

"Very funny."

"A very beautiful relationship was developing between them," he had said, "and as long as his wife didn't find out . . ." She was to speak on The Ethics of Torture, International Terrorism, and the War on Terror, a beguiling topic. The relation to Judaism was in these times obvious, he said.

"Since when has Judaism been interested in torture?" asked Oz.

"Come and find out."

A complicated and subtle point would be made, and they had gone to hear it.

The example she came up with was this: If you captured a blood-thirsty terrorist who knew the whereabouts of an anthrax cache hidden in Tel Aviv or Washington, was it ethical to torture him?

"And how!" someone heckled supportively.

There were also many nods.

And then, how should the Constitution be amended to give special powers to the State to do the torturing?

But then, "What kind of drivel is this?" someone said.

"Excuse me?"

"What kind of drivel is this?"

There was quite a to-do. Natch Perle, the buck-toothed communist doing entry work in the NDP, still, at his age, who wore a scarlet orthodontic retainer, at his age, then asked the terrorist expert if it was ethical to torture a five-year-old girl in front of her father because he might know the whereabouts of a dissident, who is suspected of having terrorist contacts.

"Don't be ludicrous," the terrorist expert told him.

"What kind of torture would you contemplate for a five-year old?" said Perle, shrugging his baby shoulders.

A voice from the back whined, "Shut up, Perle."

"How about licking the envelopes for an anthrax mailing?"

But then another: "Some of us are losing our patience, Perle."

"Seriously," continued Perle, facing down his hecklers and then addressing the speaker, "how about electrodes on a five-year old?"

The speaker opened her mouth as if for the doctor's depressor, swivelling on her chair in search of complicit looks.

"Hey, I'm talking to you, sister. Where would you attach them?

Take your time, I can see your expertise grappling with this."

"Don't be ludicrous," the terrorist expert told him again.

"Why? Can't two people be ludicrous in the same place and time? Do you have a monopoly on the ludicrous?"

There was a bitter exchange until his retainer flew out.

And later, outside in the parking lot, as Perle was getting into his crappy old Pontiac, people drove by, opened their window, and spit at him. Perle shook his fist at them and shouted, "Invaders invariably come to grief!" Sammy had seen it.

Next week's topic was Human Shields, the Dupes, and the Ocher-Yisrael.

Sammy felt all the eyes on him. It could not be denied. He'd see. They know, he said to himself. They'll spit on me, like they did on Perle.

"The talk will be led by our very own Barry Bond."

Talk about torture . . . Sammy was sitting in it. Being in your seventies meant you had nothing left to fear from other human beings, didn't it? They'd already done their work on you. What was left to suffer through?

Then it occurred to him that life was like a barbecue, and that after the first half, you were just turned over on the grill.

Once the announcements were finished, Sammy found himself carrying cups and saucers to the industrial-size kitchen sink. Dr. Hellman, his plump frame balancing against the edge of the sink, much of his paunch overhanging it, soaking up the suds, was washing while Mannie Hershberg dried.

"Really," Hershberg said, "go look in any company, any office, you always find one."

"One what?"

"A Shrimp Woman."

"What's a Shrimp Woman?" asked Hellman.

"A woman with a great body, and I mean something outstanding, but an ugly face. Like a shrimp, you don't eat the head."

Hellman reflected on this for a minute, recalling the nurses and staff at the hospital where he toiled until he came up with a shrimp woman in his memory.

"You're right. Helen Mills. Helen Mills."

"There you go."

"Helen Mills. Shrimp Woman."

"Did you hear that Sammy Ostrove's son is a human shield?" Mannie said, after waiting for Hellman's acknowledgement of his shrimp factoid. "*Ocher Yisroel.* Did you see him on CNN — you've got cable, don't you?"

Mannie's son was a lawyer, with an MBA.

"My son's a lawyer, with an MBA, working for the community, liaising with the hoi polloi, and his son's a human shield. He's a human shield for Arafat. Did you see him on CNN with the PLOs? First he has an affair with a rabbi's wife and then he's in Israel protecting terrorists. I wonder why the Israelis don't bomb them all. What's *shtupping* them?"

Hellman sniggered. He always did when Mannie used the "*shtupping*" pun.

Sammy's face was hot. Slanders about his son.

"Actually, I think his son is a male nurse."

"A male nurse? What's a male nurse?"

"It's like a female nurse but with *batzim* and a *shmuck*." They both sniggered through their noses.

Dr. Hellman, gossiping with Hershberg, his glasses having steamed up, had to soap and rinse by looking down through the space between the rims and his cheeks.

"There was always something wrong with that kid."

Dr. Hellman passed the Hersh a hot saucer.

Sammy stood still, listening from behind, unnoticed, the rage bubbling up in him. Hershberg and Hellman were slandering his kid so cavalierly.

One option could be to pretend not to have heard. That was option one.

"Sammy's daughter Marilyn is no angel either. You know why she divorced Max Lerner's son Jack?"

"I heard she was a tease."

"Worse. My son told me she was running around with half the city."

"The male half, I hope," said Hellman.

The Hersh snickered.

"How did he know, my son?" Mannie self-asked before self-answering, "He was one of the men who got in her pants. He laid her. After all," he paused, "if everyone else was doing it, what was *shtupping* him?"

"What was *shtupping* her?" Hellman quipped.

"He was," sniggered Hersh.

Hellman also sniggered.

Hersh received solemnly the saucer Hellman passed him and held it to his chest and waxed, "A hot lay, my son said. She screamed. He even buggered her."

This was the trifecta. Sammy's heart thudded and he started to shake. He could hardly suck up enough air to keep standing.

So then there was option two. Option two could be a mistake, could bring consequences. But he could cope with them. It was tempting. *I don't have to take this,* he said to himself.

Mannie Hershberg got clipped but good by option two and it sent him flying. He didn't know what hit him.

Sammy stood over Mannie lying stunned on the floor by the *Pesach* cupboards. He had flown and skidded about eight feet from the sinks. Mannie looked up, shocked and awed. A profuse stream of blood poured from his nose, "in all directions," people said later. Sammy had not committed a violent act since the war until now and he felt delighted. Even with the bad toe, he thought he would kick Mannie in the teeth now that he had him on the ground. He could always use the side of his foot, like in soccer, or his heel, or stomp him with his sole. He licked his lips. Oz, his true friend, came up from behind and grabbed his elbow, like you do with your grandmother before tucking her into a taxi cab, and swung him around.

"Sammy!"

"I'm going to kick his teeth in."

"He's on the ground," Oz chortled. "You clobbered him. He's losing blood." Oz made an exaggerated, unnecessary, nervous adjustment to his big windsor.

"It's just a nosebleed."

"Sammy."

Mannie scuffed his shoes weakly on the floor in a dithering attempt to stand up. You could see his hairless calves about his anklets. He tried to mask the rising nausea but couldn't and burped up a bit of the kiwi fruit cheesecake.

Sammy felt limber. One good kick in the teeth to shut up Mannie Hershberg's big mouth, he thought. "Just one," he said to Oz.

Oz shook his head.

"It'll be manslaughter if he passes."

Sammy looked at Mannie's mouth, slightly slavered with cheesecake vomit, those baby jowls quivering, crying out for a good swift kick.

"He's smearing my children," he said to Oz, his eyes stinging with two heavy tears resisting gravity.

"Sammy."

"He shouldn't have said those things about Marilyn."

"What did he say?"

"He shouldn't have said them," Sammy snuffled.

"What did he say?"

"Atrocious things about Marilyn."

"Like what?"

"He said she was a hot lay. And . . ."

"And what?"

"And . . . a sodomite."

"Now that was uncalled for. Let me kick him. Marilyn's a *shtick* gold."

"Your aneurysm."

"So what? They're going to operate."

"No, this is my business."

"You're right."

This was one of Oz's typical expressions. In fact, his most typical. Whenever people made fun of him, they would always imitate the way he said "You're right," and the way he said it, bringing a heavy worker's index finger down from his cheek to shoulder height, giving what people called Oz's finger of agreement.

There was a refrigerated hush in the synagogue kitchen, except for Sammy and Oz talking about whether to kick Hershberg.

Sammy thought for a second that perhaps next week Oz might be gone and that kicking Hershberg might be one of his last acts on Earth. He didn't want that to be.

"He's pathetic," Oz said, looking down at Hershberg. "You clobbered him."

"And he was bad-mouthing Teddy."

"Teddy's a good kid. Too good."

"Exactly."

"A *shtick* gold."

"Let's not go that far."

"He's not worth kicking. You've just clobbered him."

Oz was applying reverse psychology. This is how he had raised his own kids, using reverse psychology.

"Teddy's a good kid. All this stuff, it's all politics."

This was another favourite Oz line, the one Anna shared. But he even applied it to political discussions, nursing his words, till the end of the conversation when he would only draw one conclusion: "It's all politics. Feh." "Of course it's politics," the others would say, exasperated. "We're talking about politics."

"And that crap about Marilyn."

Dr. Hellman gingerly crouched and duck-walked towards Hershberg, protecting his face with a hand as if in a salute, fearing Sammy's kick. His deep crouching brought on a poignant fart. Oz flinched. Hellman dropped his hand to balance himself.

"Excuse me," Dr. Hellman said, turning crimson. "The cheesecake."

Sammy moved in closer, reasserting himself, staying Hellman's outstretched hand with the toe of his shoe, just as Hellman was about to apply a paper towel gingerly to Hershberg's philtrum. Sammy then shoved his toe against the waddling Hellman, tipping him over. With Hellman cowed, effectively out of the way, he stooped and whispered into Hershberg's ear, "You are some scum."

He waited for Hershberg's nasal whisper: "Antisemiten. Self-haters. *Ocher Yisroel.*"

Self-haters?

"I told you, it's all politics," Oz said, restraining Sammy's shoulder.

"Antisemiten," gasped Hershberg again. "You people . . ." he said, stumbling over the words, ". . . are the worst kind . . . of Jew."

That was all Sammy needed. When he was there in '48, in Herzliya, where was Hershberg? Eating *kishkes* at Oscar's, probably.

Sammy had reached the boiling point. No, he had reached more than that. He was in a porcelain kiln, at 1,455 degrees centigrade, the temperature in Hell.

He heard a voice, and it wasn't Oz's. It wasn't anyone's.

"What's it gonna be, Sammy, hoof him, what's *shtupping* you?"

"Nothing." Nothing held him back, nothing was *shtupping* him, for once.

And so Sammy stomped his face once, but good.

3

When Sammy tried to think of what he had done at the Sophisticates, he couldn't. It was like staring into a blinding light.

The reprisals came swiftly.

Sammy was arraigned: assault and battery. But that wasn't the worst thing.

The worst thing was that he and his wife were told bluntly, curtly, to stay away from the Sophisticates, and then extra-officially, contemptibly, never to come back, via what Anna called "a poison pen."

It was unsigned and ugly.

They sat at the dining table in their apartment with their daughter Marilyn the lawyer, and Oz, with his big Windsor, the tips of his shoes so buffed they looked like chestnuts.

Marilyn had come in not too long before, wearing her blonde cashmere coat; she was tall, rippling in the light. Oz didn't take her eyes off her, never could.

Baba X was sitting on the plaid chesterfield next to Sammy's cognac-brown leather recliner, wearing her battered, black Persian lamb coat with the huge buttons, clutching her enormous brown purse in readiness, like a parachutist his pack, for her Alex, her favourite, the fearsome Uncle Alex, who was invariably late, to pick her up and take her out for her drive. Today he was going to take her for tea to the top of the Windermere Tower. She had never been there before, and on the phone to him she had asked:

"Are there stairs?"

"Ma, it's the tallest building in the city. There's an elevator."

Marilyn had brought her some tea, but she hadn't noticed it.

"Marilyn, sweetie, I'm dry."

"I made you tea."

"Oh, I didn't see it."

Baba X canted forward, drove her cane into the carpet almost down to the hardwood underneath, then put out her feelers for the tea.

"She's going to poke a hole through the broadloom," said Oz.

Although Anna didn't want to get Marilyn involved, Sammy insisted on calling her over, ostensibly to seek out her professional opinion. As far as Anna was concerned, as she told Sammy herself, he just wanted Marilyn to know what he had done in her honour. Sammy denied this, but it was true. He wanted Marilyn to know, and he felt sort of noble about it.

Marilyn squealed with delight when she heard about it. She was like that. Nothing fazed her, her mother always said.

"Your father really creamed him," Oz said.

Her father's behaviour, clobbering The Hersh, had been so out of character that at first she thought it might be a sign of dementia, which was worrying. But when her mother explained all the details and circumstances, her being a hot lay and all that, she laughed her head off. Then, when told about the poison pen letters, Marilyn peeled one laugh after another, cancelled her two o'clock and rushed right over.

"Believe you me, it's a poison pen," Anna said. "Read it."

"It's a poison pen *letter*," Marilyn said to Anna. "Not a poison pen."

"Don't *fardray* me. You're always *fardraying* me."

Marilyn put on her thick black reading glasses and read:

Dear Scum:
  You call yourselves Jews. Your son is ocher-Yisrael, friend to the suicide bombers, cowards without guts, that stink who kill and then kill themselves as they are true haters living in a world of hate, hating life, something they learned in the PLO school books that teach hate. And your daughter's a slut, a whore and a trumpet.

Marilyn smiled.

"Strumpet," said Sammy.

"It says 'trumpet,'" said Marilyn, pointing to the line. Oz put on his Polish general glasses and leaned over to see.

"Trumpet," he said, doing the Oz finger of agreement.

"Shh," said Anna.

Marilyn went on: "Half the city has been in her pants . . . "

"The male half, Hellman said," Oz added seriously.

Marilyn flushed, then howled again.

Baba X looked up from the commotion, thinking her son had come, trying to lever herself off the chesterfield.

"He's here, he's here, where's my purse?"

"Ma," Anna gave a *geshray* from the table, "he's not here, yet."

The old lady flopped back. "You don't have to shout."

"You can't hear me if I don't shout."

"I can hear as good as you."

Marilyn screamed at this.

"I'll tell you when he comes."

"I'll manage myself."

"You won't hear the phone."

"I'll manage."

"And stop poking your *shteken* in the carpet."

"Who's poking?"

"You're poking."

"Don't *fardray* me."

Marilyn was still in hysterics. She couldn't finish reading the letter, took off her glasses and wiped her eyes.

"What's so funny?"

"Just let her poke," said Marilyn.

"I'll take her to your apartment and she can poke your carpet."

Marilyn snickered. She had hardwood floors.

"Ma," Anna said to Baba X, who had shifted back deep in the chesterfield, "you can take your coat off because he's going to be late."

"Don't *fardray* me. He's not going to be late."

"He's already an hour late. Take your coat off. And stop making holes in the carpet."

"He's not late. I'm early. And I'm not making holes in the carpet. Where's a hole. Show me a hole."

They exchanged dirty looks.

"Take off your coat."

"I'm keeping it on."

"Keep it on. Roast! Then you'll go out and get a chill. And when you're sick I'll have to look after you, not your Alex."

"Big sacrifice. You can do a thousand things for a daughter, but . . . "

"But what?"

"Leave her alone," said Sammy to Anna. "She's out of it."

Marilyn was still laughing.

"It's not funny!" Anna blurted.

"It *is* funny!"

"He could go to penitentiary."

"He's too old to go penitentiary. They'll make him get counselling."

"They'll put him in jail."

Marilyn, knowing the law, laughed at her ignorance.

"You take my *neshome* out. You know what a *neshome* is?"

"I think it's Japanese for . . . "

"For what?"

"For overacting."

Alright. That was it. And as Baba X had started up her poking of the broadloom again with her cane Anna got up and grabbed it out of her hand, wanting to swat Marilyn with it, or her mother, or both, but then slammed it down on the couch and stormed off to the bedroom.

"Ladies and gentlemen, Elvis's mother has left the kitchen-dining area," Marilyn said softly.

"Anna!" called Sammy, giving Marilyn a soiled look, but suppressing the snigger.

Baba X was startled by Sammy's shout, mistaking Anna's exit and the commotion again for her Alex's entrance. She started shifting to get up again, feeling for her cane and clutching her purse. Marilyn crossed in front to save her the effort of levering.

"Sit, he's not here yet, Baba."

"So what's the big parade?" Baba X said, flopping back again, losing her breath.

By that time Anna had reached the bedroom and slammed the door. Sammy flinched as if an earthquake had rolled underneath the broadloom. Marilyn wished she hadn't laughed so much or so loud. She got up and went to the bedroom door to apologize.

"Ma!" Marilyn called appeasingly. "Ma."

"Anna!" Sammy called from the dining table.

"Ma, come out. Ma."

It was hopeless.

"Ma, I'm sorry."

It was really hopeless. So Marilyn went back and joined the men at the table.

Oz looked at Sammy commiseratingly and said, "kids." Oz always said the word "kids" as if the word had the power to reduce Freud's entire opus to one word.

"You always say that."

"Kids," said Oz.

Marilyn came back and joined the men at the table.

Sammy took up the letter. Marilyn giggled.

"It's not funny," Sammy said to Marilyn.

"Ma!" Marilyn shouted one more time. But there was no answer.

"We've lost her," Sammy said to Marilyn, knowing Anna's moods.

"Sorry. It's all just so stupid."

"But he really clobbered him," said Oz.

Sammy didn't know why Marilyn was taking it so lightly. He continued reading:

". . . half the city has been in her pants . . ."

Marilyn flushed again. "You read that already."

She's probably diseased with the AIDS. Second-hand goods. A pig is what she is. Don't come back to the Sophisticates. You belong in a mosque for sluts and scum with PLOs.

Oz said, "It's articulate. I'll grant you that."

Marilyn howled at this.

"Get a hold of yourself, Marilyn," admonished Sammy.

"They don't mention Teddy and the Rabbi's wife," Marilyn added when she got a grip on herself.

"Not a real rabbi. They were from San Francisco or something."

"She was a lesbian," said Oz.

"So what if she was a lesbian," said Marilyn.

"It's not natural — being a lesbian."

"You like pickles. Are pickles natural?" asked Marilyn.

"What's pickles got to do with lesbians?" asked Sammy.

"You're right," went Oz.

"It's a metaphor."

"It's just not natural," said Oz. "It's homosexuality. It's not normal."

"It's not the norm, but it's natural alright," said Marilyn.

Sammy didn't like the way she said "alright," as if she knew something about it.

"Anyway, it all blows over. Short fuses, short memories. It's just politics," said Oz.

"Read me the other one, yesterday's. But no more laughing, okay?"

Marilyn picked up the second letter.

Dear Scum:
  We saw your son on CNN supporting the PLOs. We don't want you at the curling rink anymore. Go curl with the PLOs. Or get into your daughter's pants, through the backdoor, if you're bored. Just stay out of the Jewish community. We've suffered enough. Six million worth. Everyone will get wind of you. We're sending this to all the members.

"He's smearing you," said Oz.

"Who?"

"Hershberg, he's probably behind this," Oz said. "The Hersh and his scheming. He always uses the expression 'getting into someone's pants.'"

"You mean the Hearse," said Marilyn.

"Good one."

Oz said, "I heard him in the *shvitz* saying how he once 'got into Betty Ackerman's pants.' Remember Betty, the blind girl. A *shtick* gold. He was a real pig, that Hershberg."

"Aw, he's a bullshitter," said Sammy.

"A bullshit*teer*," said Oz.

"What's the difference, Oz?" asked Anna.

"A bullshitter is anybody who bullshits, but a bullshitteer does it for personal gain." Oz felt satisfied.

"Remember Betty Ackerman's brother, Schnitz? He was blind too," said Sammy. "He used to stand on the puck when we played hockey. We'd all scream at him, 'Schnitz, pass the puck!' 'Where is it?,' he'd say. 'You're standing on it.'"

Marilyn laughed. She was getting a sore throat. She'd heard the story before, but it always made her laugh.

"I remember when the Hershbergs didn't have a pot to pee in. None of the Hershbergs."

"When they were on relief, his entire family, he always ran around with snot dangling from his nose."

"From both nostrils."

Marilyn cracked up.

"That's how poor they were."

"She wasn't totally blind," Sammy remembered.

"Who?"

"Betty Ackerman."

"She had a certificate or something," said Oz.

"Betty Ackerman was a sweet girl," Sammy said. "A *shtick* gold."

"You're right," said Oz, innocently, naturally, bringing down the Oz finger of agreement.

Marilyn trapped a giggle at Oz using "the Oz" and shot a look of complicity at her father, who acknowledged the Oz doing "the Oz" with just a wink, which released another giggle, which she suppressed because she thought she might have caught Oz realizing they made fun of his Oz finger of agreement.

"I know I'm right," said Sammy.

"He's just sore you broke his nose. And his front bridge. You shouldn't have hoofed him, or Dr. Hellman. You'd clobbered him, why kick him?"

"Something came over me," said Sammy. "Something so strange. I mean the first punch was a gut reaction." The expression made Sammy feel younger. "But the kick, it came from I don't know where, from deeper down if that's possible."

"I've never seen you get violent, not even with your family."

"Dad, why did you really beat up Mannie Hershberg?"

"I didn't beat him up — I shut him up. I had to stop that mouth of his. I knocked him down and hoofed him one in the face. To shut him up."

"Why did you do it? You've never been violent in your whole life."

"He said some things about Teddy."

"The human shield crap?"

"Yes."

"And so you kicked the shit out of him for that?" Marilyn said smiling, her tone combining incredulity, scolding and pride.

"Not just for that."

"Why then?"

Sammy shrugged.

"Why did you knock him down?"

"He said some things about you, too."

"What did he say about me?"

"You know. Some pretty mean things."

"What exactly?"

"You don't want to know."

"I do."

"He didn't tell me to my face. I heard him talking to Dr. Hellman while they were doing the dishes at the Sophisticates. He wouldn't have told me to my face."

"What did he say?"

"Things."

"What kind of things? What?"

Only by a miracle had Sammy come this far. Once on a diving board, as a young man, Sammy had felt like this: terrified, not jumping yet but knowing that he would jump, that vital sensation pumping through him. But he didn't like it now.

"What did he say about me?"

"Hellman, the asshole, said he heard you were a tease."

"So you punched out Mannie Hershberg?"

"No. Not then. There's nothing wrong with being a tease. But I think that's the limit for a decent girl. They should have left it at that."

"But they didn't."

"Then Mannie Hershberg had to say that his son Max said you were running around with half the city and that . . . and that . . ."

"And what?"

"That you were ..."

"... What?"

"A hot lay."

Marilyn laughed again, and blurted out, unable to hold back, "You say that as if it's a bad thing."

Sammy looked at her, monumentally pissed off. Oz sniggered and Marilyn laughed with him.

"Sorry, Dad."

"And a screamer. Quote unquote."

"Max Hershberg said that about me?"

"According to his father Mannie."

"So you punched the shit out of him?" Marilyn laughed, delighted. "For saying that, you beat him up?"

"I shut him up."

"So for that you 'shut him up'?

Sammy was tempted to say yes and finish it then and there.

"So you decked him for that?"

"That wasn't all," said Oz.

Sammy shot Oz a look, but remembered his aneurysm and turned back to Marilyn.

"No, actually. Up till then I had held back."

"So why did you assault him? They're going to ask you that in court. Just for calling me a screamer?"

Marilyn thought about this. Her father, who used to trap flies in a glass with a playing card and shoo them outside instead of killing them, had punched Mannie Hershberg, then kicked him because he said she was a screamer.

"He told Hellman that his son ..."

"Max ..."

"He told Hellman that his son, Max, said that he, Max ..."

"That he ... what?"

"That he buggered you."

Marilyn roared.

"And that was the last straw: one punch and I decked him. There are certain things you don't say about other people's children, especially their daughters. It's in the Torah."

"It is?"

"It should be."

"And then you kicked him?"

"Not right away."

"I tried to hold him back," said Oz. "Horatio to his Hamlet."

"Why did you kick him?"

"Oz tried to hold me back."

"That's the truth."

"We discussed it, but then the Hersh, under his breath, said I was *ocher Yisroel*. Me, who fought in '48. So I gave the Hersh a swift kick in the mouth."

"There will be an upshot," said Oz.

"There has already been an upshot," said Marilyn. "Do you have any idea what you're going to do about all this?"

"I know that if I see Hershberg again, I'll belt him one right in the kisser."

Marilyn squealed, and her eyes began prickling.

Oz looked worried.

"But here's a caveat for you, Dad," said Marilyn.

"What's a caveat?" asked Sammy.

"If you belt him again, you'd lose your bond, and they might even put you in jail."

"No, I meant what's a caveat?"

Laughter tears bubbled in the corners of her eyes. But she managed to say, "A warning."

"Caveat emptor," said Oz, "Let the buyer beware." Saying this in front of Marilyn made Oz feel the warmth of self-esteem.

"You're right," said Marilyn, almost daring herself to do a kind of half-Oz of agreement, suppressing the tears and giggles, withdrawing in time so that he wouldn't catch the parody.

"Why didn't you just say 'warning'?" asked Sammy.

"Why don't you eat the same thing every day?" said Marilyn.

"I do."

Marilyn squealed again with delight.

"Anyway, what am I going to do?" asked Sammy.

"You need a lawyer," said Marilyn.

"I don't mean that."

"What do you mean?"

"About these letters?"

"I was talking about the assault charge," said Marilyn.

"I'll get a lawyer. I'll plead hereditary insanity. The type of insanity you get from your kids."

"I'll find you a lawyer."

"But what can I do about these letters?"

"To hell with the letters," said Marilyn.

"Prosecute?" posed Oz.

"The letters are not the issue, Oz," said Marilyn.

Sammy and Oz looked at her as if she had missed the point entirely.

"I can't go to the Sophisticates anymore," said Sammy.

"Me neither," said Oz, "they've blacklisted me too."

"Oz, you're going to have an aneurysm removed from your heart. You'll probably never make it through the operation," said Sammy, partly in irritation, partly to make light.

"You're right." And down came the finger of agreement. "I'll probably never make it into the operating room."

"Alright, I'll have a talk with Max," said Marilyn with familiarity. "Get him to get his father to drop the charges."

"Talk to Max?"

Sammy didn't like the sound of that. He wondered for a second if what Hershberg said had actually been true. He looked at Marilyn, so grown up, so sophisticated, so beautiful, so intelligent, and a dynamite dresser, and then thought of Max Hershberg. Nah. Her and Max Hershberg? Nah. Just not possible. But then he wondered about the timing. Someone had come between Marilyn and her husband Jack. Could it have been? Nah. Impossible. The Hersh had slandered him. Marilyn, actually. And Teddy, too. He was right to kick Hershberg.

Sammy just left it at that. They had caucused and, as usual, they followed Marilyn's advice. She would talk to Max. Marilyn's presence had put the poison pen letters into perspective. And Sammy then put them in the garbage.

"Hey, that's evidence," said Oz.

"A thing like this can't go to court," said Marilyn to Oz.

Oz nodded, but he didn't know why not.

They all sat in silence after that, listening to Baba X poking the broadloom with her cane.

"Why not?" Oz asked moments later. "Why can't it go to court?"

"I don't need the publicity, Oz," said Marilyn.

Baba X, oblivious to everything, shifted on the couch.

"I'm in *galus*," Baba X said. "Where is he? Maybe he's had an accident."

"*She's* in *galus*," Sammy said, as if Baba X had never known what real suffering was.

At this point Anna left her room and came back. The party was over. The three of them felt guilty for having had so many laughs.

Anna looked so hurt, and she really didn't want to sit down with them, but she had a mission.

"Does Marilyn know about Teddy?" asked Anna, to dampen the party mood.

"Ask her? Why ask me?" said Sammy.

"What about Teddy?" Marilyn's brow crinkled in concern. "What happened to Teddy?"

"Tell her," she said to Sammy.

"Tell her what?"

"He's a human shield. He's on the side of the Arabs."

"Well, so is Chomsky," said Marilyn.

"Who's this Chomsky?" said Sammy.

"Teddy's going to have a baby, with an Arab girl. The little shit," said Anna.

"I know that," said Marilyn, relieved. "And don't call him that. Not in front of me."

Anna got cut by that. She wondered why she bothered to come out of her room. They would all soon be pounding her.

"And she's a Palestinian," said Marilyn.

"She's a fucking Arab."

This got her back.

"She's a Palestinian. Say it. The word won't kill you."

Marilyn always took Teddy's side, protected him, spoiled him, Anna thought.

Six years his senior, Teddy, in Marilyn's imagination, was almost more Marilyn's baby than Anna's. The complicity she shared with him had even made Jack the nebbish jealous.

"How do you know?" asked Anna.

"Ever heard of the Internet? E-mail?"

"Don't get smart with me."

"Well, I think it's great. I'll be an auntie."

"Who asked for your say-so?" went Anna.

"Since when do I have to be asked?"

"That's your problem," said Anna.

"What's my problem?"

"You don't know when to shut up."

"I think you've got it the other way around."

"Say something," Anna said to Sammy. Sammy unsealed his mouth, but that's as far as he got. In a nick of time, he remembered he never got involved in these skirmishes between Anna and Marilyn.

"Say something!"

"Kids," Oz said to Anna, in commiseration.

"Not you."

"You're both crazy," said Sammy, thinking he had handed down arbitration. Immediately he knew this was a mistake. He had been looking forward to sex that night and now he would get none. He did his best to rectify things.

"Marilyn!" he said sharply, then looked to Anna for approval. "That's enough."

"Alright buster," Anna said standing up, pissed off at Sammy, "alright buster." She went back to the bedroom.

Oz shifted in his seat. He looked at his watch. He was starting to get restless. It was almost time. He had purplish swags under his eyes from not sleeping last night.

"You guys should drive to the hospital if you want to beat the rush hour," Marilyn said.

"Now?" said Oz, startled.

"Now."

"You're right," said Oz, without using "the Oz."

Oz looked at his watch, then at the dependable Sammy. The last thing he wanted to do was go to the hospital. The operation on a heart aneurysm was always high risk, and actually, at his age, "any operation was," he had been told. And then there was the pacemaker already in there. Did they know how they were going to operate around the pacemaker? Would they turn it off? He wanted to have more tea with cream and more of Anna's trifle and just not go.

"You're not supposed to eat after two."

"I know."

Marilyn clutched Oz's hand and laid her head on his shoulder. He had a clean but unmistakably old man-ish smell.

"You'll be okay."

"I really appreciate your taking me, Sammy."

Before leaving, Sammy went to the bedroom and stood in front of the closed door. He knew better than to go in.

"Anna?"

"Go away."

"Anna Banana?"

"Up yours!"

"I'm taking Oz to the hospital now." He laid the pathos on thick, hoping she'd cave in, come out, and say goodbye to Oz. "Are you going to say goodbye to Oz or what?"

Sammy's bulletin was met with silence. Anna was going to ostracize him, "fully ostracize him completely," as she sometimes put it.

"Anna? Anna? What did I do? Anna? Anna Banana?"

Anna didn't utter another word, so Sammy went back to the living room where Oz was saying goodbye to Baba X.

"She's probably fallen asleep," Sammy said to Oz, with the type of lie that typified his life.

By the time they left, Baba X was still sitting on the chesterfield, waiting for her Alex. He was already two hours late, but she bore it well, clutching her big brown purse and poking the broadloom with her cane.

■ ■ ■

They had Oz on a gurney and were wheeling him down the hall. Sammy's eyes were watery.

"It just hit me. I won't be able to testify at your trial."

"Marilyn says there probably won't be a trial."

"What are you going to do if you can't go curling or to the Sophisticates?"

"Who says I'm not going curling or back to the Sophisticates? Let them stop me."

"You're right," Oz said, giving him the prostrate version of Oz's finger of agreement. Sammy smiled.

"What happened to your tie?"

"They wouldn't let me wear it in the operating room."

"Buggers."

"Yeah."

"If I don't make it, you can give my ties to Teddy."

"He can't tie a knot."

"Show him."

Sammy smiled. It was true. He had never shown Teddy how to tie a tie knot. Least of all a big windsor.

"By the way, who's this Chomsky?"

"Wasn't there a Chomsky family on Enniskillen Avenue or Enniskillen Boulevard?"

"Boulevard."

"You're right." And down came the finger of agreement.

They wheeled the gurney through the doors that were supposed to bar Sammy from accompanying him further. Sammy paid no attention.

"The pearly gates," called Oz.

"They're just swinging doors," Sammy said.

"You're right." Again, the finger of agreement, perhaps Oz's last. Sammy's left eye began tearing.

Sammy gave Oz the Oz gesture back. "You're right!"

"Quiet, sir," an orderly said, bounding at him from up the corridor, finally bearing down, and then pulling gingerly at his coat sleeve. "You can't come past here." Sammy's hand had been pulled off the chrome of the gurney.

"Fuck you," Sammy said watching Oz roll away.

"What did you say, sir?"

"Fuck you. I said, Fuck you, quote unquote."

Oz's feet were all he could see and he tried to sidestep the orderly, who grabbed Sammy now by the patch on the elbow of his coat.

"Watch the coat," Sammy said, irritably.

"I'm going to have to ask you to leave, sir."

"I was leaving." Oz was out of sight.

"And not come back."

"You can't ask me that. This is a public hospital."

Sammy yanked his sleeve away and walked to the elevator. Oz was gone. The orderly took after him and grabbed the back of his coat this time, just as Sammy pushed the elevator button.

The jerking of his coat made his knees bend and he almost lost his bearings.

"What's with the coat?"

Sammy turned around and decided to get a good look at the orderly.

"You're going to have to leave, sir."

"I am leaving."

"But because I said so."

"What are you, four years old? I'm leaving because I say so, not because you say so. Even if you asked me to stay, I would leave."

"This is a hospital, sir."

"Is there anything else you can say besides the obvious?"

"I'm afraid you can't use that language with me."

"If you leave me alone, I won't. Now let go of my coat." He tried to yank his coat but the orderly held fast.

Sammy was struck by his own word choice. The elevator doors slid open. A celestial chime was heard. Sammy yanked his coat hard out of the orderly's hand and stepped inside and pressed G. The orderly hesitated and jumped into the elevator at the last second. The doors closed and the two were alone. They rode down together, with the orderly clutching the patch on the elbow of Sammy's coat sleeve.

"What's with you and my coat?" Sammy asked.

"I'm showing you to the door."

"I know where the door is."

"Just in case."

"What's with the coat? Chrissakes."

He raised his arm yanking his sleeve out of the orderly's grip again, but this time the patch almost ripped right off, exposing how threadbare the sleeve was. The coat had been given to him by his friend Stevie, before he died.

"You ripped my coat."

"It's just the patch."

"You'll pay."

"Sue me."

"I'll sue you alright." He cut the orderly between the soft underpart of the jaw and the windpipe with his two biggest knuckles and the man went down gagging.

"Do you want me to punch you out?"

The orderly, astounded, could barely breathe let alone speak, and his astonishment blended into a hurt look.

"We'll call it even. The coat for the punch. Nod if it's a deal."

The orderly opened his eyes wide and nodded, which buoyed up Sammy. He left the elevator smartly when the doors opened, elated and slightly baffled, fingering the fabric of the hanging patch as if it were a scab ready to come off. The orderly didn't budge and the doors closed on him. Sammy strode past the front desk and out the door.

He dug deep into the pocket of his pants for his car keys and wad of cash. Lately he always carried a thick wad of cash, at least five hundred dollars in fives, tens and twenties, in both Canadian and American. It was a gesture to style, to show that he was not giving in. And now that he was always carrying it around with him, he was always checking to see that it was there. Closing his fist around it, he thought the wad too small and so before going to meet Anna for supper at Rikki's, he went to the bank and withdrew another two hundred dollars from the cash machine and wrapped it around the wad.

All of a sudden in the parking lot outside the bank he remembered punching the orderly in the throat and he heaved once, twice onto the pebbled side wall of the bank like a filthy rummy. He spat the last fibres and bile and then got into his car, weeping.

He thought about his son the male nurse, the human shield for Arafat, who should know better, and wept some more. He thought about the minnowy *yasel* in the belly of this Aïda person and wept even more.

4

That afternoon Marilyn stood outside on the frosted steps of the law courts building in the freezing cold when she saw Mannie Hershberg's son, Max, come up the stairs with some of his buddies. She called him over. "Max, get over here."

"Hi, Marilyn," said Peter and Snib.

"Pete. Snib. Max will join you guys in a second."

"Bye, Marilyn."

Max's buddies scurried up the steps without him and into the warmth and glow of the vestibule.

She couldn't remember a colder February. The sky was a block of enamelled blue ice. The wind whipped into her cheeks. As Max approached her, he took off his toque to look cool and she saw his head was shaved like a coconut.

"What happened to your hair?"

"I got tired of it long."

His lobeless ears were turning hotter and redder by the second.

"Marilyn, it's freezing out here." He wouldn't look her in the eye. She saw the red pulp lips smack together.

"So put your toque back on. I want to talk to you."

"It's freezing out here. I've got a hearing in five minutes."

"You're such a prick."

Max was stunned.

"You're such a prick, Max."

"Your father's a maniac," said Max. "And your brother, if he comes back here, we've decided we'll beat the shit out of him."

"You're such a fucking prick."

"What's going on, you want to apologize for your father's assault on my father?"

"Did you tell your father I was a hot lay?"

"What?"

"Did you tell him I was a hot lay?"

"What?" He still wouldn't look her in the eye. He had another spot to look at: across the street from the law courts, where a drunk in a T-shirt lying on the packed snow, trying to get up.

"Is that why your father assaulted my father? My father said it was this human shield thing, this ocher-Yisrael business about your brother, what an asshole."

"So you did tell him?"

"Marilyn."

"Max," she mimicked.

"Marilyn."

"Did you tell your buddies too? What have you been telling people about me?" She poked him hard on the shoulder with her fur mitten.

"I didn't say a fucking word to anyone."

She poked him again.

"Maybe your wife would like to hear I'm a hot lay?"

"Whoa. Hold on. We both agreed she was not to know."

"We agreed no one was to know. Did you tell your father that I was a hot lay?"

"Of course not."

"That you buggered me?"

"Marilyn."

"Max."

Marilyn pulled off her mitten and took out her mobile phone. "I have your home number on my memory card. Look."

"It's fucking freezing out here."

"Doesn't affect the phones."

"I'm going to be late for my hearing."

Marilyn pressed a button and a menu of names flickered on the screen.

"I didn't tell anyone."

She knew that if she pressed "call" he would break.

He stared again at the drunk trying to get up off the icy sidewalk, rolling down the snow bank.

She pressed "call."

"Alright. Alright. I told my dad."

"You are such an egregious liar."

She cancelled the call.

"We were at the hockey game and talking about my marriage. He knows that Naomi and I are having trouble in the sex department. Even you know that. She's a bit squeamish. She shudders when I touch her, I told you that. It disgusts her. Anyway, he asks me if I'm getting something on the side, to tide me over. I told him not to worry because I was getting something on the side. I thought that would be it, but he asked me who with. With a Jewish girl? I said yes, yes, a Jewish girl, to put him at ease. Who? he says. I didn't want him to worry that I was with a shicksa or that I was going to get AIDS or something. So I told him it was you. And I didn't say I buggered you. I swear on the Jewish Torah. I just told him that we were having an affair."

"You call it an affair?"

"Yes. Why not?"

"It was just once. Once means nothing. And I did it because I was bored. I wouldn't have an affair with you."

"Why not?"

"Because you're not a hot lay, Max. Hasn't anyone told you that?"

He hesitated.

"No, no one's told me that."

"You never noticed for yourself?"

"No."

"You never noticed that you ejaculate prematurely."

"I do not."

"I've had sneezes that lasted longer."

"It's not funny."

"Yeah, because you're not fun."

"Marilyn."

"Max."

"Well why did you go out with me?"

"I told you I was bored. Why did you call me?"

"Terry. Terry from your office. She told me you told her you thought I was funny."

"I told Terry I thought you were goofy."

"She said funny."

"She probably said goofy, you heard funny."

"Marilyn."

"Max. Where were we? Oh, right, your sexual performance. First, you couldn't get an erection, then once you did, you couldn't keep it. Then, when you finally got something going, ffffttt."

"I was nervous. I'd been drinking."

"Who else did you tell?"

"Nobody."

Drawing out the phone from under her arm she set up the menu again until "Naomi" flashed on the tiny blue screen.

"Just Snib and Peter."

"Just to show off?"

"I suppose so."

The two stood, watching the drunk trying to scale the snow drift. Max thought about putting his toque back on, but didn't. He thought he was in love with Marilyn.

"What do you want from me? I'm freezing."

"*Primo*: I want you to get your father to talk to the police, say he had provoked Sammy, drop the charges, whatever."

"Why should I do that? Your father smashed his bridgework."

"Because if you don't, I'm telling Naomi."

"Naomi's not well."

"I don't give a fuck."

"She'd divorce me."

"She'd be a lot happier."

"And what else?"

"*Secundo*: I want you to get your father to ask the Sophisticates to lift the sanctions against Sammy, and stop sending the poison pen letters."

"Alright. Alright, I'll talk to him."

"And thirdly, I want you to shut up about what happened between you and me. You know, Max, I don't mind being known that I'm a hot lay. I don't even mind people knowing I'm liberal about anal sex. But I do mind people knowing that I had sex with you."

"If you thought I was pathetic you shouldn't have let me put this" — he held up an index finger — "into this." He made an "o" with the thumb and forefinger of his other hand and tried to slot his index finger into the "o," but as he was wearing gloves he had a hard time of it.

"How mature."

"Well, you should have thought about how pathetic I was before doing it."

"Max, you're hurt."

"Save the sarcasm."

"You know, I didn't really know you were pathetic until afterwards. I had heard rumours, but I had always given you the benefit of the doubt."

"Rumours?"

"Rumours."

"Marilyn," he whined pathetically.

"Max," she mimicked.

"Alright, alright, that's fair. I shot my big mouth off. Where's the remedy?"

She knew he'd roll out the legalese.

"For you, there is none. Just do what I asked re the Sophisticates and your father."

"What are you doing this weekend?"

"Get over yourself."

"No, really. Are you busy?"

"You're such a narcissist."

"How do you mean?"

"You're proof that Freud was right, that you can be your own preferred love object."

"Fuck Freud."

"Who's the buggerer now? Or is it the buggeree?"

"I told you I never said that. I never told him I buggered you."

"Then your father has quite an imagination. You should have a talk with mummy."

"Forget that. What are you doing this weekend?"

"I have a date."

"Who with?"

"Wouldn't you like to know."

"Yeah, I would. You know, I had the weirdest dream about you."

"Well, you are the weirdest person."

"Can I tell you my dream?"

"I thought you were late."

"I am."

"Just go inside, Max."

Then he canted and grabbed her, tried to kiss her. Tried to nuzzle her. She wriggled out gently, decisively.

"Would you fuck off!"

"Sorry."

"Maybe you're not a narcissist. Maybe you're just not very bright, I think that's your problem. Now get inside. Go."

"I'm not your dog. You can't tell me what to do."

"Just get inside. I don't want to be seen walking in with you."

Max stood still, unwilling to obey, yet really wanting to get out of the cold and get to his hearing.

She knew this and twisted the knife. "Just get inside."

"You go in first."

"Max. Just get the hell inside."

5

That night, at supper time, Sammy sat in Rikki's with his Anna Banana having his Rikki's usual: bacon, eggs and white toast with marmalade and pancakes. It's what he'd had for the last twenty years at least. The waitresses in their pink blouses and black pleated skirts doted on him but, as Anna said, he had his beady-eye look, and she knew he would be giving them trouble.

"You're not going to sleep if you eat pancakes at this time."

"I always sleep."

Sammy scooped out some whipped butter from the crenulated cupcake butter container with a spoon and spread it on his pancakes.

"Use your knife."

"Too late."

Then he poured the maple syrup.

"You don't eat sensibly. You're getting your timing all mixed up."

"What timing?"

He pocketed a wedge of toast into his mouth.

"Your day for night. You'll mix up your day from night."

"You're the one who doesn't sleep. I can sleep standing up."

Normally he never gave his wife an argument. He was marriage compliant, even uxorious. If he disagreed with her he usually gave in, or, on the odd occasion, just ignored her. But now he was giving her arguments right and left. What's more, he thought, she was getting old, and he felt her to be less desirable sexually. Why now that she was 61 and not 60, or now that he was 78 and not 77, this he didn't know. All he knew was that up to this year, for thirty years or so, being in bed with her touched off a powderkeg. A powderkeg. His word.

That afternoon Anna had gone to the food bank where she did volunteer work. She had found its stocks heavily depleted, especially top-shelf items to which customers were restricted to two. The other volunteers and the full-timers were in a panic. It seems that that morning there had been a "run on the food bank," as one of the hippie staffers quipped, and people were already lining up ten deep. The manager was an enormous, florid ex-Trotskyist named Barry Bronstein-King, AKA "B.B. King," who spent the afternoon screaming into the telephone, shaking his fingers out in front of himself, sending out urgent calls for people to donate food. He was on the phone to the more sympathetic radio stations that would give a free plug, to the human affairs departments in the ministry and Safeway or Loblaw's or Superstore or whatever, as well as to churches, synagogues, Sikh temples and ashrams. He stood in the small office at the back of the food bank, a cigarette hanging from his bottom lip, with a silver worm of ash about to collapse, shouting abuse at the other people on the line. When the bank's stocks were depleted suddenly like this he had to get bolshy, he would say.

"Bread!" he would scream into the phone. "I've got people here who are actually saying they'd settle for bread. And this is a rich country."

There was a pause while Anna and some other unpackers stood up to listen. Barry always gave a great performance at moments like these.

He cupped the phone and shouted to the staff, "These people at Safeway are actually offering cake." You needed no genius to unravel the irony, but the "dumbfuck manager" at Safeway didn't get it.

Into the phone: "What you're telling me is to tell them to eat cake?"

To the staffers: "He still doesn't get it."

"Let them eat cake? — Marie Antoinette? — The guillotine?" Huh.

"Never mind. If you've just got cake from yesterday we'll pick it up. But you can't make cake into peanut butter sandwiches for your kids. What other rotten shit have you got? I've got fifty people in line here and I'm going to have to send them home with a can of tuna. We've got nothing on the top shelf!"

"What? ... Dogfood?! We don't give away dogfood. These people don't have dogs, they have children. Okay, okay. Now you're talking. Beans. What else you got? More tuna. Okay. Microwave popcorn. You're a prince." To the staff: "He's a prince." To the manager: "We'll know who to go to next time the Samaritans are engaged. When the revolution comes I'll tell them not to put you against a wall and shoot you, if you throw in the microwave for popcorn."

Pause.

"I was just kidding. Hey, I know how to be diplomatic — who are you calling undiplomatic?"

Pause.

"I'm to blame? The food bank's to blame that there are people in this city who don't have enough money to buy food?"

Pause.

"It's the bloodsuckers like you who are to blame? Maybe we'll shoot you today. Why wait for the revolution?"

Pause.

"What do you mean you're taping this conversation? Do you think if I gave a shit, I'd be working here? Just have the stuff ready. Barrels of it."

When he was holding the line he would answer questions, do the accounting and direct the staff. Anna felt intimidated by him, but she respected the way he managed to scrape all that food together from so many uncaring sources. In some way he reminded her of her mother, who was a cook at the Jewish orphanage during the Depression, and would have "heated polemics" with the Board of Trustees about the food budget, and had to combine her unspeakable love and kindness for other people's abandoned kids with a stern attitude towards the trustees, rich men who seemed to spend their time feasting on bagels and pickled herring, and drinking scotch at their endless board meetings at the orphanage. These were the men who sat on the *bimah* at the synagogue, had more than their fair share of being called up to the Torah, were always being honoured with a roast or a toast or whatever, or a newly named pew, or having a small forest in Israel named after them. But their admonitions of Anna's mother were useless. "I'm going to buy what we need here," she'd say. "Barrels of it." She spent the entire food budget and bought on credit from the butchers, bakers and dairy farmers. They would never humble her, or break her will to fatten up the orphans, who, in fact, were better fed throughout the Depression than the kids living at home. Anna's brother Alex, whenever anyone asked him what he wanted to be when he grew up, would say, "An orphan."

Since Anna was the only one with a car that afternoon, Barry asked her if she wouldn't mind going out to make the pick-up at one of the major supermarkets, the one with the manager Barry had suggested executing either before or after the revolution. The truck was already making pick-ups. Anna didn't dare refuse. A small, wiry boy called Snake, forehead and nose acne-enraged, rode with her to do the lifting.

"This young man, the Snake, has tattoos up his arms and on his bum," she told Sammy.

"How do you know he has tattoos on his bum?"

"What kind of stupid question is that?"

"It's a logical question. How do you know he has tattoos on his bum?"

"He told me in the car."

Sammy called the waitress over and asked her to take back the bacon and make it crisp. For some reason, the crisper the bacon the less unkosher it seemed.

"The bacon's not crisp — take it back, please thank you."

"You never send anything back. Only Stan would do something like that. What's come over you these days?"

"Nothing's come over me."

Stan was a Chinese friend from work he used to go to the track with years ago and who, once at the Shanghai, their favourite Chinese restaurant, sent the food back because it was cold. For Anna and Sammy this was the height of bravery.

"I asked for it crisp. I want it crisp."

"She's just a worker. You didn't have to be mean."

"I wasn't mean. I just wanted it crisp."

"Making it crisp doesn't make it any more kosher."

"We haven't kept kosher for years."

"Whose fault is that?"

"Am I blaming anybody? Actually, if you want to blame someone blame Bernstein, the butcher. He priced everything sky-high. He gouged us. He was responsible for hundreds of Jews going *trayf*. He worked at it, at the gouging."

During the drive out to the Safeway, Snake had explained to Anna how she was a petit-bourgeois element. It was his favourite expression: petit-bourgeois element. Anna didn't really understand. She was living on a pension, so that made her a pensioner.

"You're a petty bourgeois," said Snake.

"I'm a pensioner."

"You're a petty bourgeois. In the revolution it's not clear which way you'll lean."

"Don't worry, I'd lean to the left."

"In a revolution the workers have to lean to the left, but for the petty bourgeois, it's up to them individually."

"Trust me, I'll lean to the left, so don't call me a petty bourgeois element."

Anna and Snake had pulled up to the back of the Safeway and waited fifteen minutes for the manager to come out in his long green apron that rose up to his button-down shirt collar and the thick trendy knot in his paisley tie. He took one look at Anna and Snake and Anna's crappy car and laughed, showing his unblemished incisors, as if he thought them unfit to put him against the wall and shoot him.

"So, you're the firing squad?"

Snake snorted. "I wish we were."

Anna felt ashamed, like they were actually begging.

The manager noted this, relishing her humiliation.

"The stuff's way back in there," he said, thumbing towards the depths of the warehouse area and smiling.

He actually enjoyed tormenting them.

"Can we drive the car in?" asked Snake.

"Not that piece of shit. It's busted a cam or something. It's leaking oil."

"You a mechanic?"

"No."

"So mind your own business," said Snake, mustering gallantry to defend Anna's car and honour. "You know nothing about cars. If it had a busted cam we wouldn't be here. If it leaks oil it's because ... Oh, fuck it. It isn't leaking oil. Fuck it, fuck it, fuck it. Look, we don't have a lot of time, can't you get some guys to help us? The food bank's fucking empty, man. We're a bit desperate."

"No. Either you two desperadoes go in and haul it out yourselves or you go home. We're generous, but we're not the ones running the charity, you are."

"He's the type who hates the poor," said Snake to Anna.

"What?"

"Nothing. Look, just let us drive in, or let someone help us, it'll take five minutes."

"No. Why should I?"

"'No, why should I?'" mimicked Snake.

"Look, I couldn't give a fuck about the fucking food bank. People are poor, it's their own goddam fault."

"Fuck you, mister," said Snake, flicking a cigarette at the manager's eyewear.

"The Snake has a discipline problem," Sammy said.

"They tell me he's bipolar," Anna replied. "They found him the job in the food bank to help him out a bit. He's a bit of an alcoholic, too, which doesn't help."

The cigarette had plunked down under the manager's green apron and sent the manager into a spin and dance.

"Snake," she said. "I think we should go."

"Not until I punch the crap out of this bitch," he said. "He's a petit-bourgeois element."

"I don't understand why he called him a bitch," Anna said to Sammy. "Or a petit-bourgeois element, which is what he calls me."

"*Bitch* is a thing the kids pick up from watching *Bad Boys*."

"It's not called *Bad Boys*."

"What's it called?"

"*Bad Boys* is the theme music."

"Theme song."

"Theme song. I stand corrected."

"You stand corrected."

The manager finally located the hot butt with one hand thrust down his apron. He fished it out and stood up. It was then that the Snake jump-kicked him in the chest and sent him stumbling backwards until he landed painfully on his tailbone. Anna thought this shouldn't be happening. She wanted to know who this Snake was and why Barry had sent her out with him. She did not like his name or his tattoos. God forbid anything happens to me, she muttered.

"Who is this Snake?" Sammy asked. "Did they fire him?"

"No. Barry got him out on bail and he's probably unloading tuna fish as we speak."

"Did they arrest him?"

"Yes. But he's out on his own cognizance. He didn't just kick the manager, as the Snake said himself on the phone to Barry, 'He drop kicked him.' The Safeway guy was winded. Everyone came up to watch. They looked at me as if I was the mother of Snake."

"I like that: Mother of Snake."

"It was very embarrassing for me."

"I could see how it might've been."

"As if it wasn't enough being the mother of a human shield for Arafat, the little shit."

"You're telling me?"

Sammy cut into the last eighth of his pancake stack just as the waitress appeared with the bacon.

"I'm almost finished," he said. "Did you have to slaughter the pig? You can take it back. I de-order it."

"Sammy."

"I ain't taking it back, hon."

"I'm not eating it."

"Sammy. Just take it."

The plate banged down on the table.

"Why did you make me take it?"

"Sammy."

"Would you like more coffee?"

"Just half a cup please, thank you."

The waitress filled his cup to the top and left.

"Believe you me, she's tired," Anna said. "She's just a worker."

"She's tired?"

"And how was your day?"

"I took Oz to the hospital. He told me to water his plants. I got my coat ripped."

"Let me see."

"How did you rip it?"

"I didn't rip it."

"Who ripped it?"

"Some orderly. He ripped off the patch on the sleeve in the elevator. So I punched him in the jaw or the windpipe or something and left him in the elevator."

Sammy didn't even think Anna was mad about it. And when reconstructing a story, Sammy thought, the wilder the better. He thought he'd make it a little more interesting. But then Anna, who was facing the front door of Rikki's, saw something.

"Sammy."

"What?"

"Look, but don't turn around."

"Look at what, then?"

"It's the Queen."

"Of England?"

"You know who I mean."

"Sophie Ruben? Or her son?"

"Sophie Ruben."

At that moment Sophie Lerner née Ruben and her husband Ernie and the Weinsteins had just walked into Rikki's, saw Anna and Sammy and walked down the aisle, between the tables, right past them — snubbing them. It was an outright snub, a gauntlet-throwing snub. A snub that launches a thousand future snubs.

The animosity from the Lerners, Sophie and Ernie, they could understand, because they were friends of the Hershbergs and the former rabbi, even the rabbi's former wife, and they also had a daughter, Annette, who had married a zealot from New Jersey and was now living in a Jewish settlement in the West Bank. But the Weinsteins, Minnow and Gertie, were a bit more of a mystery. Why would they snub them? Anna's mother practically kept Mitzi Weinstein, Minnow's mother, alive when she was at the orphanage, when she was Mitzi Sokoloff. Are they just playing up to the Lerners? He could understand them sucking up to the Hershbergs; the Hershbergs were worth two million and had a home in Palm Springs. But the Lerners? What were they good for? They even had to sell their cottage last year. And then there was that hilarious thing with their silverware.

"They snubbed us," Sammy said. "They went right past without saying hello."

"Believe you me, they said something," Anna said. "Under their breath."

"Antisemiten."

"You heard it, too?"

"Antisemiten. It was very clear."

"Which one said it?"

"Sophie."

"She looks like a whale in designer cords."

"Just about."

"Did the *goye* come today?"

"No."

"Why not? Never mind. What does it matter? She never cleans anyway."

"She has a bad back."

Sammy pounded the table.

"'*Antisemiten.*' Me who fought in '48 in Herzliya," Sammy said. "Just Sophie said it?"

"Don't get up, Sammy."

"I won't."

"Is that where you were?" said Anna.

"And other places. A lot of other places."

"You've never once talked about it. Since I met you."

"I've never talked about it in over fifty-five years."

"Don't get up, Sammy."

"You know about Sophie and the silverware business?"

This had become mythical news in the community. Sammy knew the story but he let Anna tell it again.

"She was bragging that she bought a thirty-six-place Christofle silverware set."

"Thirty-six pieces."

"No. Thirty-six place settings. Do the math: if there are eight pieces of cutlery per person that's thirty-six times eight."

"I wonder if everyone gets a helmet and breastplates, too."

"But what she didn't know was that it was silver-plated. She thought it was solid silver, but Christofle only sells silver-plate."

"Now she knows."

"And how."

Sammy canted and swivelled to get a look at them. There was an undergrowth of pleasure in the eye that cast its gaze at the Lerners and Weinsteins.

"Sammy."

"What?"

"Sammy, don't go over there. Turn around. Sammy, look at me."

"I'm not going over there."

"Where are you going, Sammy?"

"I'm going to go to the bathroom."

"You never use public toilets."

"I've got to go."

"Don't go over there."

An arm shot forth across the table, tried to clamp a sleeve.

"Why's everybody grabbing my sleeve?"

6

"*I'm going to* tell her anyway," Anna said, as punishment. After all, Sammy wasn't too old to punish.

"Don't. Tell. Marilyn."

"I will. I told you not to go over to their table."

"I wasn't going to. I was going to the bathroom. But they looked at me phoney."

"I told you. You didn't listen. I'm telling Marilyn."

Anna was in a bad mood. And as usual, when there was a disagreement, she felt she was to blame. Even though it was Sammy's fault, again, she bubbled over with guilt. Go know why. He was the one who went over to their table, even after she had told him not to. He was alienating all their acquaintances. They couldn't go out anywhere, not to the Sophisticates, not to the rink.

Not even to the hairdresser.

She had been at the hairdresser that morning and had sat beside Sylvia Yamron under the hair dryer, two dyed blondes among a row of elderly ladies with maple-coloured hair. The rotten-egg smell of permanent had lodged up her nostrils. Sylvia, with her smoker's voice, had spent the better part of the morning there *fardraying* her head about her ingrate of a son-in-law and his *grine* parents, how they were making life miserable for her Sheila. So it was Sheila this and Sheila that for a good hour, with no regard to what Anna might be going through.

Then Sylvia got on to talking about Belle Pearlmutter, an old foe, but by that time, they were under the hair dryers and it was hard for Anna to hear her with the whirring in her ears.

It was from Belle that Sylvia had heard about Teddy. When she finished off the gossip on Belle she was ready to let Anna know she knew.

"Anna," Sylvia said, lifting her hair dryer, almost getting under Anna's, sounding like a child with croup, "I heard about Teddy."

"Just a second, I can't hear a thing." But she heard the word Teddy. Anna flipped up her hood and inserted her hearing aid. "What did you say?"

"I was at the curling rink, with Belle. They have cable there."

Expecting Sylvia to mention the human shield stuff, her skin sizzled with resentment and denial.

"Belle told me Teddy was marrying an Arab girl."

Now how did people know this? Go know. Her heart stopped for a full five seconds. This hit her hard. Go know how Belle Pearlmutter knew this. Her body shook and the curlers shuddered.

"She's a liar. Teddy's not getting married to anybody."

"So Belle's got it wrong?"

"She's a liar. Come on, you know how the *grine* are."

"But he is with someone, isn't he? Belle said Mushy's son saw Teddy in Jerusalem. He was with a girl. Not a Jewish girl."

"They're such liars. That's how most of them got into this country."

People had no right to that rumour.

"It's a lie. Belle's a liar, like all the *grine*, you know that."

Sylvia took Anna's hand. Anna gripped the arm of the chair, and asked, "But he is a human shield, isn't he?"

Anna made a face. "It's all lies. He's doing humanitarian work."

"In Israel?"

"Yes."

"Where in Israel?"

"In Israel. Here and there. It's a big place. You know he's there."

"You never talk about him."

"What's to talk?"

"Why he's there. What he's doing there? You never mention it."

"It's part of his medical studies." This was one of her lies to herself that she sometimes shared with others. In her imagination Teddy was doing a very long pre-med, taking his time, developing humanistically, first as a nurse, before going back to med school. It's what kids do these days, she would say. They need to find themselves. It was, of course, a lie. Teddy had no intention of going back to medical school. Firstly, he didn't like the other students, who were there for the money, and, secondly, he was frightened by the responsibilities, the fact that medicine implied settling down, while nursing meant he could go gallivanting.

"Imagine saying or even imagining something like that about someone else's kid; but that's the *grine*," said Sylvia, taking Anna's side unconditionally, but knowing full well that Belle was right.

"They're like that."

"Who?"

"The *grine*?"

"Don't I know," said Belle.

"Belle said this Arab girl was expecting," said Sylvia, pushing her luck.

"Expecting?"

"So, it's not true?"

"How would she know?" said Anna. "These are personal things."

"Expecting in September. That's what she heard. Her son saw Teddy in Jerusalem."

"Her son the *fertzl*, that little shit?"

"That one."

"She should talk."

"She does."

"It's all lies. They're all bullshitters. There's no Arab girl. No one's expecting. There's no human shield. It's all gossip."

Irked with Sylvia, she took out her hearing aid and pulled down the hood of the dryer. At that moment she wanted to flatten the curling rink with an atomic bomb, or get her hands on Teddy, the little shit. Christ, how she resented him for inflicting complications on her.

When she was driving back from the hairdresser's she was in a foul mood. The pert blonde girl she had had cut her hair too short and the perm was too tight. All because she wasn't attentive, due to the upset. Even before she got home she had wanted to cry — again in front of her bathroom mirror when she saw the results. And she did cry.

"You made the perm too tight," she had told the pert hairdresser.

"No I didn't."

"It's too tight."

"No it isn't, lady."

I'll give her *lady*, Anna thought, the little shithead.

During the drive home on the slushy streets she had almost hit some pedestrians, a woman pushing a baby carriage and her husband. The man banged his fists on her hood in anger.

Sylvia's reports from the curling rink had made her feel ashamed of her son. It galled her that people like Masha's son and Masha and Belle and even Sylvia were talking about Teddy. And she couldn't even get her hair permed properly. Everywhere she went was an ordeal. The next person who spoke ill of Teddy would get it from her. Get it good. She sympathized with Sammy for having kicked in Hershberg's bridge work. He should have kicked him in the *batzim*, she thought. Should have driven them up into his *kishkes*. No, up into his *gorgle*. And if she saw Belle Pearlmutter on the road right now she'd run her right over. Then she'd back up and run her over again until her brains squirted out.

Sammy saw by the way she was filling the kettle to make tea that he'd better get out of the apartment. It was still two hours before his appointment with the shrink the judge had ordered him to see. Even though Hershberg had dropped the charges, he still had to go to court. He decided to go to his visit early, the waiting room was comfortable and had magazines. Both eyes were tearing slightly as he put on his coat.

After his visit, Marilyn picked him up in front of the psychiatrist's in her hotshot-lawyer's BMW. Her perfumed kid leather gloves touched him softly as she settled him into the front seat. She smelled dynamite, his daughter. The collar of her coat set off her face just so. And what a face! A countenance. Appealing, magnetic, confident. He couldn't understand why people were so mean talking about her. But people talk. Dogs bark and people talk. They have nothing else to do. Not in this world.

Why can't they just shut up? The Hersh wouldn't be at the dentist's every week if he had just shut up.

It was the decision of the court to impose upon him a sentence of six months therapy plus the payment for the damages to the

Hersh's bridgework. His lawyer thought that he didn't come out of it all too badly, having avoided jail time. His biggest worry was that they wouldn't let him cross the line to go gambling at the Indian casinos, but that was something his lawyer couldn't figure out.

"Were you ever a member of an international communist organisation?" his lawyer asked him smugly.

"No."

"Then you'll have no problem crossing the line. Even if you're a convicted felon you can cross the line, but not if you're a member of an international communist organisation."

"It has to be international? What if it's national?"

"No problem."

"Am I a felon?" Sammy asked.

The lawyer couldn't resist. "Yes, Sammy, you are, but you're a nice felon."

Marilyn's car drove beautifully, Sammy thought, not like his clunker. Although he was proud she had it, still, it was a German car. But then, bygones are bygones. It was a car for the prosperous. And even if you weren't, you felt prosperous riding in it. It had amenities, the kind the confident people got used to. It was the kind of car you used just for going for a drive. He remembered when the kids were little and they went for a drive in the old '71 Chevy to see the Christmas lights decorating the houses on the Crescent. The yellow and green sparkling facings, the platoons of enormous evergreens wound round and round with fairy lights, the glowing red candle ornaments in the front windows, a glowing Santa or a Rudolf, sometimes even an electric Chanukah menorah signalling the odd bourgeois Jew. The houses were smothered in snow, the kids awed in the back seat, the heater purring from under the dash. The car drove slowly on the packed ice and snow through a wonderland.

"Did you see Teddy on CNN again?" Marilyn said. "They keep running that clip."

"Did you?"

"I don't watch the news."

"Why not?" said Sammy, a bit stunned.

"It takes too much out of you. They give the news and you have to imagine the truth."

"What do you mean?"

"Never mind."

"Well, why did you ask me if I saw Sammy on CNN? How did you see him if you don't watch the news?"

"Did you see him on CNN or not, Dad?"

"I saw that clip before."

"No, I mean last night's clip. It was a longer clip"

"A longer clip?"

"Being interviewed. Standing in front of Arafat's Mukata, with some people from an organisation called Gush Shalom."

"No. I didn't see that. What's Gush Shalom?"

"An Israeli peace group."

"The only peace group in Israel is the army."

"Dad."

"I don't want to hear about it."

He sat strangely helpless, thin, in the midst of her gardenia scent. She took off her gloves, and he stared at her long fingers He couldn't understand why she was getting a divorce. Why people were saying vicious things about her. He was on the verge of asking, but he restrained himself. He had never asked her a personal question in his life. It was not in his line, so to speak. And frankly, he didn't think he should. But he was curious. It was she who broke the ice and asked him a personal question, which he tolerated because it had nothing to do with Teddy or human shields or the coming of the *yasel*.

"How was your visit?"

"They don't call it a visit — they call it a session."

The third-degree about his therapy was coming. This sank him in gloom.

"What's his name?"

"Lipschitz. Horhay Lipschitz."

"Horhay? You mean Jorge."

"Something like that."

"Is he Jewish?"

"He's Argentinean or Spanish."

"What's he like?"

"Vertical."

"What do you mean?"

"Vertical. He's a vertical man. Some men are horizontal, like your Uncle Alex, he's vertical."

"You mean he's tall. Like you."

"He's vertical. That's my impression. A vertical person."

"How long did it take?"

"They don't punch you in. They charge by the session. A session is a session. It's not a matter of time."

"And today's session?"

"Ten minutes and then he threw me out."

"How so?"

"How nothing. He sat there and I sat there and we stared at each other."

"You're not on a couch?"

"Couch? I'm lucky he lets me sit on a chair. And he's in a recliner, a $5,000 recliner. Real leather, not fake."

"What did you tell him?"

"I didn't tell him anything. I'm not a Catholic; I don't go to confession. I'm Jewish, Sunday morning we go for brunch at Rikki's, or dim sum. And I'm not a fink, so I don't talk about other people."

"Did he ask you why you kicked Mannie Hershberg?"

"Yes, he did."

"So."

"So."

"So what did you say?"

"I told him I did it because he insulted my children."

"What did he say?"

"He asked me if he really insulted my children. I told him he did. He said that was the eruption of the real."

"What else did he ask you?"

"Nothing."

Actually, this was all lies. He did get to lie on the daybed. And while he didn't talk until the end of the session, which lasted an hour, he cried all the time he was there. He was confused, his mind like a tackle box that had been really shaken up. He recalled lying in his stocking feet on the tubular stainless steel daybed, which was so narrow he thought he would fall off, crying, yet on the verge of fury.

"I can't believe you said nothing else."

"Don't believe it." Not on his life would he tell her anything else.

"Nothing? Nothing at all?" Marilyn probed and poked as if

she were stirring ashes.

"Oh, he wanted to know about my desire, but the way he said it was with a capital D, my Desire, or maybe all capitals, my DESIRE. What's your DESIRE? What do you DESIRE?" Sammy felt his face flush.

"What did you say?"

"I said I don't have desires. I have my routine, my usual. That's what I told him. My usual. And since today is Tuesday, right now, I could go really for my usual at Abosh's: a lean corned beef sandwich, pickles and coffee. All that not talking has made me peckish."

He expressly did not mention the Boston cream pie. But he would order it anyway. "The cream pie beckons as the corned beef beckons," Oz used to say. Poor Oz. All tubed up. No solids. Tube into the stomach, tube up his dick, tube in his wrist.

"Abosh's?" asked Marilyn.

"Please, thank you."

"What about Mummy? She'll be expecting you."

"Let her wait. She's in one of her moods. Where does it say I have to spend every minutes of the day with her. Is it in the Torah?"

■ ■ ■

He was served his Abosh usual by the Abosh grandson, whom they, as a family, called the Happy Rodent — happy because he was surly, and rodent because he looked like a mouse.

The corned beef was divine, because it was a bit fatty, as he liked it. He had ordered it very lean, as usual, but the boy cocked up, luckily. Divine were the pickles as well, cut lengthwise into fours, perhaps attaining the perfect crunch. Nothing worse than a limp pickle.

He also ordered rye bread and butter, and clutched the slice of bread and butter in his left hand while he ate the sandwich with his right. Oz would enjoy this.

"Why are you eating bread with your sandwich?" Marilyn asked.

"I eat bread with everything, except toast," Sammy replied.

"Even sandwiches?"

"Even sandwiches."

He ate everything up with gusto, quickly, before his coffee went cold.

"Do you want your usual pie?" went the Abosh boy.

"Yes please, thank you."

"More coffee?"

"Please, thank you. And bring me some half and half."

"Why don't you have whole cream?"

"I prefer half and half."

"Why?"

"Because it's light without being heavy."

The kid brought the Boston cream pie and Sammy groaned in ecstasy at the size. Marilyn loved that pre-satisfied groan Sammy gave in approval of a big portion. Ever since she was a kid it made her smile.

"You can't eat all that," Marilyn snorted.

"You're right," he said, imitating Oz, giving the Oz finger of agreement.

But then he plunged his fork in, slicing down to the bottom of the crust of the Boston cream pie and ate even more heartily. Stopping after three bites to drink his coffee.

"I can't drink this."

"Why not?"

"It's . . ." he said.

She touched the cup.

"Is it?"

"It is."

After drinking her first coffee Marilyn had ordered a second, which hadn't come. She hadn't ordered any food.

"You're not eating."

"I never eat lunch."

"All that figure business," he said.

Marilyn watched him go after the Boston cream pie again, loading his fork with his fingers.

"Just use your fork, Dad."

"It's too small, these forks."

"Just hold it higher up."

"I'm sorry you're not eating. Not nothing?"

"I'm not hungry."

"Ask him for more cold coffee."

"I will. And you don't be so sarcastic."

Marilyn beckoned and the Abosh kid came over with the beaker of coffee. She knew her father would say something sarcastic.

"Don't say anything sarcastic."

Too late.

"Remember us?"

The kid said nothing, just sort of smiled stupidly with squinted eyes. He began to top her off. He looked at Sammy's coffee cup, which was three-quarters full, and hesitated.

Sammy spoke. "Don't you have colder coffee?"

The kid didn't know what to say.

"Is it cold?" said the kid.

Sammy made a face, as if he were playing the piccolo. "Yes, it's cold."

"Would you like some more?"

"More cold or more hot?"

"More hot."

"Please, thank you."

"I'll bring you another cup."

"Now we're doing business."

The boy brought Sammy back a fresh cup of hot coffee. Sammy ripped open a sachet of Sweet'N Low and then hung back in his chair in despair.

"I can't drink this."

"It looks hot to me."

"I can't drink this. Where's that kid?"

"Why not?"

"Do you see a coffee spoon? I don't see a coffee spoon."

"Here, use mine."

"That's not the point."

"Dad," she beseeched.

He stirred his coffee with her spoon. His right eye was tearing slightly.

"Drink it before it gets cold."

The coffee scalded his tongue as he zooped. When he finished he sat there po-faced, looking at her.

From the counter the Abosh boy, who was reading the sports page, lifted his head. "Hot enough?"

"No."

The kid went back to the sports page. He sipped the scalding coffee and stared at Marilyn, who looked suddenly absent, even sad.

"Is there something bothering you?" he asked. "Something I should know about?"

Immediately he regretted asking.

Marilyn hesitated, making him fear that she would actually confide. She lowered her head and stirred her coffee. Yes, it did look as if she was going to answer him.

He realized this was the first time he had ever asked her such a question. Normally his wife handled all these personal problems with the children — with anyone, for that matter — and reported back to him. The debriefing, they called it. It was an arrangement that suited him. The truth was that he didn't want a real answer from Marilyn. In fact, if Anna hadn't got upset at the hairdresser's they wouldn't be here together. His wife would have picked him up.

His own question had given him heartburn, and he wished his wife were with him. Anna always carried Tums.

Why did he ask her whether there was something bothering her? Look at her, she was lifting up her eyes like she was going to tell him something.

"Have you got a Tums?" he asked her.

She, like her mother, always carried everything. Tums, Valium, Tylenol, chewable Aspirin, all the necessities.

She shook the Tums out on the table and he crunched one between his molars. They didn't do any good, but they had a good taste, like a healthy mint.

"They remind me of the mints at the Nanking, the restaurant for North End Jews. The Shanghai, the restaurant for South End Jews, hoi polloi, didn't serve mints."

"The pastel pinks and blues. With the minted toothpicks."

"Do you remember the fried wontons?"

The mutual reminiscence couldn't be stretched much further. He wondered what had happened between her and her nebbishy husband, Jack, whom she called the harmless herbivore (he was a vegetarian). Ten years married and now nothing.

Anna had summed it up: "It's the failure of the sexual revolution." But that was about all she said about it, and it had become her nostrum.

What was the point in getting married in the first place? he wanted to ask. And now what would she do?

Marilyn was in a ruminative mood. She stared out the window.

"It's starting to snow," she said.

"Well, it's not going to snow in here."

Sammy's curiosity had started to stir, after all these years. What had gone wrong with her *knish* of a husband?

"Did he cheat on you?"

"Who?"

"'Who.' Who do you think? Jack, who else? Men do it."

"Women do it, too."

He was in over his head. His spirits drooped. He should never do this again. What's wrong with a father and daughter sitting at Abosh's and not saying anything? Just sitting. Just eating. That's what they had done just when they sat down: him eating, her sitting in meditation, wistful maybe. A little chat. What's all this sincerity business anyway?

"Maybe it's unnatural, but I never think of him."

"Who?"

"Jack."

"Nobody thinks of him. That was his problem. He was a *knish*. Why did you marry him? Your mother told you not to marry him."

"The rebound. Big mistake."

"The rebound. From who?"

"You know from who."

There was that other one. The cool cookie who broke her heart. They both remembered how their mutual pride was hurt. But that was a no-fly zone, definitely.

"Marilyn, about Teddy?"

"Yes, about Teddy."

"So far, we've decided to deny it."

"You're crazy. How can you go around denying it?"

"It's not something we're proud of. They way we see it, and knowing Teddy, he may get cold feet, or the girl might have a miscarriage."

"Denial won't make it go away."

"Who knows?"

"Dad, you're going to have a grandchild. Teddy's not going to get cold feet. He's changed. Dad, look at me."

"What?"

"Dad, Moshiach is coming."

"The *yasel* is coming."

"We'll have to get T-shirts made," she said.

"The *yasel* is coming."

"We'll get some T-shirts anyway. Did you see Teddy's human shield T-shirt on TV?"

"Were you thinking of something like that?"

"Yes, but in a beige."

"You're being very cavalier about this, Marilyn. It's not funny."

"Where did you learn that word?"

"Cavalier? I read it."

"But Dad, it is funny. You send Teddy on this incredible all-expenses-paid Zionist youth trip, five-star hotels, disco parties, speed dating to get the kids to fall in love with Israelis, the soldier chaperones, the works — "

"The Israeli state paid for everything."

"Whatever."

"We wanted to encourage him to move out. To be independent. To get over that nonsense. That involvement. He seemed depressed. He was reading poetry, Anna told me."

"So you send him to Israel through Hagshama or Hagshaoma or Hag-whatever, and the WZO, because he got caught running around with a rabbi's wife and once he's there he falls in love with a Palestinian princess. That's funny."

"They weren't married and she isn't a real rabbi."

"But Aïda's a real princess."

"*Pritzteh*, you mean."

Marilyn laughed.

"No, I mean princess. I looked up her family name on the Internet. I did some research. She's really a princess."

"Marrying our Teddy?"

"Your Teddy. Relax. It's not the end of the world. Actually, it's the beginning. Isn't that why we're on the earth? To procreate?"

"Apparently not you."

"Under the circumstances, I think it's better I didn't, and don't."

"And not a *yasel*. There were enough problems with the last *yasel*."

"Stop calling him a *yasel*."

"You're right, it might be a girl. A girl-*yasel*. Why not. Way things are going."

"*Yasel* or no *yasel*, what's the difference? A child's a child."

"When you're all your life expecting a little Abraham and you end up with an Ibrahim, there's a big difference."

"So you're having qualms about the pregnancy?"

"Qualms, you call them. I'm having shit fits. I can't sleep. I'm punching and kicking people. I'm crying in front of another man. I lie on a couch in front of another man, whose name I can't pronounce, and cry. It's not normal."

"It's not the norm. But it's normal."

Sammy shrugged. "You've said that before."

He lifted his spoon to stir his coffee but then set it down. His coffee cup was empty and the Abosh kid was still reading the sports spread over a chest freezer. Sammy cleared his throat and the boy looked up.

"More coffee?"

"Yes, please, thank you."

The boy came over and poured, making a bit of a mess, wiping it up with a sodden rag so that Sammy couldn't put his right elbow on the table.

"He can't even wipe a table. I'm going over there to ask him for a napkin to dry this."

"Dad. Don't go over there. I'll get the napkin."

Sammy turned swiftly and caught the Abosh boy listening to their conversation. He half rose and the boy scooted back to the kitchen.

"I'm going to get that kid."

"Dad. Sit."

"I'm not a dog."

Sammy sat. "I guess I'm old and foolish," he said. "Maybe we shouldn't have had you and Teddy so late in life."

Sammy often said this without meaning it. But today he meant it.

"You can't take us back to the store."

"I know I'm old. But something's coming over me now. I have no tolerance. So who else knows about Teddy and the Palestinian princess?"

"Probably everybody."

The Abosh kid came over and left the check sticking to the wet table top. Sammy pulled out his wife's Liz Taylor top-smoked reading glasses, which he had been carrying for half a year since he had lost his, and studied the check.

He called the kid over and said, "What's this?"

"Dad."

"What's this?"

"That's the Boston cream pie."

"How much does it say here?" Sammy, peering down his nose, pointed to where the pencil marking was smudged.

"Three fifty."

"For how many?"

"For the one."

"Three fifty for the whole pie or one slice?"

"One slice. One unit."

"One unit?"

"Dad."

"It used to be thirty-five cents."

"Thirty years ago," said Marilyn, apologetically, looking at the Abosh kid, who looked back at her as if she were going to be tonight's jerk-off fantasy.

Sammy didn't like this look, and drew the kid's attention to the check.

"When your grandfather, who wasn't a crook, was alive . . ."

The Abosh kid just walked away.

"When the coffee was hot . . ." he continued, raising his voice.

"Dad."

7

Teddy's mother had rights. "The witness has rights," she remembered Tom Cruise saying in that movie, referring to Jack Nicholson.

Teddy's mother knew she had rights. She knew it. She was his mother. She had rights. The mother has rights.

Sammy was watching a hockey game in the bedroom, so she fitted her hearing aid tight into the well of her ear, toted the cordless into the bathroom, shut the door, sat down on the fluffy blue toilet seat and hit the memory button and got connected long distance. The witness has rights, she heard the voice say, until someone spoke to her in what she thought was Arabic and she hung up. She hit the memory button again, her heart pounding, determined to ask for Teddy no matter who picked up the phone.

"Teddy?"

"Just a second."

"Teddy?"

"Hold the line."

"Teddy?"

"He's coming."

"Teddy?"

"Hello," said Teddy.

"Teddy?"

"Ma? Is everything alright?"

"I've had vomiting. I took some baking soda and water. It cleans out the stomach."

"Maybe you should see a doctor."

"It's just a little vomiting."

"How long have you had the vomiting?"

"Just this morning."

"Oh, I thought you've had it for a while, the way you said it."

"So I took some baking soda and water."

"Good."

"So what's doing with you?"

"I'm okay."

"That's what I wanted to know."

"There was a suicide bombing in Jerusalem. I phoned because I was worried."

As his mother was hard of hearing he knew it would be a conversation of non sequiturs.

"I'm not in Jerusalem. I'm in Ramallah."

"There was a suicide bombing in Jerusalem."

"I'm not in Jerusalem."

"I was worried."

"I said I'm not in Jerusalem."

"It's very dangerous in Jerusalem."

Teddy raised his voice. "I'm not in Jerusalem."

"You could get killed there."

"Ma. Turn it on."

"What?"

"Turn it on! Turn on your hearing aid. You haven't heard a word I've said. I'm not in Jerusalem."

"I have an affliction."

Teddy stifled a giggled.

"You don't have an affliction. Just turn on your hearing aid."

He heard some feedback from her hearing aid that sounded like a fax machine.

"Can you hear me now?"

"I can hear you."

"I said I'm not in Jerusalem. I'm in Ramallah."

She heard that for sure, because then she said, "With him?"

"Yes. There are about forty of us here. People from all over the world. A third Jewish."

"Human shields?"

"Some are."

"I don't want to hear about it. I hear enough about it. People are saying terrible things about you here."

"How are you?"

"I'm having some bone loss."

More like hearing loss, he wanted to say.

"And Dr. Peters won't give me extra estrogen."

"What do you mean extra?"

"I don't know. That's what he says. And I've got some uncontrolled twitching in the heart."

"Fibrillation."

"What's fibrillation?"

"It's a quivering of muscle fibrils."

"I have that. I have that. What should I do?"

"Defibrillate."

"He won't give me anything for it. I asked him for a patch, but he won't give me one. He told me he's heard some things about you. Mind you, who hasn't?"

"What's he heard?"

"That you're in the PLO."

"You say it like that's a bad thing."

"Don't be smart."

"Ma, I'm not in the PLO. Actually, there are some Jews in the PLO. Descendants of pre-Zionist Jews who in '48 — "

"Don't pound me with your propaganda," she interrupted him. People are giving your father a very bad time, and he fought for the State of Israel in Herzliya in 1948. He's got into fights here because of you."

"Sammy?"

"Sammy."

"What kind of fights?"

"Physical fights."

"You mean kicking and punching?"

"Kicking and punching."

"Sammy?"

"Sammy. They've slapped a restraining order on him. He can't go to the rink or the Sophisticates."

Teddy laughed.

"He can't go to the card parties."

"Is the restraining order only about the card parties?"

"And he won't go to the curling rink or *shul*. We've been ostracized. Isolated. And my car was impounded."

"The Sophisticates impounded your car?"

"We have to depend on your sister for rides. Or taxicabs, which cost us an arm and a leg. I'm taking it out of your inheritance. And people have seen you on CNN with a Palestinian flag on your T-shirt."

"It's a Gush Shalom T-shirt. With Israeli and Palestinian flags crossed. Even Arafat wears this pin. I'm sorry, for you. They're wrong. They're wrong to attack me and even more wrong to attack Sammy."

"Every time there's a suicide bombing they mention you. Your father's so ashamed."

"I'm not O.J. Simpson."

"O.J. didn't kill Nicole."

"Of course he killed Nicole."

"That's not what the jury said."

"Forget O.J. I'm trying to do some good here."

"You're protecting him! You're protecting Arafat! And he's doing the bombing."

"We were with him this morning and we didn't see him do any bombing."

"I can't believe that."

"Believe it."

"Look, buster, I was born at night, but not last night."

"Ma, he's not doing the bombing."

"He orders them."

"I didn't see him ordering any bombing."

"He sends messages."

"Ma, all his communications are monitored by the Israeli army."

"It's done on TV, with hand signals and gestures."

"Come off it."

"Well, he does nothing to stop them."

"Ma, the man's under house arrest. He can't even go to the toilet."

"He should be arresting the suicide bombers."

"Ma, I told you the man is under house arrest himself."

"He should be stopping the violence. Arresting the suicide bombers."

"How can he arrest someone if he's under arrest, and how can he arrest someone who's already blown himself up?"

"You know what I mean. He could arrest the ones who prepare the attacks."

"He can't. Even if he could he'd have nowhere to put them. There isn't even a jail left standing. The Israelis have bulldozed everything on the ground."

"He could put them underground, six feet underground."

"If Arafat could do it, as you say, while under house arrest, with the few resources he has, then the Israelis could surely do it. Why don't they? They have the run of the place. They have tanks everywhere. Every town is surrounded with razor wire and trenches. Why can't the Israelis stop them?"

"How should I know?"

"Because they can't. No one can. Could the British stop the Irgun from bombing the King David Hotel? No. Did you know there are waiting lists to be suicide bombers? And if Arafat was really responsible, why don't they just arrest him and put him in their own jail? What's stopping them? It doesn't make sense to blame him and yet keep him alive. Unless they keep him alive just to blame him."

"Stop pounding me with your propaganda."

"It's not propaganda. Just think. Is the occupation worth it, yes or no?"

"It's a buffer zone."

"It's the twilight zone. And people live here. And if the Israelis don't want suicide bombers, they should stop the occupation."

"They wanted to end the occupation."

"When?"

"At Camp David. Why did Arafat reject Barak's generous offer?"

"What generous offer?"

"At Camp David, with Clinton."

"That's a canard."

"What's a canard?"

"What you just said: 'Barak's generous offer.'"

"No, I meant what's a canard. What does it mean?"

"A prevarication."

"What's a prevarication?"

"What they say about Barak's generous offer."

"A canard?"

"Yes."

"But what's a canard? Why do you use these words long distance."

"A canard is a falsehood. Deceit. Prevarication."

"You have such a rich vocabulary."

"Don't change the subject. Have you seen this offer? Has anyone seen this offer?"

"I don't have to see it if it exists. They offered him the moon."

"The moon, yes, because they don't have settlements on the moon."

"He offered them ninety-three percent. Ninety-three percent. They don't even deserve that."

"No one knows what they offered. There was nothing written down. But the people who participated, the people who were there, they said that this ninety-three percent was just a series of islands surrounded by Israeli settlements and connecting roads and army checkpoints. If something was offered, verbally, it was pretty shitty."

"And then Arafat ordered the Intifada."

"Not true."

"I read it in the *Jerusalem Post*."

"The *Jerusalem Post*. At home you've always hated right-wingers. You work at the food bank, for Chrissakes. And besides, Arafat doesn't control Hamas. In fact, in the eighties, when the PLO was outlawed, the Israeli government set up Hamas, funded it, like the Americans did Bin Laden in Afghanistan. Now the chickens have come home to roost. It's all the work of the neocons."

"That's neo-*mishegoss*. Arafat controls them all. I'd like to cut his balls off."

"No, he doesn't."

"Yes, he does."

"No, he doesn't."

"Shh, I hear your father coming."

"Where are you?"

"Shh."

"Ma?"

"The coast is cleared."

"Where are you?"

"I'm in the bathroom. Your father would have a conniption fit if he knew I was talking to you on the sly long distance. Now you listen to me. I'm not telling you what to do, I'm just making a suggestion. You have to get out of there. They're going to bomb you."

"How do you know that? Are you in contact with the Israeli defence ministry?"

"I just know it. Because that's what I would do."

"Then why haven't they done so already? They could just come in the front door and arrest him. There are only two rooms here and some sandbags in front."

"Those people won't stop until they've annihilated us."

"Why are you so hawkish? You were against the Vietnam War. I don't get it. Just give them back the occupied territories and be done with it. What do you care?"

"If we give them back the occupied territories they'll want more and more. They'll want Tel Aviv. You can't trust them. Scratch a German, you get a Nazi. Scratch an Arab . . . look at the Mufti of Jerusalem and Hitler."

"Actually there is an Arab I can trust."

"And apparently you've done more than scratching."

"Yes, and underneath is your grandchild."

"Don't get smart with me."

"I'm not getting smart."

"How are you going to raise a child over there?"

There was a pause. Teddy knew that tears were coming.

"There's nothing. No sewers, no roads, no schools, nothing. They live in filth and crap."

"Whose fault is that?" asked Teddy.

"Theirs! They live in muck. They breed in muck. And you'll end up in muck."

When she hit the word *muck* the first time, the anger and frustration reared up in her and she started sobbing, which hurt Teddy, especially long distance.

"It hurts me so much," she heaved, "to think that you're suffering, because of them. How do you go to the toilet there? I've read the toilets are backed up. It must be crawling there."

The sound of an old woman crying is unique, thought Teddy. But he wouldn't relent. He would let her weep for twenty seconds and then he'd break it off. And he did.

"Where did you read that? Not in the *Jerusalem Post*?"

"No. In *Time*. How do you flush the toilets there?"

"It's no picnic. It's like the outhouse at the beach."

"Do you know what a *neshome* is?"

"Yes." He was expecting this part.

"*Neshome* is Yiddish. It means the soul."

"I know that."

"You're taking my *neshome* out."

"Sorry."

"It hurts a mother so much to see her son suffer."

How often she went from the particular to the general, Teddy thought.

"But I'm not suffering. I'm happy. I'm in love."

"And when the love fades for this Palestinian *pritzteh*?"

"Why should it fade?"

"Where did you meet this person? We have no information. Other people know more about what's going on with your life than we do. Marilyn knows more."

"What kind of information do you want?"

"Anything. A bit of information."

"It's funny but when I was in Jerusalem, on the Hagshaomar tour *you* sent me on, they assigned soldiers our age to keep us company, minders, sort of, to take you out pubbing and so on. One of these soldiers, Avi, the nicest guy, he had all these post-Zionist friends —"

"Post-Zionist? What's that?"

"Just what I said — and he invited me to a party in West Jerusalem. That's where I met her. Right there at the party. My Palestinian princess."

"*Pritzteh.*"

"Princess."

"I don't want to hear about it."

"I thought you wanted information."

"I want to hear good things. I want *nakhes*, not nonsense."

"Do you want to hear what happened or not?"

"Alright."

"You're going to let me finish?"

"Finish."

"It was an incredible thing: all of them together, against the occupation. The Holocaust industry has less of an impact here than back home, believe me."

"The only thing industrial about the Holocaust was the numbers of the dead."

"Don't bait me. I thought you wanted information."

"I do."

"Really, she's great. You'll love her. Like I do."

"The way you loved that rabbi's wife."

"It wasn't a real rabbi. And they had an open marriage. At least that's what they told me."

"There's no such thing as open marriage."

"You can say that again."

"And that's not the way the story plays around here."

"Who cares, really?"

"I care. We care. We have to live in the Jewish community here. And the child? You're going to bring him up in all that mess over there? In the *shmutz*, the filth and crap. They don't have sewers. It's crawling there."

"They had sewers. But Sharon dug them up. They even had sewers before the Zionists even came eighty years ago."

"They didn't have sewers. They lived in muck and crap. They had nothing. They came from Egypt to live off what the Israelis built. That's when they had sewers."

"They had sewers. They had irrigation. Read the reports of the British agronomists about Palestine in 1900. And they've been here for thousands of years."

"Ah, the British. Don't give me the British!"

"You think they made up it back then when they wrote about how cultivated the land was over a hundred years ago?"

"You're pounding me."

"I'm not pounding you."

"You're pounding me with your ideology."

"No, I'm not. What about your ideology?"

"Mine's not ideology. It's conviction."

Teddy looked at his watch, which wasn't there.

Anna went on. "Believe you me, when he's ten he'll be throwing stones, he'll be illiterate, and then he'll get shot or he'll end up a suicide bomber. And for what? For nothing. There will never be a Palestinian state. They've missed their opportunity, like always, like Abba Eban said. They don't want peace. Besides, the Jews are there to stay. They won't be budged. You know how many reasons we have to stay?"

"Yes."

"We have six million reasons to stay."

"What do you mean 'we'? You don't live here. You wouldn't live here if they paid you."

"You know what I mean."

"Anyway, what makes you think Aïda and I are going to live here in Ramallah?"

"Where are you going to live? Israel is just as dangerous. More dangerous. You go out for pastry and you get suicide-bombed."

"Well, actually that's not true. Three times as many Palestinians have been killed since Sharon waddled across the esplanade of the Al Aqsa mosque with his 1,000 armed guards."

"He went alone."

"He didn't go alone."

"In the picture in the *Jerusalem Post* he's alone."

"He wasn't alone."

"Anyway, he had the right to go wherever he wanted. That mosque should be open to anyone."

"Did he go to pray?"

"How should I know why he went."

"He went to provoke. And your generous Barak let him."

"Stop pounding me for a second. Just be frank with me. Where are you going to live with this Palestinian *pritzteh* of yours?"

"Princess."

"Okay, princess."

"Maybe here."

"There?"

Anna held on to her heart so that it wouldn't leap out the bathroom window, which it was trying to do.

"You think my *neshome* is a *rozhinke*. Well, it isn't a *rozhinke*. Do you know what a *rozhinke* is?"

"I know."

"A raisin."

"I said I know."

"So you think my soul is a raisin?"

"The expression translates badly into English."

"Okay, have the baby there, because you won't be welcome here, I can tell you that."

"What?"

"You'll be a persona non grata in my house."

"Ma."

"Don't 'Ma' me. I'm going to lie down on the chesterfield now. You've made me very upset."

"Ma."

"You have. I'm going to lie down on the chesterfield. You gave me one heart attack last year, now you're giving me another one. You pound me. You all pound me. You, your father, your sister, your Baba, my brother, you all pound me, you and your canards and your Arafat."

"Ma."

"I'm hanging up."

"Ma."

"What's your business with those people?"

"You don't understand."

"I'm going to the chesterfield. I don't know what to make your father for supper."

"Just go out for supper."

"Where? It's hard for us to go anywhere. Everybody looks at us."

"You don't need those people."

"Those people are our people. They're our friends."

"They're not your friends if they can do this to you."

"You did this to us and you're our son."

"It's not the same thing."

"Are you going to find us new friends?"

"What about Oz?"

"Oz's still in intensive care."

"How's he doing?"

"He's in intensive care. Don't you listen?"

"What's the prognosis?"

"Not so good. He looks like shit."

"He's always looked like shit."

"I give him two weeks."

"What about Molly? Or Sylvia. They can't all hate you just

because of me."

"I'm going to make your father supper. I'm very upset. I'm getting the fibrillation."

"I thought you said you were going to lie down now."

"I'm hanging up now. Do you need money?"

"I'm okay."

"I sent you some black jeans. A 32-leg."

"I'm okay for clothes."

"I'm hanging up now. You've made me very upset. If you're going to have that baby where it's crawling and filthy. In the crap and muck."

"Ma."

"Don't 'Ma' me. I'm hanging up now. I'm addled. You've addled me."

8

After Teddy hung up the phone he reflected on how it had started.

All the kids from the Hagshaomar junket were sitting in a long meeting hall in the basement of the five-star hotel in Jerusalem clapping their hands and stamping their feet shouting, *"Aliyah! Aliyah! Aliyah!"*, smiling to their left and right, giggling uncontrollably at times, as Ariel Sharon waddled to the podium to speak.

Avi, in the last row, one of the soldiers assigned to Teddy, rolled his eyes, and said, "I am not enjoying this."

"Huh?"

"This is like Nuremburg. Just like Nuremburg." Teddy was puzzled by Avi's attitude.

Sharon began his spiel.

"It's pure Riefenstahl. It's Triumph of the Will." Avi said, pulling his tam out of his epaulets, rolling it up, then stuffing it back in.

What?

"Aliyah really just means *colonization.* That's really what they're shouting: 'Colonization! Colonization! Colonization!' Of course, *aliyah* sounds cooler, you get one when you read the Torah, but what they're really shouting is *colonization."*

"They're just expressing their identity," Teddy said.

"At someone else's expense. What kind of identity is that? What about the Palestinian identity?"

Teddy stopped clapping and stomping.

"You think this is a shaggy dog story," said Avi," but it's really a shag-the-dog story. And the Palestinians are the dog."

Sharon paused to drink from his water glass and smiled nervously, generating a hectic gaiety in the air. All the kids started giving the "Yes!" sign, grasping an imaginary clothesline with their fist and dragging it down to chest level.

"Yes! Yes! Yes!"

Sharon smiled again shyly, modestly.

"Yes! Yes! Yes!"

"It's like they're auditioning for a fucking porn film." Avi said to Teddy.

Teddy swallowed.

"This entire fucking country was inhabited by the Palestinians before we came. We expelled 750,000 of them and either flattened their towns and cities or renamed them. You know what the word used for the operation was?"

"No."

"*Ticher* — cleansing. The first ethnic cleansing."

"You're exaggerating a bit, aren't you?"

"It's been proven. By Israeli historians: Benny Morris, Avi Schlaim, Tom Segev, Ilan Pappé. We're still in denial, but it's true. We shouldn't be shouting *Aliyah, Aliyah, Aliyah.*"

Teddy looked at him in shock.

"So what should we be shouting?"

"We apologize." Avi repeated the words, then raised his voice. "We apologize! We apologize! We apologize!"

Avi's chant irritated two kids from New Jersey sitting in the row in front, a boy and a girl, who had fallen in love on the tour. They turned around with the only Hebrew word they knew, "*Sheket,*" spinning out on the swivel of their necks with nasty looks following, but when they saw Avi's uniform they froze in their stares.

"What are you looking at, bitch?" Avi snapped, the hip-hop vocabulary he used with Americans always on the tip of his tongue.

They could not respond verbally, but the girl did smile inanely.

"Are you enjoying this, bitch? I'm not enjoying this," Avi said evenly, looking at them.

The New Jersey kids looked as if flies were trying to settle on their faces, but the girl still kept smiling.

"What are you staring at, ma nigga?" Avi then said to the boy.

"Nothing."

"We're Jewish," added the girl.

"What?" said Avi.

"We're Jewish."

"So?"

"We were trying to listen," said the girl.

"To that fat shit?"

This also took them by surprise.

"We're Jewish," the girl repeated.

"We're both Jewish," said the boy, "and this is our land."

"And he's our prime minister."

"He's disgusting," said Avi.

"He's the King of the Jews."

"He's a fat cunt. A murdering fat cunt, bitch."

The two kids remained frozen, staring at Avi's uniform. They couldn't turn around now if they tried. They were completely paralyzed, the girl's smile so tightly cut into her cheeks that she couldn't relax it.

"What's that smile for, bitch? Relax. You'll leave here feeling like you've just given someone a five-hour blowjob."

The boy gave the girl a signal to face the front again.

"Don't turn around, ma nigga." Avi said.

Now the boy also tried to smile, to break the tension, like in a mugging, but Avi was relentless.

"You come here, you shout these slogans, you get laid, meantime, we are brutalizing the Palestinians. We shoot ten-year-olds in the occupied territories because they don't give us their soccer balls. We bulldoze their houses. We tie them to the front of our tanks. We cut off their water and electricity. Close their schools. We terrorize them night and day."

"No, you don't," the boy said.

"And we do worse things than that."

"No, you don't."

"We drag people we suspect from their homes and shoot them in the street. No arrest. No trial."

"No, you don't."

"The kids we arrest we take them to jail and strip them and then the girl soldiers come in and laugh at their dicks, bitch."

This time she didn't say "no, you don't."

"We drop bombs on apartment blocks where we think a Hamas leader is living and massacre everyone in the building."

"Okay, I heard about that. But you regret the killing of innocent people. The Palestinians rejoice when a suicide bomb goes off."

"So, the fact that we regret killing innocent civilians is justification for killing them?"

"Yes . . . No."

"Which is it?"

"No. But at least you can express yourself here. Israel is the only democracy in the Middle East. Under Arafat . . ."

"Do you think uprooting someone's entire olive grove, bulldozing his house and putting a canvas bag someone has pissed in over his head is an ethical act because its done by a democracy?"

"No. But they're terrorists."

"All of them?"

"No. Yes." The girl was finally having trouble keeping the smile from cracking.

"We're Jewish, I don't even want to have this conversation."

"You keep saying that."

"I do?"

"So what is it, are they all terrorists?"

"They're terrorists."

"They weren't until we started stealing their land and humiliating them. If you knock down a wasps' nest, don't be surprised if you get stung. And don't say the wasps started it."

"They started it," the boy said.

"We started it."

The boy made to face front again.

"Hey, don't turn away from me, ma nigga. Look at me." Then, to the girl, "and lose that fake smile."

The two kids didn't know what to say. The girl stopped smiling. Her jaw was sore and it looked as if she were going to cry.

"That's it. Get rid of that fake American smile. Don't you realize it's so fucking stupid?"

"You're so mean," the girl said. "All you Israelis are so mean."

"Fuck off and turn around then. The bag of *kishke* is talking. Come on. Stop staring at my uniform. Turn around."

They obeyed Avi and the girl started crying.

Avi had released them just in time as Sharon started talking about the corruption of Arafat, how an audit was needed of the Palestinian finances.

"An audit," Avi heckled, but only to Teddy. "Sharon wants an audit. It's like Michael Corleone calling for an audit of Oxfam."

The Hagshaomar kids, most of them thinking about the hip hop party after a supper of hot fish and *knishes*, sensing Sharon had come to another high point of his speech, began once again to chant:

"*Aliyah! Aliyah! Aliyah!*"

Avi couldn't stand it anymore.

"Fuck this, let's go get high," Avi said to Teddy. "That guy's a bloody murderer. More Israelis have been killed since he came to power than in some of our biggest wars. He's been murdering people since he was fourteen years old. Even his own soldiers in '74. Then thousands of Lebanese and Palestinians in the eighties."

Avi made a reefer gesture with thumb and forefinger against his lips to these two others on the tour with Teddy under his charge, one an Argentinean and the other a Catalan, astute boys, but unengaged, who had only come for the free trip, the food and the girls, but not in that order, and couldn't care less about *aliyah*, although they cynically laughed and shouted it.

"We're not even really Jewish," they laughed, shouting "*Aliyah! Aliyah! Ali Akbar!*"

"How did you guys get on the tour?"

"Just our fathers are Jewish," they said, explaining something for the umpteenth time that week.

Avi made the reefer gesture again. They nodded.

Sharon wasn't going to stop speaking just yet, and the four snuck out.

As Teddy closed the back door the sound of "*Aliyah! Aliyah! Aliyah!*" filled his ears.

After a quick call on his mobile phone, a friend of Avi's, Tom, another soldier, picked them up in an old red Deux Chevaux.

"You toke up?" Avi asked Teddy, after they dove into the car, its open doors like the flapping wings of a giant ladybug. Teddy was in the front with Tom while Avi, Carlos, the Argentinean and Carles, the Catalan, with bunched and raised shoulders squeezed in the back.

Tom cranked the volume of Fatlip on the car stereo before licking a joint and lighting it, not forgetting to pop the clutch and shift into a grinding second.

"Listen to this shit, ma nigga."

Tom was on a furlough after two weeks of checkpoint duty and grunt work outside of Nablus. He was lean like a racing dog, aggressive like Avi, and seemed like someone who would never go out of his way to make friends. He had the pallor of the shtetl ghetto, frizzy hair and thick, sharply bevelled lips, and was as white as Art Garfunkel.

"You get into trouble here, you call me," Tom said sincerely, handing the joint to Teddy.

"Why should I get into trouble?"

"Your face. You look like the type of guy who asks for trouble. Just remember, anything happens, you find me."

Teddy took two tokes and passed the joint to Avi who passed it back to the Argentinean everyone on the tour was calling Che, "because Che's mother wasn't Jewish either." And then to Carles, the Catalan, whom everyone was calling Gaudí, "whose mother wasn't Jewish either," and then to Tom. Tom took another toke and started reciting a poem:

> *We celebrate independence*
> *on the backs of another people*
> *we feel completely free*
> *to kick them around*
> *and cut down their trees.*

"Yehonathan Geffen," Tom explained. "You know this poet?"

"No," Teddy said. "I don't know any Israeli poets. I don't know any poets. Period."

"Are you getting off?"

"Uh huh," Teddy said. "But another hit'd be good."

"How come you guys are on this trip? You're not even Jewish."

"I'm Jewish," said Teddy.

"Our fathers are Jewish," said Carlos again.

"We suspect," added Carles.

"They must be scraping the bottom of the barrel."

"The trip was free. The food's great. The girls here put out. And we're dudes in flux," Carlos said, taking a massive hit. "Getting in touch with our Jewish " — long toke — "roots."

"You mean Rastafarian roots."

"Whatever," Carlos said, exhaling with a squishing sound.

Teddy took up the joint and flicked the ash, which fell onto the black muzzle of one of the two Uzi machine guns lying inside an open hamper with hard-boiled eggs, schnitzel, some bottles of beer, half a roast chicken, flake bars and a thermos. Tom was always ravenous because he was always stoned.

"We're going to Sandra's house," Tom said to Avi, passing the joint to Teddy. "They're having a party for Zev."

"Why are you driving so fast?"

"Gotta get there before Zev passes out. Want some more?"

"I shouldn't have any more," Teddy said to Avi, passing him the joint after taking a long heavy hit, just as they curved around a monument bathed in yellow light. They bounced over a speed bump and Carlos banged the crown of his head on the roof. The Uzis jumped up, alarming them all.

"*Mierda puta. Boludo, el tío,*" Carlos said to Carles.

"Hang on."

"*Está gilipollas total.*"

"See that monument? It's Palestinian," said Tom.

Every time they passed an object that had been there before 1948, Tom said, "Palestinian," the way obnoxious back street drivers often say "green light" to daydreamers at the wheel.

Avi leaned over from the back seat and fast forwarded Fatlip till he hit a song he liked.

Avi said: "Tom drives like a taxi driver, fast in the city and slow on the highway."

"See that?" The car swung around another monument at incredible speed for a Deux Chevaux and the Uzis bounced once more. "Palestinian."

They passed an ancient gate lit from below.

"Palestinian."

Then a stone tower.

"Palestinian. Palestinian. Palestinian."

He then folded up the window of the Deux Chevaux and shouted: "This whole bloody city, fucking Palestinian." And like that all the way to Sandra's house.

The car came to a halt, the Uzis jumped one last time. Looming above them was an immense cream stucco building. Teddy slammed the car door shut and stared up. Immense black clouds encased the tower block.

After being buzzed in, they padded down blue broadloom tucked into blue baseboards under yellow walls with baby blue trim.

Sandra, tiny with a big bust under a tight T-shirt, a face full of black freckles, opened the door saying, "Bring the stuff?"

"Yes," said Tom.

"Is it good?"

"Only the best."

Tom was smooth.

Sandra's parents' apartment already smelled of skunk weed and spilled beer and was chock-full of kids: hippies with dreadlocks, clean-shaven soldiers, smart girls and some retro this-and-that. Lambchop was playing on the stereo.

"Smells of feet in here," Tom said.

There they were: the upper end of the food chain, only fifteen kilometres from extreme privation and misery, 72-hour curfews, electricity and water stoppages, checkpoints, closed schools, the works, the spiteful works.

Teddy was puzzled by the normality of it all.

The party was for a mutual friend, Zev, a conscript who was going to jail tomorrow because he refused to serve in the Occupied Territories. Zev had already passed out under the Ikea daybed in the corner, but the party went on anyway. His brother was supposed to take him home but someone had slashed the tires of his car, which sported a bumper sticker against the occupation.

Sandra, barefoot, led the four of them to her bedroom to get "seriously" stoned. Her parents were in London visiting her sister who had married an English guy and bailed out of the Zionist madhouse, she told them. "I doubt she'll ever come back."

All but Teddy settled down cross-legged on Sandra's bedspread, Carlos having gingerly manoeuvred his knees against Sandra's thigh.

Teddy noticed Sandra had a short neck. He had a peek at her T-shirt again, her tits, actually. In the mood for love, he thought.

"I even have my doubts as to whether my parents will come back," she added after a beat.

Tom burst out laughing.

Carlos took the plunge and made his first in a series of moves on Sandra, asking, "Are they post-Zionists, too?"

"Nah," she answered, still unaware of his intentions. "Just cynical. My father always has the same cynical line: the only thing wrong with the Middle East is that it's full of Jews and Arabs. If you got rid of them there would be no problems. Ha, ha, ha."

Tom pulled out his bag of dope and started rolling a joint.

The Argentinean made his second move on Sandra. Parents in London, home alone. He told her he liked her toes.

She still wasn't wise to him and she giggled.

"I like your T-shirt, too."

"Oh, yeah?" she said. "What's so special about it?" she asked.

She had him there because there was nothing special about it.

"Come on, what's so special about it?"

She could see he didn't expect her to repeat the question either.

"It's cool."

"Fuck off."

Sandra's walls were plastered with photographs of Israel, although on closer examination, which is what Teddy was doing, tilting up the lamp attached to her study desk, still a bit too shy to sit on Sandra's bed with the others, Tom setting to work on the weed, with his "Amsterdam technique," he saw that these were actually pictures of pre-'48 Palestine. There was a big photograph of the old towns of Tantura, and Jaffa, Ijlil, Sarafand, Jaba, Ayn Ghazal, Lydda, Ramla.

Tom got the joint going and they all sat in a circle on the bed smoking in silence until Sandra used her stereo remote and flicked on another Lambchop CD.

"What's with all the Lambchop?" Carlos said to Sandra.

"It's my party."

"Lambchop's so melancholic," said Carlos.

He still had designs on Sandra, but was determined to be a bit more suave. Teddy saw how he caught hold of her eyes, held them, made as if to let go, didn't, which brought her eyes closer into his snare, then he released her, feigning disinterest.

"Why are you are so fucked up?" she said to him.

The hinge of his jaw dropped. She had stopped him cold and he put more concentration into the world of dope. "Okay, chill."

"Chill?"

It was then that Sandra's friend Aïda walked into the room and sat with them on the bed, wedging herself between Sandra and Carlos.

"This is our Palestinian Princess," Sandra said. "Aïda."

"A real princess?" asked Carlos, almost smacking his lips.

"That's right."

"What are you doing here?" Teddy asked her. He was now checking out Sandra's CD collection, his head on one side, reading titles.

"My family used to live on this block. Seventy years ago. The house was demolished to build this building. What are you doing here?"

"Helping with the colonization," Tom said, pre-empting him, knowing that Teddy was not going to know what to say.

Aïda had the loveliest high complexion, and was striking in a black miniskirt and grey tights. Emerald earrings matching an emerald cashmere sweater. His mother used to say that only beautiful women could look nice in green, invariably when she wore green herself.

Aïda took her turn and filled her lungs with pot smoke.

Teddy kept staring at the photographs but he really wanted to look at Aïda. His head canted and he looked at her weed-slitted eyes. She was wearing vermilion lipstick. Her straight black hair was combed in a part and tucked up into a bun. It reminded him of photographs of his grandmother's auntie Chassa, the beauty and the Bolshevik in the family, who had been imprisoned in Baku after the 1905 revolution. That was his first dangerous mental transference. The second dangerous transference came hard and fast: she was wearing silver earrings, not gold. Silver was his grandmother's favourite metal. He then noticed Aïda's narrow stockinged feet, the first thing he wanted to touch of hers. He wanted to hold them between his palms. He stopped observing her, in fact, because his imagination was racing far ahead of him.

But she did give him a look before the Argentinian made his move, the latter's lightning-quick reaction to the no-go Sandra situation.

Teddy looked back again at the posters, then back at her.

Aïda looked back at him and it gave him a funny feeling in his stomach. Like being a child again in an elevator.

But the Argentinian had his hooks into her. What Teddy learned about her he picked up from their conversation. Her grandparents were Palestinian refugees, expelled from Jerusalem. Part of the family went to live in refugee camps near Ramallah. Her parents were raised in Lebanon and then settled in London. They separated when she was fourteen. She grew up between London with her father and Paris with her mother. She was now working in Ottawa as a research lawyer on the World War II War Crimes Commission. She had come to see her ailing grandmother in Ramallah, to bring her some packages and stuff.

The Argentinean made a crack about if he could be the big bad wolf.

Should he cut in?

They got on to politics. The Argentinean said that things would never, ever get better. And that he would stick by that.

She neither nodded nor shook her head, just stared through her slitted eyes rotating her head slowly to snag Teddy's eye and smile.

Teddy got that funny kid-in-an-elevator feeling again, funnier than the last time, actually.

Should he make a move? Should he?

He could wait. There's still a lot of time, he thought. The party's not ending just yet.

9

She wasn't in the crowd. Damn! Maybe the Argentinean was with her.

He had been scanning the hundreds of faces, asking himself why he hadn't reacted last night, talked to her longer.

Aïda.

He was in a taxi with Sandra, Zev's brother and Avi. The taxi had crawled to the first checkpoint. At every bend in the road, the driver got on his cell and phoned to see if the coast was clear or if there were snipers.

They passed houses with blistering fronts and then the odd pile of rubble where a house had been demolished. Sometimes there were children playing in the ruins.

As they approached the next checkpoint, the driver made with his hand and everyone went quiet. Teddy held his breath.

"What's the big deal?" someone said.

"Checkpoints are not toll booths."

At the first checkpoint, a soldier had poked the nozzle of his Uzi in the window and all their shoulders jumped in unison.

Another soldier was holding a litre-and-a-half plastic bottle of Coke and taking sips.

They were forced to get out, run through the checkpoint, walk a kilometre, and then get another taxi.

It was a warm, dry day. The crowd of mostly young Israeli peaceniks had congregated in the middle of nowhere it seemed. They seemed fresh and full of vigour. Many of them carried knapsacks and plastic water bottles from which they swigged. T-shirts prevailed. The younger the girls, the more belly was exposed. There was an atmosphere of celebration.

The demonstration started moving slowly towards Salem, an

army camp with Palestinian detainees from the latest roundup. At the back were ten aid trucks carrying food to Jenin.

An old Palestinian lady, wizened to a husk, who was trying to get to the next village, halted the demonstration.

She explained where she was going and asked for support. Her robe was shiny from wear and her shoes shabby, barely clinging to bony feet. She was carrying two plastic shopping bags.

And so the demonstration had to move even slower, with the old lady at the front. It was mostly made up of Jewish Israelis, some Arab Israelis and a contingent of foreigners, some Canadians, a few British and Americans and some Catalans. They chanted two slogans in Hebrew: "The refuseniks are heroes!" and "Corrupt occupation!"

When they got within about a hundred yards of the camp the tank turrets swivelled and aimed their cannons at them. The demonstrators stopped. The old lady kept on walking ahead, oblivious to the fact that the demonstrators were no longer marching with her.

Some people called to her but she must have been deaf for she kept on walking.

Aïda appeared in front of Teddy, her skirt billowing, violet shadows under her eyes.

"Hi!"

The funny feeling returned. So funny that he couldn't think of anything to say right away. The wind blew her hair and she brushed it from her eye. Finally, Teddy hit on something to say.

"Hi!" And then, "My parents would kill me if they knew I was here."

"No they wouldn't."

"How do you know?"

"If they were parents like that, you wouldn't be here."

"Actually, they sent me here. Well not here, exactly."

"Why's that?"

"I had some problems back home. Relationship problems."

"Have you worked them out?"

"I think so."

"So you left your tour just to be here."

"And all the gratis five-star hotels down to Eilat."

"Tom convinced you."

"No. You did."

"We hardly talked last night."

"Didn't have to."

"Are you in this for the girl?"

This stopped him short. He didn't know if he should admit it. Last night he spent hours in longing, deliciously awake thinking about her, yet he hadn't been able to conjure up her face, try as he might. This is the one, he had thought. You know it is, you just do.

"Sounds bad if I say yes, but it might sound like a lie if I said no."

"So which is it?"

This also threw him.

"Yes."

"I'm glad you said that."

"You are?"

"Can't believe your luck?"

"No."

"Will you come back to Sandra's tonight? I'm staying there. Or are you going to try to catch up with the tour?"

"I'll be there."

A crackle of loudspeaker talk was heard. The demonstrators were on the move again, in spite of the tank turrets.

Once about ten yards from the camp gates, the demonstrators stopped again. The old lady had disappeared, engulfed in the crowd.

A flap in the border hut, draped with the Beitar football team flag, opened in a wall and a barrel-torsoed guy started waving to the demonstrators, clapping his hands above his head, waving and throwing kisses in support. Judging from his age, he must have been a reservist. A roar of approval went up from the crowd.

The reservist jumped on top of the sandbags and waved again, booming in Hebrew, "Corrupt occupation! Corrupt occupation!"

The crowd chanted back with approval: "Corrupt occupation! Corrupt occupation!"

There was a silence for a moment. The reservist adjusted his buttpack then wailed again: "Corrupt occupation! Corrupt occupation!"

"Corrupt occupation! Corrupt occupation!" the demonstrators answered back. They surged forward a few yards, until the tank turrets swivelled again.

After a few minutes, the reservist's commanding officer came out. "Bevakashá, Mordechai!"

The reservist jumped down and the commanding officer gave him hell for a few minutes and sent him back behind the flap.

No one knew what to do or what would happen next.

Suddenly another soldier, young, with movie-star looks, came out from under the flap of the guard post and gave the crowd the British two-finger finger.

The crowd roared in defiance.

He tugged on the buckles of a pair of Blackhawk sternum straps, pulling his buttpack higher, pointed successively at three people at the front of the demonstration, in a sort of mock gay nasal English, "Fuck you! Fuck you! And fuck you!"

It was hard to believe that the reservist from before and this smooth-looking guy were in the same army. He pointed the muzzle of his M-16 assault rifle in the air, stared at the front line of the demonstrators, then levelled it.

"We're going to fuck you good!"

"No need. Your wife did last night" shouted a trim, fit, white-haired man, maybe seventy years old, standing at the front of the demonstration.

After laying down his rifle, the soldier humped over the sandbags and landed on the dirt in front of the white-haired old man, who had just moved forward to meet him by ducking under the barrel of the tank's cannon. The soldier adjusted his buttpack and assault vest and came face to face with the old guy, staring at him with grim amusement.

There was a standoff.

"What did you say about my wife?"

"Since you're doing your duty for the occupation, someone had to do your conjugal duties."

"You know what it's like to be shot?"

"Yes," the old man said. "I was shot in the stomach four times in 1948 when I was eighteen."

"Fucking liar."

"Would you like to see where?"

"I'm not interested."

"Don't you want to see?"

"I told you I'm not interested where you were shot."

The old man untucked his shirt to show his scars and followed the Israeli soldier around until he would look at him. The soldier finally glanced at the scars, the size of burnished lipstick kisses, then raised his fist to strike him.

"You'll see that I am immune to your threats," the old man said.

"The fuck you are."

"The fuck I am."

The blow came down, and so did the old man, who sprang up from the dust, grabbing the soldier's assault vest and pulling him down to scuffle in the dust.

The commanding officer came out again and pulled the young soldier away from the old man and ordered him back inside. The flap with the Beitar football team flag lifted and swallowed him too.

"Are you going to let the convoy through?" the old man, shouted to the commanding officer.

"This has been declared a military reserve area."

"Since when?" the old man tut-tutted, lifting his chin and lower lip. "It wasn't yesterday."

"Since this morning," the commander tut-tutted back.

"Let's see the order."

The commanding officer disappeared behind the flap.

The demonstrators waited three hours for the commanding officer to come out from under the flap with a document he didn't have. In the meantime, Jewish settler SUVs and sedans had been allowed through. In response, the crowd sat down on the road and stopped the settler traffic as well. It wasn't long before military vehicles arrived at the camp bearing the document declaring the zone to be a military reserve for the next twenty-four hours. The demonstrators were to be cleared and the settlers allowed through.

The commanding officer showed the demonstrators the document.

"Okay, clear out," he said.

"We just want you to let the supply trucks through. Then we'll leave," said the old man, who appeared to be one of the protest's leaders.

"Turn around. Even if we let the supply trucks through they'll be stopped up ahead and sacked. So just go home."

A tall soldier from the regiment that had just arrived stepped into the conversation, looking stern. A camera shutter clicked, then another, which slowed him down.

"You people going home, then?" he said, looking at the photographer, suddenly accompanied by a Palestinian cameraman.

"Once you let the trucks through."

"We're not letting the trucks through. This is a closed military zone."

"How come they're going through?" The old man gestured towards the settlers' vehicles.

"They have authorization."

"Show me."

"I don't have to show you anything."

"You just showed us this document."

"A courtesy to you. Now show some courtesy to me and go home."

"As soon as you let the trucks through."

"We're not letting the trucks through."

"Then we're not leaving."

The solider left the conversation.

The commanding officer said, "You'd be better off listening to me than dealing with him."

"If it's our welfare you're worried about, we'd all be better off if you let the trucks through."

"Can't."

"Can't or won't?"

"Can't and won't."

The officer withdrew to talk to the solider and the two of them disappeared behind the flap. The settlers' car horns were honking in rhythm.

Suddenly there was a chemical tang in the air. The first tear gas canister had been lobbed, followed by another. A shot rang out from the direction of the newly arrived soldiers, and the crowd retreated behind the aid trucks.

In the panic Teddy got separated from Aïda. Nauseous and foggy-eyed, he wandered inside the battered gas cloud until he stumbled over a clod of earth and down into a ditch where some settlers who had gotten out of their cars, ready to help the soldiers, were now just smoking, having decided to watch the fray instead. Teddy's arrival gave them the chance to execute their original plan. They pulled him up off the ground by his shirt collar, which choked him until his shirt ripped down the front. One of them slapped him. He fell to the ground again and found himself being kicked.

He was protecting his head and trying to shout at them in English to stop, but fear filled his mouth with saliva. He took a stinging hit above his eye that made him feel as though he was bleeding from his ears.

"Get — the — fuck — out — of — here," one of the settlers yelled, getting the hour's wait out of his system, kicking his point syllable by syllable into Teddy's thigh. The guy had a New Jersey accent.

The reverberative wallops set his teeth chattering.

"Corrupt occupation," Teddy managed to mumble, "corrupt occupation."

"You and the Arabs, you're the occupiers," someone said with a Boston accent, his knitted *kipe* askew, hanging from the bobby pin.

The settlers were coughing now too, as the wind veered, and were slowing down their assault.

Teddy got to his knees, scraping his shin on a chalky stone.

"Alright, alright. I'm going."

One of the settlers gave him a kick in the ass and he landed on his elbows.

"Fuck out of here!" said the guy with the Boston accent.

"Are you from Boston?" Teddy managed to ask, legs splayed, lifting his head out of the dry ditch side.

"Maybe I am."

They surrounded him again and got back to their kicking.

"Stop kicking me."

"Maybe. What are you doing here?"

"I'm on the Hagshaomar tour."

"Stop kicking him!"

The kicking stopped, but there was no apology.

Teddy rose to his feet and looked at the faces of his assailants. The faces were very North American and even seemed familiar. There was a kid maybe fourteen or so with them. His eyes were bloodshot from the gas.

"What are you doing here?" the Boston guy said, more with curiosity than reproach.

"I told you. I'm on a tour sponsored by the WZO."

"You should be in Eilat, not South Hebron."

"I got separated from the group. And wound up in the occupied territories because one of our soldier chaperones brought us here."

"The only occupied territories are the Jewish territories occupied by Arabs. This is the *Yesha*."

It was then that Teddy noticed their Uzi machine pistols, and that Tom was walking towards them, looking taller than last night. Wearing a different uniform, with the Lavi regiment insignia, ironed to perfection on his sleeve.

Tom tried to talk to the guy from Boston in Hebrew, but the guy from Boston would only talk to him in English. Tom didn't seem impressed by the machine pistols and spoke curtly to the settler.

"Did you touch this guy?"

"Touch him? We kicked the shit out of him."

"Here in this ditch?"

"Yeah."

"What if I kick the shit out of you?"

The settler and his buddies didn't expect this.

"You want to get the shit kicked out of you? And you? What about you?" This last bit he said in Hebrew to the teenager.

"I said what about you?"

"No," said the kid.

Teddy couldn't understand why these armed guys were so intimidated by Tom, who was only carrying a bottle of water, with which he was now flushing out his eyes.

"Did they hurt you?"

"They were a bit rough, but everything's been cleared up."

Tom wiped his face with the back of his sleeve.

"Tuck your shirt in," Tom told him, and the kid obeyed.

"Now tell me, why were you kicking this guy?"

The kid said nothing, looking this way and that, at the adults, baffled.

Tom then picked the kid up by the hood of his sweatshirt and swung him around.

"You're going to rip the hood. My mum just bought it."

Tom swung him around again and again, holding him by the hood. Teddy heard the ripping quite distinctly. So did everyone. But the men didn't make a move.

"Why were you kicking this guy?"

"I wasn't kicking him," the kid spoke up, just as he passed Tom on his flight.

"Were you watching?"

"Yeah."

"Which ones were kicking this guy?"

"Tom, it's okay."

"No, it's not okay."

"I don't know," said the kid, spinning through space.

When the hood ripped off completely the kid fell into the ditch and scrambled up to his feet, then wobbled forward.

"Come here," said Tom.

Tom steadied the kid by his hair, and gave him a good dig in the chest with three fingers.

"They were all kicking him," the kid said, looking at his hood in the ditch.

"We didn't mean any harm."

"By kicking him?"

"We weren't kicking him that hard."

"I'm alright, Tom."

"For fuck's sake," said the Boston guy.

Tom backhanded the Boston guy. The slap was louder than it was hard, yet it drew a heave out of him.

"You were all kicking him in this ditch?"

The Boston guy moved backwards out of Tom's backhand swipe until he had his back up against the SUV. Tom let go of the fourteen-year-old, came up quickly behind the Boston guy and thumped the guy's sternum with his knuckles, as if he was knocking aggressively at someone's door.

"You were kicking him in this ditch?"

Tom thumped him again, harder, but at too close range to hurt. The Boston guy was frozen. Bobbing a bit, looking to get around Tom, but realizing that he was pinned to the SUV. His friends didn't move to defend him. Tom bore down on him.

"You're the cause of all our problems. If it weren't for you settlers, there'd be peace. People are getting killed just to defend you shits."

"God gave this . . ."

Tom thumped him again on the sternum, pressing into him.

"Sorry," the Boston guy said.

"You're a shame. You're not worth punching in the face. Why don't you go back to your country."

The Boston guy was dying to say something.

"I swear to the Torah that . . ."

Tom gave him a fast stab to the sternum again and he shut up.

"So?"

"So."

"So, what's it going to be?"

The others started piling into the SUV.

"Get out of here!" Tom said, lunging at him one last time.

As they drove off Teddy stared at Tom.

"What?" said Tom to Teddy.

"I'm in awe."

"Don't be. In a land of bullies, never be bullied. If you are, you're lost."

10

Teddy looked at Tom afresh. He saw his ruddy cheeks, thick lips, thin frizzy hair. He'd be bald in ten years.

"Why were they so intimidated by you?"

"They thought I was from the Lavi regiment."

This was supposed to be self-evident. Teddy didn't pursue it.

"It's the settlers," Tom said. "And their *Yesha*. Wouldn't you agree they're fascist scum? Coming here from fucking Boston. Fucking university towns."

"I would."

"Thank you."

Teddy hobbled alongside Tom up out of the ditch. His body was starting to ache.

"So now you understand?"

"I do."

"I'm glad."

"But there are more of them than you. And they have the support of the government, the army, the Shin Bet, the government of the United States, the CIA, the Israeli population at large, the international Jewish community and my parents."

"Don't forget the silence of the rest of the world."

"Believe me, if my parents saw this, they would change their minds."

"Would they?"

"Yes. They just get the wrong kind of information. When I tell them what I've seen . . ."

"They won't believe you."

"Yes, they will. They're honest people. They've always rooted for the underdog. My mother thinks O.J. is innocent."

"They won't believe you. They wouldn't believe it if they saw it with their own eyes."

"They'll believe me."

"No, they won't. The lie has been lodged too deeply."

"But if the Jews don't change, there's no hope. The Palestinians have nothing."

"They have the one thing we don't have."

"Which is?"

"They're in the right."

He picked up a stone and chucked it at a settler pick-up truck speeding by. The driver slammed on the brakes, rolled down his window and looked back at Tom, who just waved him on.

"No matter what atrocities the suicide bombers commit, they'll still be in the right. We know it and they know it. In the end, it's the hard thing that gives way. This crap occupation is getting too expensive, the ideal of Greater Israel is so stupid anyway, and it will collapse."

"How can you be so sure?"

"The Palestinians will never give up."

"How do you know?"

"Come with me."

Oz was playing solitaire all tubed up. Sammy just sat beside him watching, his eyes watery. He rubbed them slowly with the lower inside of his palm.

"Red seven under the black eight."

"Didn't see that."

"It was right there. Now you can put the ace up."

"You're right," Oz said, lifting his finger to his cheek and bringing it down characteristically.

"How's it going, Sammy?"

"I can't even go to the curling rink."

"Did they let you back into the Sophisticates?"

"Yes, but you should see the dirty looks. I can't go there either." But why were they talking about him. It was Oz who was really trapped. "Don't worry about me, Oz. It'll pass."

"Let's hope so."

"We should be worrying about you."

"You're right."

"But don't you worry," Sammy said. "We'll get you out of here."

"One way or another."

Teddy and Tom couldn't find Aïda amidst the people taking refuge behind the aid trucks, well back from the gas. It seemed that almost everyone had dispersed. He remembered, though, they had a date tonight back at Sandra's.

Someone noticing Teddy's tattered shirt pulled a Gush Shalom T-shirt out of its plastic wrapper and threw it to him. He put it on over what was left of his shirt.

Tom had promised to take him somewhere. But he didn't know where.

For a while they just loped down the empty road, then trudged across a rubbly field until they came to a dusty house on the outskirts of a village. The sun was setting.

Tom knocked on the door and he was let in by an unshaven youth in a wheelchair, Adreez, who out of the wheelchair, he knew, would have been tall and sleek. A stout, raw-faced woman in a headscarf and a long neon blue burnoose came out of the kitchen, smiled, but was not introduced. She sounded out the situation and went back into the kitchen. Tom and Adreez spoke in Hebrew for a while, feeling relaxed.

"I dynamited his house," Tom said, "with him in it."

"Why?"

"Orders. The government wanted their land to expand a settlement. Now they're here. They have relatives in Los Angeles who want them there, but they won't go. They refuse to leave. That's why they'll win."

Adreez's mother returned with some tea and sesame seed cookies and sat silently on a high-backed sofa, rubbing her chalky palms.

Teddy had forgotten how hungry and thirsty he was, even that he had had a headache since getting kicked in the ditch.

Adreez asked Teddy how he had got a black eye, which Teddy hadn't realized had become visible.

Tom told him the story and Adreez laughed, raising his hands to his forehead so jerkily that he pulled his catheter out. Then he roared with laughter as urine sprayed the room.

His mother put her hands to her cheeks in despair and then anger, as if she was going to smack him, but then she just cried.

Teddy offered to do the recatheterisation, and had a feeling for a second that he was showing off or compensating.

"No, we'll ring an ambulance," said Adreez.

"That could take hours," Tom told him.

"I'm a nurse," Teddy said.

"We have nurses, " Adreez said. "This is not Africa."

"I know."

"But for a moment there you thought you would have to do it. Look, we live in cities here. It's logical we have the medical expertise."

"Yes, I just thought . . ."

"You Westerners, you are wanting in logic." Teddy admired Adreez's arch British locutions.

"Right, but I just thought it wouldn't take me long, if you have a new tray."

"I was just taking a piss."

"I knew it."

"Yeah, sure."

"No new tray. The ambulance is the only solution."

Teddy looked at the catheter that Adreez was holding in his hand. It was an Aetna indwelling catheter which seemed to have a malfunction in the balloon or had been obstructed.

"How often do you change the catheter?"

"About once per month, if that is possible. Mobility is difficult for me," said Adreez, laughing.

"Maybe we should call an ambulance. He should be refitted in a sterilized environment. Or maybe you've got an insertion tray?"

Adreez shook his head. "There is no insertion tray."

Teddy took off Adreez's vinyl leg bag and checked to see if it had a gel matrix. He noticed at that point that Adreez's penis was leaking urine. His mother brought a towel.

"What should we do?" Teddy asked.

"Well, for one thing, he shouldn't drink any more tea," Tom said.

Teddy examined the drainage and thought that Adreez had some sort of cystitis.

"Hospital would be a good idea."

They sipped tea and waited. Adreez's mother adjusted the shutters. Blades of the last vermilion sunlight slipped through.

The ambulance arrived in about an hour and Tom, having to return to his unit, said good-bye at the ambulance doors.

"You go with them. Sit up front with the ambulance driver. You'll be the human shield. This way you should get to the hospital in about four hours. Without you there's no telling when you'll arrive, or if you'll arrive."

"Human shield?"

"You've got the T-shirt for it."

"Hey, don't leave me on my own."

"I'll give you my cell number. If anything happens, call me."

So began their journey to the nearest hospital, in Ramallah. What should have taken twenty minutes took almost four hours, as Tom predicted. It required taking bumpy by-roads and passing three checkpoints. At each checkpoint, they all had to get out of the ambulance for body searches. Adreez had soaked the towels they had diapered him with and the soldiers were not pleased by the smell.

At the last checkpoint they were made to wait. During that time, Teddy checked the supplies in the ambulance to see if he could do the operation, although he found a catheter tray and some irrigation tubing, there wasn't enough sterile saline or water. He also thought it would be a better idea to use an irrigation solution with antibiotics, but there was nothing of the kind. He grew impatient.

After about ninety minutes he had had enough of waiting and approached the soldiers at the checkpoint. He noticed, for the first time, the rifle barrels sticking out of the sniper posts.

"Can we go through now?"

"You, the human shield?"

"Yes, I'm the human shield. Can we go through?"

"No."

He got back in the ambulance and they waited for another half hour.

The snipers fired into the air and a soldier whipped open the back of the ambulance doors.

"OK, now the dogs can go," he said.

The ambulance driver turned the engine over.

"No! Not you, I said dogs!"

The ambulance driver turned off the motor and after a rumble it sounded as if the engine had dropped to the ground.

"Okay, now humans can go."

The ambulance driver, tilting his chin so he could see the soldier through the rear view mirror, started the engine again and scraped into first gear.

"No! I said humans."

Still not having taken his eye off the mirror, the driver took his foot off the clutch and the motor thudded and died.

Teddy turned to look at the soldier, which made the driver nervous.

"Why have you kept us here so long?" asked Teddy, rising, bending to get out of the ambulance.

The soldier ignored him.

Adreez tugged Teddy daintily by the sleeve of his shirt.

"Why are you doing this?" Teddy asked the soldier.

"Teddy," Adreez called softly from the ambulance as Teddy stepped out, stretching his legs.

Teddy looked at the soldier, who couldn't have been more than eighteen and who wasn't paying attention to him.

"What's with this sick joke? Or are you just a prick?" Teddy said, keenly aware of the sniper posts, the guns and gear on the soldier, the blood rushing to his own face.

"Just a prick. We have to be."

"You have to be or you want to be?"

"Depends. Me, I want to be. You don't know these people."

"And what do you know about them?"

"Just what I have to know."

"And what do you have to know?"

"That they're not really here."

"What do you mean they're not really here?"

"For me, they don't exist. I don't see them. They're like people in a dream. One day, they'll be gone. So I don't think about them as real. It makes life easier."

"For whom?"

"Who do you think?"

Back in the ambulance Teddy talked to Adreez about external urinary catheters.

"You really believe this is Africa, don't you?"

"Have you tried them?"

"Of course, I've tried them. All types."

Teddy looked a bit shocked.

"I told you," Adreez said, "this isn't Africa."

"What was the problem?"

"First I had the non-sticky kind with the wrap. Big mess. Then the latex, something called the Texas catheter, but I got a rash. So then I changed back."

"You should try Clear Advantage. You can wear them for twenty-four hours. Put on an aloe gel first."

"Thanks for the tip."

A half hour later the back doors to the ambulance opened again. The soldier poked his gun barrel in.

"Okay, bugger off."

The ambulance wheels bounced in and out of potholes until they finally made it to the hospital in Ramallah. The city looked ravaged. Deep tank tracks had pocked the asphalt. Small craters exposed damaged sewer pipes. The solid urban texture was pocked by gaps filled with mounds of rubble where houses once stood. When they arrived at the hospital, Adreez was rolled out of the ambulance and wheeled through a throng of impassioned visitors awaiting news of family and friends shot in the latest army incursion.

Teddy waved and Adreez, going cross-eyed, in his best George Bush imitation, shouted, "Leave no cripple behind."

Teddy smiled as Adreez disappeared. He would never see him again, and the encounter, he would later realize, was like so many he would have there.

Off to one side there was a group of people he recognized from the noon day protest, but Aïda was not among them. He felt sure she was back at Sandra's by now.

They dragged him and a small crowd along to the Mukata, on

which, rumour had it, the army was about to make an attack.

Odd decision, really, tagging along like that. Knowing that he had to be back at Sandra's that night for something on which the rest of his life might depend.

But he found the pull of the crowd irresistible. Having seen how his presence at the checkpoints with the ambulance did in fact make a difference, he thought he was somehow invulnerable, if not invincible.

The lights of bulldozers and at least a dozen tanks flanking the Mukata lit up what was left of the building and the throng of protesters in front of it.

When he reached the vast esplanade of rubble, he fell behind a group of Israeli human shields speaking before the spotlights of a CNN reporting team. The lights held him in thrall as he listened to the articulate white-haired spokesman from the afternoon being interviewed, an interview that would never be aired, he thought. For a brief moment he saw the lens of the camera panning left to right. He stared the cameraman down and it panned away. Suddenly \a pair of F-16s above shattered the sound barrier.] It made his heart muscles quiver. Surely he would die. Everyone around him cowered in fear. The cameraman, a guy in his fifties, slipped off his shoulder video unit and crouched. It was duck and cover as two more F-16s swooshed down and belted out another pair of sonic booms. There was panic now and people bumped into each other as they rose off the ground from crouching positions.

Surely he must die.

But no bombs were dropped, as everyone soon realized. The sonic pop had pierced the massive bruise around his eye and dazed him with a pain that scraped against the inside of his skull.

He finally let out a bellow of fear.

Some of the PA police let off rounds into the air, laughing in relief or maybe anger, it didn't matter anymore.

The cameraman humped the video unit back on his shoulder as he straightened out.

Teddy surveyed what could have been carnage, but which just looked like a mosh pit, thousands of arms up in the air, shaking their fists.

The CNN reporter approached him and asked him who he was, where he was from.

"You a cop?"

"What?"

"You a cop?"

"No."

"What's your name? Where are you from?" Teddy was a bit shocked by his own aggressiveness.

"Hey, I'm asking the questions."

The CNN reporter was a funny looking, tiny, freckled British guy with a patch of fawn hair in the way of bangs that he flicked back expertly and who could only talk, it seemed, when he rose on the balls of his feet at the beginning of a sentence and fell back down on his heels for the punctuation.

"What are you doing here? Why are you standing outside the Mukata? Do you think they will attack Arafat tonight? Deport him? Kill him?"

Teddy shrugged. "How should I know?"

"What are you doing here? You're wearing a Gush Shalom T-shirt. Are you a member of that organization?"

"No. Someone just gave it to me. Some settlers ripped my shirt."

"What do you hope to accomplish by being here?"

"Nothing."

"Then why are you here?"

"I'm not sure."

It was like conversing with a machine gun.

"Do you think suicide bombing is justified?"

"Explainable maybe."

"Could you explain it to Americans back home after 9/11?"

"I doubt you'd give me enough air time." Now he was talking like Tom.

"What would you tell the parents of the Jewish child on the bus who was blown to bits this afternoon?"

So that's what this was all about.

"Corrupt occupation," Teddy said, in Hebrew.

"What?"

"Corrupt occupation," Teddy said, in English. Definitely sounding like Tom.

"That's it? Corrupt occupation?"

"That's it. Corrupt occupation. Two words. Would you have air time for that?"

"Wrap."

The reporter turned his back on Teddy as you would after you flushed a toilet.

"Some tic you've got there?" Teddy said, almost shouting at his back amid the din.

The cameraman sniggered, bouncing the video unit up and down.

"What?" the report asked, not yet turning around.

"Some tic."

The reporter wheeled about. "What?"

"That thing you do, standing on tip-toes and then falling back on your heels."

The reporter reddened.

"Bugger off."

"Don't you ever watch yourself?"

The reporter ignored him and spoke to his assistant, with whom he was discussing his positioning for his broadcast. The assistant inched him into position and just as he was about to commence ...

"Don't you ever watch yourself on TV?"

The reporter reddened again with irritation.

"I'm trying to work here."

"Try doing it without rising on your tiptoes. Just for me. It would be like a signal. I would know that you were saying hi. Just once."

"Would you just bugger off. We're going live here!"

The small crowd that had formed to listen to the interviewer screamed with laughter, which helped relax the tension created by the Israeli jet fly-bys.

The reporter began a run through of his piece with professional aplomb, rising on his tiptoes and falling back on his heels. The little crowd laughed.

The Palestinian kids, with their enormous smiles, and some of the Israeli human shields began imitating the reporter's tic. When the reporter rose, they rose and hooted softly. When he came down on his heels so did they, sighing, slowing, dropping the hoot an octave, as if they were riding a roller coaster.

The kids looked at one another and started laughing. They said one word to each other, which Teddy didn't get, but thought must have been Arabic for "asshole".

The CNN guy got the signal; he was going live. He began his report, rising on the balls of his feet. This time a small group of women shields, mostly Americans, surrounded him. The heaviest one in the group gave the reporter a disco bump and knocked him out of the shot. Her friends held up a sign and shouted its contents: "End the occupation!" The Palestinian kids roared.

"Jesus, I'm live here."

The women shields were delighted. One of them wiped her eyes, giving Teddy a wink. He winked back.

The women flashed a placard which the assistant wrenched out of their hands.

The reporter ordered his team to move away, but the kids followed them, the women shields followed, and so did Teddy.

It wasn't long before the rapid thumping of a US Apache helicopter appeared in the sky, which meant the F-16s had gone off elsewhere.

The reporter was unable to run his report so they decided to broadcast the interview with Teddy and then try again in a half hour.

The huge crowd started shouting at the helicopter and then the tanks slowly encroached another ten yards. No one ran off. The mass moved in closer together, swallowing the reporter, his team and equipment before they could sneak off. Surely Teddy would die without seeing Aïda.

He wanted to see Aïda and he wanted to die.

13

A sleepy-voiced Sandra buzzed him in and pointed out Aïda's room. Apparently they had discussed the affair and Aïda had been loaned the parents' room.

The room had a lot of satin, much in the style of a demimondaine who had either lived in Dallas, or had watched *Dallas* before decorating the apartment in the seventies.

It was almost four in the morning.

"Is that you?"

"It's me."

"Come here, I can't see you."

Teddy went over the bed and sat down on the edge, surprised that she had waited for him.

"Why are you crying?" he said.

"I'm just sad." She said this in a totally unaffected way.

"Why?"

"Neurosis."

"I sort of got detained. It was hard to make it back."

"I'm glad you're here."

"Stop crying."

"I can't help it."

"What's wrong?"

"I don't know. I'm just happy." She was also unaffected when she said this. "I'm a romantic."

"Curable or incurable?"

"With you, curable, I hope."

"So stop crying."

"I can't. I'm too happy now."

"You're sad, you're happy. What's it going to be?"

"Both."

That was okay with him, really.

Their faces were only inches apart. They studied each other. She raised a slender hand to touch his cheek. He could see himself fully reflected in her.

"Ouch."

"What's the matter?"

"I got a bit roughed up today. My eye is swollen."

She cupped his face. "You're lovely," she said. She raised her hands and flipped his hair off his forehead and tucked it back behind his ears.

Teddy thought that no one he had ever met, or ever would meet, was — would be — like this girl. He liked all this emotion — and the clash of emotions — in her. He thought he would be the one to turn this sadness around. Yes, he would be the one for her as she was the one for him. Everything was so clear now. He'd never miss a night with her if he could help it.

Bliss filled the night, or what was left of it, that and shuffling and tender shoving, for he was sore all over, and rasping sheets, gurgling; listening to her breath.

In the morning, while she was showering and he lay in bed, listening to his own breath, he thought: so that was bliss and this is bliss. It was odd that such a word existed, especially here.

When she came out of the shower, her black hair combed, still wet, she sat on the edge of the bed, her back towards him, and asked: "What are we going to do?"

"Today?"

"No. I don't mean today."

"I was hoping you'd say that."

The night they had shared had allowed him to be known, and he thought: I want to sleep with her every night of my life and be known like this. I want her to hold my hand when I die, with her acknowledgement before I depart, that she had known me. That's what he should say. None of that getting to know each other, that modern coyness, the calculations.

"I was thinking marriage," he said. "Fuck it. Marriage or something like it. Definitely."

She lay down, her cheek propped on her palm, her elbow at a right angle, facing his profile, the hem of her bathrobe having ridden up to her round thigh. He caressed it.

"What will your parents think?" she asked.

"No problem. They'll adore you. They're great. They're fair people."

"But I'm Palestinian."

"Believe me, they won't mind."

"You're sure?"

"I know them. What about yours? We're the villains here."

"Dad lives in London now, Mum in Paris. Nothing fazes them. They're thoroughly cosmopolitan. They pride themselves on having Jewish friends. My Dad dresses like an English dandy."

"Edwardian?"

"Edward-Saïdian."

"Have you known many boys?"

"Some."

Satisfactory response.

"And you?" she probed. "Many girls?"

"A few."

"I'd say more than a few. You seem to know what you're doing."

"Was it that good?"

"Let's just recall Julien Sorel: 'His virtue was equal to his happiness.'"

"I loved that book."

"I'm sure you did. But I'm not a big fan of Julien Sorel."

"You're not?"

"I prefer Fabrice, from *The Charterhouse of Parma*. Fabrice doesn't have such a chip on his shoulder, isn't so mean. He's just loving and lovely."

"And he doesn't murder his lover."

"Definitely a plus. Anyway, back to my third degree. So, how many girlfriends, ex and current, floating around in here?" She knocked on his skull.

"Ouch."

"Sorry."

"Not many. I mean, my fair share, but nothing spectacular, at least not by today's standards. But I've always known I'd find what I wanted."

She: "No regrets?"

"About quantity? None. About quality, yes."

"What do you do?"

"I'm a nurse." For a slight moment he thought it would be great if he could say something else. But that's what he was. She didn't seem to mind. He was going to say he had done a year of medical school, but it wasn't necessary. She would find out some day.

"And you?"

"Guess."

"Well, you're not tall enough to be a model, but you're beautiful enough. Your fingertips are a bit calloused so you could either be a typist or play the cello. You're smart enough to be a lawyer, but I don't think you enjoy lying to people, not even for their own good."

"Do you know any lawyers?"

"My sister."

"I'm sort of a lawyer. A researcher, not a litigator. At the War Crimes Archive in Ottawa."

"Lots of laughs."

"What's been your biggest obstacle to having a real relationship?" she asked.

"The other person," he said.

"Oh-oh."

They never loved me enough, he thought, now that he was faced with it. That was the truth. But he wouldn't tell her this.

"They never loved me enough," he heard himself say anyway. "Or was it less than I loved them. It was always tentative, wait-and-see. Wait and see if something better would come along."

"Did it?"

"For them it did. And now it has for me."

14

They were all at the airport waiting for him, Sammy and Anna and Marilyn and his Baba X, in a jungle-green African shift with an enormous orange date palm on the back and elephants on the front and her white hair in a tight perm. The plan was to drive out to the cottage and spend part of the summer together until Aïda arrived, but first they would go to Saturday morning service to say *Yortzeit* for Sammy's father.

When it came time for the rabbi's speech, for some reason, everyone tensed up except Teddy.

The rabbi was an excellent orator, and proud of it, but a bit too shrill when he wanted to drive home his points, sometimes getting red in the face and shaking, his voice rising an octave almost into a comical yodel, but he really knew how to give a speech. He was in his late thirties and wasn't bad looking, but really just someone you wouldn't notice if he weren't yodelling from a pulpit.

As usual, his speech was about Israel and atrocities committed against the Jewish people, appealing to the congregation to support Israel by taking a junket there. Some of the *minyan* regulars, who were quite poor and could never afford such a trip, had stopped listening to the speech and were thinking of the *kiddush*, of hot coffee and bagels and lox. The people who could afford the trip were too terrified about the suicide bombings to go themselves or to send their children. But that hadn't stopped the rabbi himself from a twelve-day trip, staying in empty hotels and lunching in empty restaurants, sans customers, sans tips, sans everything. "And who's responsible?"

And then came the shrillest yodel of all: "Arafat!"

As if one body the congregation sat up alert as if wakened in the night by a bad dream. The rabbi's voice went up an octave. "Arafat!" And what does Arafat want?

"He wants.

"He wants.

"He wants the Jews to disappear. He wants the Arabs to have the right of return. His Arab brethren couldn't take them in so now he wants to flood Israel with Arabs and for the Jews to become a minority in the Land God gave to them, to us.

"God help us if we abandon Israel in her time of need.

"God forbid it.

"So if you can't make *aliyah* to Israel, defend Jewish soil, then be a tourist!

"Yes, be a tourist!" Up an octave he went.

"Put away the brochures to Palm Springs or Yoruba or Cuba." Down an octave.

"Be a tourist!" Up an octave.

"Next time your travel agent shows you pictures of coconut groves and Caribbean beaches and tropical drinks." Down an octave.

"Be a tourist!" Up an octave.

"Because if you don't. If you abandon Israel, someone we know will be there to get his hooks into the land we built from nothing. And we know who that someone is."

And then the shrill cry again: "Arafat!" Up two octaves until his voice cracked and the feedback rippled through the PA system and back up the mike and the everlasting light shook over the *bimah*, and even the doors behind which the Torahs slept shook with the reverberations.

"If you want to be part of the war on terror, if you want to support Israel so that when this wave of anti-Semitism that's sweeping across the world leaves you no choice but to take refuge there, then be a tourist!

"Because if you go to Cuba, which is no friend of Israel, then you're shooting yourself in the foot.

"When my Israeli friends inquire of me why their hotels are empty, why their restaurants are empty, their souvenir shops empty, what should I tell them? When they ask me where is your congregation? Why don't they come to Israel? What should I tell them? They're in Cuba? They're slurping down mojitos and listening to Cuban salsa music? They think you're doing a good job of defending the Jewish people but Israel's just too dangerous — they prefer a nice relaxing Communist dictatorship that has voted against Israel in the UN every time it gets a chance.

"And when they inquire of me to whom they are going to sell their souvenir T-shirts, what should I tell them?

"Should I tell them they're buying T-shirts of Che Guevara? That you people prefer Moncada to Massada?

"And when Arafat sends his suicide bombers into a Haifa restaurant and our Jewish holy men are picking up pieces of flesh and skull bone in the street half an hour later, a hand here, a foot on the roof of a car there, and they inquire of me what support we are giving them, what should I tell them?

"They'll send you a cheque when they come back from Cuba?"

Teddy thought this would be a good point to wrap up. But the guy squeezed his brows and paused. There wasn't a guiltless heart in the congregation.

Teddy saw that his father was getting nervous and hungry and was just waiting for the guy to finish and for the *Adon Olam* to start. But this was not to be.

"You know, today's passage from the Torah was about compassion. And before I came here this morning I read it again, just after reading an opinion poll taken of Palestinians which showed that seventy percent of the Palestinian population support the suicide bombers." He paused.

"Seventy percent. Almost an entire people without compassion for the innocent. These are people who don't want peace, with a leader who has never wanted peace. They were offered peace on a silver platter at Camp David and they refused it. They were given the most generous offer possible, and they refused it.

"Seventy percent. Remember that number. In your memory of numbers, put that number seventy beside another number: six million.

"How can there be peace when you think of the number seventy?

"Remember: seventy percent think that it's okay if a person straps a bomb belt to his body, yes, there is a name for it — a bomb belt — packs it all around with ball bearings to maximize the atrocity and goes into a crowded restaurant and massacres Jews.

"Seventy percent think that's okay. They approve."

"Seventy percent." The rabbi's final "ent" went up another octave.

Teddy had had enough. He stood up.

"I'm surprised it's only seventy percent," Teddy said, his voice carrying cleanly up to the menorahs and their flickering electric bulbs.

Sammy froze the moment his son stood up. He had just wanted to say *Yortzeit* and drive to the cottage at the lake. Then when he heard his son's words, a cold froth bubbled in his stomach.

The rabbi had never before been interrupted in his speech from the pulpit. In fact, no one in the congregation had ever witnessed such a thing, or ever heard of such a thing.

For some reason he mustered an embarrassed grin, from the shock.

Teddy took advantage of the rabbi's stunned silence to say one more thing:

"You know nothing about the Palestinians."

The rabbi's shock rose in a crimson line up his face.

"That's right. You know nothing about the Palestinians. I just came back from Israel and its Occupied Territories. What is done there in our name, what is done to those people long before there were suicide bombers — that's why there are suicide bombers. Your timeline is wrong. Suicide bombing did not beget occupation, occupation begat suicide bombing. We're not the victims." Teddy was shaking.

The congregation looked to the rabbi for leadership. They could boo, but it would feel strange booing in *shul*.

The rabbi was deciding whether this was a time for polemics or policing. But he believed in his own charm. He knew what he would do. He would address him in Hebrew and discredit him. But Teddy pre-empted him, having decided for his family's sake to end his intervention.

"Corrupt occupation," concluded Teddy in Hebrew. "Corrupt occupation," he translated, into English, and was about to slide out from the pews into the aisle to leave.

The rabbi looked at Teddy and instead of leaving things as they

were he decided to address him in Hebrew after all. Since the
congregation was paying him good money and giving him rent-
free housing — a split-level — this was a good chance to show
them how fluent he was.

"Don't walk away, young man."

Teddy turned around and looked at the rabbi, who grinned,
facing down this nuisance with what he thought was his natural
charm.

"I would like to ask you to leave," the rabbi continued in English. "You're interrupting the ceremony."

"I was just leaving."

"We're trying to hold a service here."

"You're the one who interrupts the ceremony. I came here for
my grandfather's *Yortzeit*, to honour his memory, not to hear
you spew hatred."

"I grieve with you for your loss, but the speech from the pulpit
is my privilege as rabbi."

"All men are equal before the Torah. There are no privileges.
The Torah was supposed to be the antidote to privilege."

"I would like to ask you to leave."

"I would like to ask you to stop spewing hatred against the
Palestinians."

"Should we be praising them?" the rabbi spluttered.

"We should be apologizing to them. Plain and simple. We
should say this: 'We were on a burning plane and we bailed
out. We had no choice and bailed. Unfortunately, we landed on
you.'"

Teddy's father sat there, paralyzed, his face waxy, perspira-
tion beading along his hair line, one hand gripping the flexible
leather *siddur* and the other the pew in front.

He felt a shame that burst in him like a grenade. He felt a longing for annihilation. "A *shande*," Sammy said to himself. "A
shande."

The rest of the congregation was getting restless. It was almost
noon and they were famished. The rabbi realized this and decided
to cut the young man off by summoning the beadle to do the job
for which he was paid, although nothing compared to the rabbi's
sinecure with its free rent.

But before he could:

"*Shabbat shalom*," Teddy said softly in Hebrew; and then "Peace," in English, flashing up two fingers at the rabbi. He then squeezed his way out of the pew into the aisle. He gave a curt bow to the rabbi and left the synagogue.

15

"*It's like sitting* shivah." Teddy said. "We're supposed to be celebrating. And she's coming tomorrow."

Sammy shot him a dirty look.

"Shiva? Isn't that a Hindu god?" said Marilyn.

"Marilyn!" said Anna.

"Where are the candles?" asked Marilyn.

"He doesn't want any, believe you me, he's despondent," said Anna to the kids.

"I'm not despondent," said Sammy. "Don't tell people how I feel!"

Anna got very offended and decided she wouldn't say another word that night.

Sammy's birthday cake sat on the table, and damned if she would fetch and light the candles for him now. Let him find his own bloody candles.

It was Marilyn's idea to go to the cottage, to escape the heat and celebrate Teddy's homecoming and Sammy's birthday, and Aïda's pending arrival. Big mistake, she thought.

■ ■ ■

Teddy loved the cottage, in spite of the clouds of mosquitoes and fishflies, biblical insect plagues and the intermittent smell of skunk. It was the site of the best times of his youth, his games with friends, late suppers of egg sandwiches on the beach, the pampering by his sister who took him everywhere with her, especially into the company of her perfumed girlfriends who babied him, or into that of her suitors, who treated him deferentially. It was where he fell in love for the first time, and the second, and the third, and then had his first sexual experiences, his encounters with books and music.

The cake was on the table, looking rococo, overladen with pink and white buttery, sugary flowers.

Outside, several billion fishflies the size of nickels fluttered under a streetlight. The tarred streets were already carpeted with them. An entire wall of Sammy and Anna's cottage was black with them. Here in this kitchen they had had fabulous family summer times, shrieking with laughter at the old stories, Marilyn ridiculing relatives, Sammy telling tales about the north end of town, his poverty, the petty crimes pulled off with friends, robbing their own fathers' crappy stores.

But tonight everything was so solemn. And Aïda was arriving tomorrow.

Teddy had shown them a picture of Aïda, who was enormous already, her high complexion peaking. But, except for Marilyn, the amount of enthusiasm in their voices was minimal. They lost interest and dropped the photograph on the table. Teddy had expected a more enthusiastic reception.

Aïda's picture just lay there for a long while. Teddy had thought they would be excited to see what she looked like. He was proud of her, of his Palestinian princess. Those arching Chinese eyes, the straight black hair, the oval face like a porcelain doll.

"You know, Aïda suggested you might be intolerant about this, but I defended you. I told her you'd accept her, that you were open-minded people."

"What do you know?" Sammy said. "She knows us better than you do."

"If you give her this kind of a reception tomorrow, it's going to make me look pretty ridiculous."

"Welcome to the club."

The kitchen was almost in darkness as the wood panelling absorbed the dim overhead light, with its two resident speckled moths crashing into it again and again. It was a hot night and the soft breeze brought hordes of fishflies smashing against the screens.

"Are we going to light the candles or not?" Marilyn asked.

His mother sat despondent in her chair, and waved her hand in disgust. The scene in the synagogue had unnerved her.

His father, who rarely said anything to Teddy about anything important, fretted and stared into his coffee mug, dreadfully depressed, unable to live down Teddy's latest action. He would be harassed and menaced forever in the community. He would never be able to find a card game or a friendly face. The ostracism would never go away, they were *sans* Sophisticates, *sans* curling, *sans* synagogue. He'd be lucky if they let him into the cemetery.

"Do you want some cake or not?" Anna asked Sammy. She had broken her fast of silence.

"What about the candles?" asked Marilyn.

Sammy made with the hand, waving off the candles and the cake. Nothing tasted of anything anymore anyway.

"I told you he was despondent," repeated Anna.

It was like a funeral.

"This is like a funeral," Teddy said.

"Mine," his father said. "It's like being alive at your own funeral."

"Like Tom Sawyer," sniggered Marilyn.

Teddy laughed.

"No. Not like Tom Sawyer. More like being buried alive." Sammy said.

"Oh, like the death scene in *Aïda*," said Marilyn, not being able to resist.

Teddy suppressed that laugh.

"And you two are the gravediggers," said Sammy, pointing a finger.

"What did I do?" grouched Marilyn.

"You're on his side," said Anna. "You're egging him on."

"I am not. I'm not on anybody's side."

Teddy looked at her.

"Maybe just a little."

Anna pulled on the skin of her face, as she often did when trying to imagine herself with a facelift.

Sammy caught Marilyn looking sidewise at the photograph of Aïda.

"Even now, you're encouraging him," he said to Marilyn.

"How am I encouraging him?"

"You're being nice to him."

"He's my brother."

Marilyn stood up, went to the counter and plugged in the kettle that sat next to the Lladró porcelain of a dove grey chassidic rabbi bending sveltely in prayer.

"He's not facing east."

She turned him towards the east. No one spoke for a long time. Not until the kettle started to purr and steam.

"The kettle's boiling."

"Who wants more coffee? Dad?"

Sammy turned to look at her.

"And you. Running around with other men." Sammy pointed two fingers at her.

Marilyn was hurt by this. But her hurt never gave way to weakness.

"I'm not running around."

"That's not what I hear."

"Do you want more coffee or not?"

"I don't know."

"Give him more," Anna said.

"This city is stifling," said Marilyn.

"So leave. Go run around somewhere else."

"I don't want to leave."

"Then we'll leave," said Sammy.

"You're not going to leave."

"You two are such a disappointment. Such a disappointment."

"How so?" Teddy asked innocently. He still didn't get it.

"How so? Look at you. A male nurse. A human shield. An Arab wife."

"Don't forget the *yasel*," giggled Marilyn.

"The *yasel*. Let's not forget the icing on the cake. Ha!" His father gave a sharp sarcastic laugh that came straight from the lungs.

"That's it? Four things?"

"That's enough."

"What's wrong with nursing?"

"You could have been a doctor."

"I didn't want to be a doctor. No. In fact, let's face it: I couldn't have been a doctor. It was too hard."

"You didn't try."

"I tried. I did first year."

"If you were smart enough to get in and finish first year, you were smart enough to finish the other years."

"It was too hard."

"You gave up."

"Of course I gave up. It was too hard."

"Of course it was hard. It was medicine."

"Why didn't you say anything then?"

"I felt sorry for you. I should have given you a swift kick, but I felt sorry for you." He looked at Marilyn, remembering how he had suffered about Teddy, how he had wished that Teddy had finished medical school, how he would rather have had Teddy finish medical school, than Marilyn become a lawyer. It was unfair, he knew, but he really suffered for Teddy's failure.

"Why? Why did you feel sorry for me?"

"I don't know why. She told me not to say anything."

"Me?" Anna said. "Don't *farmish* me in this."

"When I went into nursing you didn't say a word."

"Nursing. Don't use that word. You know, your mother, she didn't tell anybody for months that you dropped out of medicine, not for months. In fact, she told people you were still in medical school. She lied. For months she lied. I think she still lies about it."

"You're *farmishing* me. Don't *farmish* me."

"We didn't tell anybody, not our friends, nobody. Nobody knew. But they found out. People always find out."

"I didn't care what people thought."

"We did. We do."

"I just wanted to help people. It didn't matter to me if I was a doctor or a nurse. What's the difference? Helping is helping."

"You could have helped me. I wanted you to be a doctor. Me. You could have done it for me."

"I didn't know."

"Now you know. It killed me inside. You thought I had no pride?"

"I didn't think."

"That's it, you didn't think. You don't think."

"You should have said something."

"She told me not so say anything. That's always been her line.

You and her." On "her" he pointed his thumb to Baba X.

"I didn't tell you not to say anything," said Anna.

"Yes, you did. You know you did."

Sammy gave Anna a look with creased eyes then sat up stiffly and looked Teddy straight in the face, his disappointment having turned to anger. Teddy thought he would throw the hot coffee at someone, probably at him.

"If you had only said something," Teddy said, "I thought it was okay. You're both always helping people — the food bank."

"She's the one who works at the food bank!"

"I thought you were pleased by my decision."

"Pleased! I didn't sleep for weeks. You humiliated me. Both of you. No, all three of you."

"Sorry."

"To hell with sorry. And to hell with you. And," standing up, he blurted, "get out of my cottage." He picked up Aïda's photograph and said, "And take her the fuck with you."

Never in his life had he seen his father so enraged. Sarcastic maybe, but never enraged.

All his life not wanting to disappoint his parents but always having done so.

"Go on, bugger off."

Teddy didn't budge.

"Bugger off."

Teddy sensed there wasn't enough air coming into his lungs, although just enough to have a gasp or two.

He picked up Aïda's photo from the absurdly broadloomed floor and slid back the screen door, which stuck just long enough to allow in a fresh troop of mosquitoes and fishflies.

"You're letting the bugs in!"

"Teddy!" his mother shouted. "He doesn't mean it."

"Shut the door, you're letting the bugs in," his father said.

He managed to slide the screen door shut behind him and walked out onto the back deck to the railing. It was hard to make out the stars from the fishflies.

Not far off Teddy managed to hear the rhythmic lake noise, not quite surf, but more than wavelets.

He knew this sense of disappointment.

He was revisited immediately by a sad supper alone with his

mother at the cottage years ago, far back into early puberty. His longing to be outside nipped by bed-time regulations. Then into pyjamas and a glass of milk in the late evening summer sunlight — bed approaching — being alone, his yearning for a young girl at day camp bursting in his chest yet feeling warm and protected at home. He was still digesting the outcome of a crush that was going nowhere from his shyness.

With all the suffering in the world, he thought, the human race can count itself as lucky that melancholy is so pleasurable.

16

The next day Marilyn said cheerily, "Should we all go to the airport?"

"Are there stairs?" asked Baba X.

Marilyn laughed.

As she stirred her coffee and flipped the pages of her magazine, Teddy's mother shrugged despondently. Her mouth had been drawn down all morning in the "Big Hurt" position, as Marilyn called it at times, or the "Ben Hurt" position, at other times. The last thing in the world Anna wanted to do was drive out to the airport in this heat and bring back a pregnant Palestinian. Sammy, who was in bed, was also despondent. Dreading the day.

It was a bright warm morning. Outside things glittered wetly. It was what Anna would have called a beach day, had she not been despondent. All the insect hurly-burly of the night before had disappeared. From time to time, they heard the rumbling of cars over the lightly tarred gravel road in front of the cottage and could smell the asphalt heating up under the sun. Birds, sated from their sumptuous insect feasts, twittered from bull-rushes in the little glade behind the cottage, in front of the marshy creek that poured slowly into the lake. All was peaceful.

Teddy and Marilyn were also at the table, making their list of phoney words and expressions. "Issues" was the first one on the list.

"Yes, like 'That's a health issue.'"

"What about 'I have a problem with that.'"

"Okay."

"The Homer Simpson 'D'oh.'"

"Add 'Dude' to that."

"No, Dude's okay. Makes me think of Jeff Bridges."

"Dateable?"

"Definitely dateable."

"You keep on like that and you kids are going to run out of words, you won't be able to talk," said Anna.

"Thank god," flipped Sammy, who had just walked in looking for Kleenex, found the box and went back to his room.

"Okay, let's make up a list of conspiracy theories."

"I've got one. There's this guy, he parachutes into Buckingham Palace, fucks the queen, is whisked off to a mental institution, and never heard of again."

"That's an urban legend," said Teddy.

"Okay, let's make a list of urban legends."

Marilyn had made them bacon and French toast that morning, which she and Teddy gobbled up.

"I'm dry," said Baba X, like a TV weatherperson giving a bulletin.

"Here," she said, handing the legal pad and pen to Teddy, and got up to make some more coffee. She plugged in the electric kettle and bent down to look for filters.

In her search she pulled out seven tins of creamed corn.

"What's with all the creamed corn?"

"Sammy likes it."

"But it's summer. You can buy corn on the cob."

She pulled out an electric hamburger patty maker, for a single patty, and then another machine for a double patty.

"Why do you have a one-patty maker and a two-patty maker?"

"What?" Anna asked, looking up from her magazine.

"Why the one-patty maker?"

"I got it first," said Anna in irritation. "What's your business?"

Finally Marilyn found the filters.

"Why don't you get an espresso machine?"

Anna wasn't talking.

"You really like to buy gadgets. You've got a machine here for making a single hamburger patty and one for two. Why not an espresso machine?"

"Marilyn," Teddy admonished.

Anna just sat there stirring her coffee, trying to concentrate on her magazine. The Big Hurt. One of her best poses.

"That expression," Marilyn said to her, "is that a pose or an act?"

Anna didn't take the bait and just sat there stirring her coffee, trying to read.

"I'm dry," said Baba X.

"She's making it. It's coming," said Anna.

"So's Christmas."

Baba X got off her chair and shuffled over the broadloom in her mauve and yellow shift and into the kitchen, releasing a *baa* of farts along the way, which she didn't hear.

The kids sniggered.

"Ma!"

Baba X unplugged the kettle, feeling for the plug with her hands more than actually seeing what she was doing.

"Ma! Marilyn is making it for you."

"I can make it myself."

"Is she totally blind yet?" asked Marilyn.

"Ask her," Anna said. "She sees what she wants to see and hears what she wants to hear."

With her hands Baba X felt around the sink for a cup and began rinsing it out. She was singing softly.

"Seniors discount. Put it down."

"I thought we were doing urban legends."

"We can run two lists at the same time. Any use of the term 'the big guy,' especially in cheap TV commercials."

"Put it down."

"'Crease.' That creases me."

"No. I still say that sometimes."

"Doesn't make it not phoney, objectively," Marilyn said, spooning the coffee into the filter, making a bit of a mess, which Baba X, coming up from behind, sponged clean.

"Phoniness isn't objective, it's subjective."

"But the subjective is objective."

"Diane Keaton in *Love and Death*, or Woody Allen."

"Which one was it?"

They both roared at their cleverness, causing Baba X to raise her head. Baba X pushed Marilyn out of the kitchen area towards the nook. She would take care of the coffee herself.

"Ma!" Anna warned.

"Even a blind chicken picks a worm," Baba X said, hefting the kettle with two hands, sloshing water out of the spout, onto the counter and floor. She stopped pouring and put the kettle down so she could wipe up the water.

"Ma! You've filled it too full. You're going to burn yourself. You'll burn the house down."

"Anna, it's a kettle, not a blow torch," Marilyn said in defence of her grandmother.

"You'll see, one day she'll burn it down."

Marilyn walked to and fro in front of the nook, nervously watching, along with Anna and Teddy, as Baba X started once again to pour the boiling water from the electric kettle into the filter, a delicate operation at any age. The sagging flesh where a tricep had once been jiggled as she poured.

No one breathed out until Baba X put the kettle down on the counter.

"She's so stubborn," Anna said. "Wipe that up!"

"Alright." Marilyn wiped up the spill and squeezed the *shmate* into the stainless steel sink, looking out across the lawn to the creek, which lapped the rushes and gurgled.

"Let's make another list," said Marilyn.

"What categories?"

"Things Wolf Blitzer would say when he wants to say something else."

Anna refused to be baited.

"Okay," Teddy said. "Israeli incursions, when he means to say atrocities."

"You're not going to bait me," Anna cried.

The two stopped, with a giggle, just as they would when they were little.

"Go for a walk!"

"It smells of fishfly gunk outside."

"I don't care. Just let me have my coffee in peace."

"You've been having your coffee for two hours already."

"I can have coffee for as long as I like. I've earned it. I'm retired."

"But you never worked a day in your life."

"Whose fault was that?" Anna said, her face getting hot. "And anyways, I raised you brats."

"No, you didn't. She did." Marilyn nodded her head towards the old woman.

"You twist everything around."

"No, I don't."

"Just let me have my coffee. And don't touch my paper."

"How about a hug?" said Teddy, shifting along beside and up to Anna, purloining the entertainment section of the paper from under her elbows.

"No, I'm mad at you, too."

When she saw him peeling off the first page of the entertainment section, she wrenched it out of his hands.

"Give me back the culture section!" said Anna.

"The entertainment section," said Teddy.

"This is not working out," said Marilyn.

"Shut up, and go see your father."

"He won't talk to me," Teddy said.

"Go with your sister. Try and cheer him up."

"But we're the ones depressing him."

"Well since you're both so fucking clever, go figure it out. Let me have my coffee in peace."

"You've been having your coffee for two hours and two minutes," said Marilyn.

Anna picked up a spoon and hammered Teddy on the knuckles.

"Ow! What did you hit me for?"

"Because you're closer."

They both left the kitchen nook and caught Baba X from behind in the kitchen, as she was preparing to butter her toast, and started tickling her.

"Are you ticklish or Jewish?" they asked her as they tickled, taking yet another step backwards in this cottage-fever regression towards childhood.

The old lady cooed in delight.

Officially, she couldn't stand being tickled or cuddled by anyone over ten years old, but her resistance always broke down after they ganged up on her.

"Are you ticklish or Jewish?"

"I'm ticklish. I'm ticklish," she rasped.

The two really got into it.

"You're going to give her a heart attack," Anna berated. "Leave her alone and go see your father."

"She's jealous," said Marilyn to Teddy.

"I'm not jealous," said Anna to Marilyn. "And stop with the two-bit psychology."

Anna was angry. This was unfair, all this love for Baba X. It had always been unfair.

Baba X raised her shoulders and squeezed her arms against her bust to defend herself, crackling with old-lady giggles. "There's hot coffee here," she said to the ceiling.

The two just tickled her close to the armpits.

"You're going to kill her," said Anna.

"We're not going to kill her," said Marilyn.

"You'll kill her."

"It's good for her. Good for the circulation."

"Marilyn! Teddy!" Anna snapped. "She's ninety years old."

"Well, what's the worst that could happen to her at ninety?" Marilyn asked.

"That's enough! If I have to get up from here — ."

"But you won't, you're too lazy," said Marilyn.

"Go see your father," she said to Teddy.

"He wants to kill me."

"Go! Leave her alone."

They had Baba X rasping with laughter, practically out of breath. They themselves were laughing.

"She's going to faint."

"She's not going to faint."

They guided the old woman to the kitchen nook and sat her down in her chair. Then Teddy stretched across the counter to get her coffee. Baba X took out her plastic weekly pill dispenser and set out her mountain of pills for the day, which she would swallow later with a histrionic cocking back of the head and swoons.

Teddy brought her her toast from the kitchen after cutting it into triangles, and Marilyn spread the grape jelly.

The old woman was out of breath, but happy and giddy. The winter had been long and boring, so boring sometimes that she had actually cried, but the winter had now just sluiced away by the presence of the kids and the coming of the *yasel*.

■ ■ ■

Sammy was lying in bed, covered up. In high summer. Noon on the dot. High tragedy smouldering on the scene. Marilyn and Teddy were sitting on opposite corners at the end of the bed. Teddy wished he hadn't come in with Marilyn.

"Do you expect me to drive out to the airport with you?" Sammy strained.

"No. Just thought you might want to get out of the cottage," said Teddy.

"I can't even go down to the beach without everybody looking at me in a phoney way."

Silence.

"I couldn't go curling all last winter."

Teddy gave him an innocent look.

"There are no Palestinian curling rinks," Sammy said.

Teddy remained perfectly quiet.

"I couldn't play poker either at the Sophisticates."

Marilyn intervened after looking at Teddy. "Whose fault was that? I told you I fixed it up for you. Anyway, who told you to kick Mr. Hershberg in the mouth in the first place?"

Sammy flung off the covers and sat up in bed.

"Who told you to sleep around with his son?"

Got her there. Sammy was seriously pissed off at Marilyn. And very ashamed. He remembered the jeering behind his back at the Sophisticates and he felt a boiling in his chest.

"Who told you to sleep around? Who?"

"Nobody."

"I'd like to meet this Nobody."

"It was a mistake."

"Is that what you told Jack?"

"Leave Jack out of it. You never liked Jack anyway."

If Anna were here she'd say "It's the failure of the sexual revolution," Teddy thought, and he was tempted to mimic her, which he knew would make Marilyn scream, but he kept his mouth shut. He was maturing.

"I liked him more than Mannie Hershberg's son," said Sammy.

"Who doesn't," replied Teddy, looking critically at his sister.

"Watch it, buster. What about you and the rabbi's wife."

"She wasn't the rabbi's wife because she wasn't a real rabbi," said Teddy. "Oh, fuck it."

"Going to the airport would be the polite thing," said Marilyn, turning to her father.

"I'm not going anywhere. I haven't been able to go anywhere. I can't go anywhere. Do you see me going anywhere I want to go?"

It sounded like he was feeling sorry for himself, which is not how he wanted it to sound. And he knew it. And if he knew it, everyone knew it. He hated that. He found the remedy.

"I'm not going anywhere, not with you two."

This sounded a bit more aggressive, yet it let the door open if he wanted to go out later for chips at Dorothy's or something, or for a drive to Henderson pier; nothing but goyim there.

"You're tearing."

He used the mound on the bottom edge of the palm of his hand to wipe his left eye.

"How pregnant is she now?"

"About eight months."

"For Chrissakes."

"Dad, you're going to have to leave the cottage sooner or later," said Marilyn.

"What for?"

"Air."

"Maybe I should go back to the city," said Teddy.

"Baba X likes us all being here," said Marilyn.

"Fuck your Baba," said Sammy.

Marilyn looked at Teddy, who swung his head to look at her. Now this was news.

"Fuck Baba X."

Teddy and Marilyn looked at each other in horror, successfully suppressing a giggle. A long silence ensued which Sammy enjoyed. He had finally said it.

"You know I was really drunk that night," said Marilyn.

"A slut and a drunk. Very nice."

Teddy smirked.

"I didn't really know what I was doing."

"A slut, a drunk, and a retard."

Teddy cracked up. Marilyn shot him a dirty look.

"A real retard. Fancy retard lawyer."

"Don't shout," Marilyn said.

"And you, Mr. Human Shield? What was your excuse? Were you drunk, too?"

"Actually, I was a little dazed by all the tear gas they shot."

"They should have shot bullets."

"They did. Some others weren't so lucky."

"Yeah, they could have cut their balls off."

"You have no idea of what's going on there. You're totally blind!"

Teddy stood up.

"Don't shout," Marilyn said to Teddy.

"I'm not blind. Six million even a blind man can see."

"There he goes with the six million. Forget about that already!"

Sammy jumped out of bed as if someone had suddenly thrown a frog between his legs: he had seen an advantage.

The two of them squared off.

"Should we forget about them?"

"Oh Christ! That's not what I meant."

"Do you deny it happened?"

"I don't deny it. Who said I deny it. I'm just saying what's one thing got to do with the other. Why do the Palestinians have to pay for what the Nazis did? For all I care they could have set up the Jewish state in Bavaria. I wouldn't be complaining. But they didn't. They had to fuck over somebody else. People who couldn't defend themselves."

"It's just their bloody tough luck. Somebody had to pay. Sorry."

"Sorry, that's not good enough."

"Look, they lost the war. Right of conquest. It's as simple as that," said Sammy.

"Do you hear yourself talk?"

"Right of conquest. If we had lost, it would have been too bad for us," said Sammy.

"So what you're saying, what you're thinking is that might

makes right? That you can do anything you want as long as you win, as long as nobody stops you. So the Nazis could do what they did because they got away with it."

"That's right. That's human nature. That's what history has taught us."

"You sound like Michael Corleone in *The Godfather, Part II*, I think."

"He was in all three parts," said Marilyn.

"Which is the one with the horse's head in the bed?" asked Sammy. "That's the only scene I remember."

"*Part I*."

"Well, he's right. Michael Corleone was right: you can do whatever you want as long as you get away with it."

"I can't believe I'm hearing this."

"You can either be bullied or be the bully. There's no middle ground."

"But look at you. You haven't lived like that. That's not what you taught us. What makes us any different from the Nazis then?"

"This time we won't end up as bars of soap or lampshades."

"But others might, and that's okay with you."

"In this world, somebody always ends up the bar of soap. Just let it be someone else next time. We've been the bar of soap."

"Listen to yourself talk. Do you hear what you're saying? By your own logic, therefore, the Palestinians can use whatever methods they choose to get rid of the Israelis, and it'll be okay if they succeed."

"That's right. But since we're mightier than them, it doesn't matter. Whatever terror they use only makes us stronger."

"So there's no such thing as morality?"

"Nope. Never has been. There's only human nature. Only power."

"No law, no commandments."

"Nope, nothing."

"What kind of Jew are you?"

"The kind that's not a bar of soap."

"So you're dividing the world into bars of soap and people who make other people into bars of soap."

"Not me. That's the way the world was made. It's *bashert*."

"It's not *bashert*."

"Keep your voices down," said Marilyn.

"The screamer wants us to keep our voices down."

"You're so mean all of a sudden."

"Finally. How would you like it if people went around saying your mother was a hot lay and a screamer?"

"What do you care what people say?" asked Marilyn.

"Yeah, what do you care?" echoed Teddy.

"It's not what people say, it's what you do, the two of you. My two kids: one's a slut and the other's a retard. And that's what people see, and then they discuss it. If you're not ashamed of what you do, that's your problem. One slut and one self-hating human shield."

"No, you only care about what people say," said Teddy.

"Why do you care?" added Marilyn.

"Why do I care? This is my community. I have to live in it. Or you have some other place for me to go? Six feet under? *In drerd*? Is that where you'd like to see me?"

The two kids sort of ran out of steam here, but Sammy didn't.

"It's embarrassing to have your dirty linen paraded in public, you know. You could have thought about me, about your mother and me. Were we mean to you?"

Big pause.

"Did we deny you anything? There were other parents who were neglectful, who never played with their kids or spent time with them, or only spent 'quality time' with them, which is no time at all. Did we do that?"

No answer.

"Did we?"

Still no answer.

"Did we neglect you? Starve you?"

Nothing.

"Why did you do this to us? I only ask for one thing. That when you have children that they are exactly like you two. Tormentors."

These kids unsettled him. No, worse. They were a *shande*, both of them. They had ruined his life. He felt like shit feeling that way, but it was true. What was the point in having had them? He could have done something else with his life. He could have stayed in Israel after '48. The only thing was he was lonely there, and he didn't really like the food, or the fact that there were Jewish people in jail, Jewish thieves, Jewish prostitutes.

Anna came into the room. Sammy and Teddy were standing by the window, Marilyn still sitting at the corner of the bed. The first thing she did was shut the window.

"They can hear you screaming from Prospect Avenue."

"Can't we just discuss this rationally?" said Teddy.

"You can't discuss rationally with an anti-Semite," said Anna.

"Teddy's not an anti-Semite," said Marilyn. "He's too much of a narcissist to be an anti-Semite."

"If you criticize Israel, you're an anti-Semite."

"There should be a long line of rabbis ready to smack the crap out of you," said Anna, trawling on ahead.

Marilyn screamed with laughter.

Teddy was too hot and angry to laugh. "And if you criticize the Spanish government, are you anti-Spanish?"

"It's not the same thing."

"Or does that mean Chomsky's an anti-Semite because he criticizes Israel?"

"Who's this Chomsky again?"

"You're so ignorant, you people!"

This was a mistake, so he backed up.

"You're so ignorant when you talk about Israel!"

But it was too late.

"You think we're ignorant because we didn't go to university?"

"That's not what I said. And do you really think I'm an anti-Semite? Think! It's impossible if I'm a Jew."

"You're a self-hater."

"That's what King Ahab called Elijah the prophet!"

"Teddy's a narcissist," said Marilyn. "If you know what that is."

"I know what that is," said Anna. "I'm not ignorant."

"You say that as if I am," said Sammy, feeling that Anna had stabbed him in the back.

"There are a lot of Jews who are against the occupation," said Teddy. "Even Israeli Jews."

"It's not true," said Anna.

"It's true! There are hundreds of Israelis in jail who refuse to go into the army."

"It's not true!" shouted Anna. "We've never seen that on TV."

"I was there. I've met some of them."

"It's not true!" insisted Anna. "Don't *farmish* me."

"You're so gullible, you people. You probably believe Bush is compassionate!"

"They're crazy," shouted Sammy. "They're crazy. Any Israeli who refuses to fight in the army is crazy."

"They're not crazy. I met some of them. One of them actually saved my life when some settlers were trying to kick the shit out of me. He's the one who convinced me we were wrong, that it was time to admit our error."

"We don't like the settlers," said Anna.

"Who said we don't?" went Sammy.

"But they're all settlers," said Teddy. "The whole place is one big settlement."

"It's the only place that's safe for the Jews," said Anna.

"Do you think it's safer for a Jew right now in Tel Aviv or Toronto?"

"So now you're looking out for the welfare of the Jews," said Sammy.

"Of course I am. Who gave you people the franchise?"

"Moses."

"Let me ask you one thing: If they don't give the Palestinians a viable state, what will happen? Or if they annex the West Bank and Gaza, what will happen? Given the demographics, in twenty years there will be more Palestinians in Israel than Jews. Now if Israel is a democracy, one man one vote, the Palestinians will be a majority."

"So."

"So there won't be a Jewish state."

"Who says they'll have the right to vote?"

"Well, then it will be like South Africa. Apartheid."

"So."

"'So'! What do you mean 'so'? Would you like that to happen here. Would you like the government to take away your rights because we're a minority. Would you like to have to carry around an identity card stating that you were a Jew. Or maybe sew on a yellow star."

"Then I'd move to Israel."

"But you already lived in Israel. You left. You couldn't stand it, I bet. I bet you wouldn't eat chickpeas."

"I had a choice then. If I didn't have a choice, I'd put up with it. I'd eat something else."

"But we can't live like that. We can't."

"Why not? It's dog eat dog."

"I can't believe it. Zionism has turned you into a Nazi."

"And you're an anti-Semite. The worst kind."

"And in a time when anti-Semitism is sweeping Europe," said Anna.

Teddy turned to Marilyn for support. "Say something!"

"Actually," Marilyn began, "I don't care about the Israelis or the Palestinians. They don't concern me. I live here. You're both, no all three of you, you're just acting out. None of this is about Israel. You should all be in analysis."

"Don't go giving me your two-bit psychology," said Anna. "You're the one who needs the analysis."

"He's the one in analysis."

"But only because they force me."

"If you were in analysis they'd tell you this was all just acting out." said Marilyn to Teddy. "Dad's really apolitical. He only cares about poker and curling. He's just pissed off that you're not a doctor. Her too. You know, she still tells people you're in pre-med."

Anna looked down at her thongs.

"And you're just defensive, Teddy. You feel guilty that you're not a doctor, even though you don't want to be a doctor, and that you have disappointed them, so you get back at them with this human shield business. It's just acting out. Look at the four of us, here in this bedroom, where we might have been conceived," Marilyn squealed.

There were more eye movements than in the denouement of a spaghetti western. But in the end, the other three looked at Marilyn and told her to shut up.

Teddy had to squelch Marilyn's theory and so he picked up one of the threads of the argument pre-Marilyn. This would be the showdown. He would not be bullied. He had points to make, even though by making them stridently, it made Marilyn look like she was right. Perhaps she was, but he would worry about that later.

"I'm going to put the *kibosh* on your anti-Semitism-sweeping-Europe theory," he said quietly, pointing at Sammy and Anna with the index-finger of truth.

He wanted to sound tough and calm and not shout.

"What's a *kibosh*?" asked Anna.

"Nonsense."

"You can put your *kibosh* up your *tuchus*, if you ask me. You don't talk, you *farmish*."

Teddy ignored Anna's last comment.

"You say anti-Semitism is sweeping Europe."

"The world."

"Alright, the world. Now, according to Amnesty International in the anti-Semitic incidents in 2002 and 2003 the number of Jews killed in that period seems to be nine, almost all by Al Qaeda, which attacks almost everybody, not only Jews. Exclude them, you get one, in Morocco. Where's the anti-Semitism?"

Teddy got out the finger of truth again and wagged it.

"So where's the anti-Semitism?"

"Why wait for spring?" asked Sammy.

"What?"

"Why wait for the killing to start? It's all very subtle still."

"So subtle you can't see it?"

"We can see it. You can't."

"This is pure paranoia. Victimology."

"So we're paranoid! But you're not really paranoid if everyone does hate you, as the saying goes."

"This would be delusional if it weren't deliberate!"

"I don't have to take this!" said Sammy.

"Take what?"

"This. This shit! So you can put your finger of truth away."

Teddy looked at his finger.

"I don't need to have a son who's an anti-Semite at this time in my life!"

"I'm not an anti-Semite!" Teddy turned red in the face.

"Go ahead, when you have no arguments, scream!"

"You're like that mental retard, what's-his-name, the guy Clinton refused to pardon, who was so severely retarded that when he finished his last meal before his execution, he asked the guards if he could save his dessert for after! That's how stupid you are! You're just so fucking stupid!" He brought out the finger of truth to wag.

Sammy took out a different finger and showed it to Teddy.

"You see this finger?" Sammy shouted.

Teddy stared at it. He'd never before seen his father make this vile gesture. Veins on his temples bulged where they had never bulged before. The rims of his eyes were red.

"Do you see this finger or not?" Sammy yelled, his face bright orange.

"I see it," screamed Teddy.

Anna was screaming "Stop it, stop it," trying to fold down Sammy's finger. He kept wriggling it out of her grasp, flashing it in front of Teddy.

At this point an exasperated Baba X waddled into the bedroom thrashing her cane about the air.

Baba X was in a rage. Her voice rasping. Her cane walloping the walls, making marks on the paint.

"Shut up!" she screamed. "Shut up!"

Teddy jumped back, away from the cane. So did Sammy.

The old lady thrashed her cane up and down, side to side. "Shut up!" she rasped, "The rabbi *geyt*."

The cane smashed against Sammy's finger.

"Fuck!"

Once the cane stopped slashing the air everyone stood perfectly still, in tableau to abide her wrath.

"I'm old, I'm dying!"

She had her chin cocked up defiantly.

"Shut up already! It's enough. Finish with it! You're going to kill me!"

She canted dangerously to one side.

"There's no peace in this house! No peace!"

Then she turned her humped back, started crying pitifully, putting everybody to shame.

"I have no quality of life," she said, "no quality of life."

Teddy and Marilyn comforted her and led her out into the hall, holding her elbow. She was pooped, and glided slowly back to the kitchen to make tea.

"I'm dry," she said to Marilyn, heaving.

Marilyn squeezed her tiny wrist almost right to the bone. The skin was tanned and papery soft. She wondered where all the cane-waving energy had come from.

Baba X, now only whimpering, said to Marilyn: "I want to see you all settled down. And from you, I want to see a baby from you before I die."

Marilyn didn't say a word, and Baba X regained more of her composure as she dictated.

"I want to see you settled down. Have a baby. Let me hold him before I die."

Marilyn's eyes went up to the ceiling and fanned back and forth.

"Are you listening to me?" Baba X asked.

Anna felt envious and angry. Fuck them, she thought. She also left Sammy alone and went to the kitchen, microwaved the cold coffee until it was scalding, and without looking at them, went out into the back yard, slamming the door behind her.

Sammy was bloody well mad at the kids. They had ruined his old age. Not on purpose, of course, but then he hadn't actually instructed them to go out and do what they did. Maybe he should have had a third kid: the third child is usually good to his parents.

He had been too soft on them. Maybe he had been too interested in his own fun, his curling, his poker games. Maybe he hadn't given them the direction kids need. Or maybe they were just ungrateful cunts. Ungrateful cunts, he thought. Ungrateful cunts. He had never said the word "cunt" out loud in his life, but it sounded just right in his head, so he ventured to the doorframe, took a deep breath, and shouted down the hall in the direction of the kitchen.

"You're a bunch of ungrateful cunts," he shouted from the bedroom, before getting back into bed, and back to his brooding. He covered himself up with the sheets and lay there, a bundle of irritation. But then he flung the covers up and got right back up again and went to the doorframe and hollered, "I said you're a bunch of ungrateful cunts! And you can all just fuck off!"

Teddy and Marilyn froze.

"Ungrateful fucking cunts! A pair of ungrateful cunts."

■ ■ ■

"He's really pissed off," said Marilyn.

"I doubt he'll come out to the airport."

Marilyn laughed. "You are so jejune."

"I wasn't being facetious," Teddy said. "Maybe mum will come."

"She'll relent. I'm sure. She's the soft one. Far too heavy on the self-commiseration though."

After making coffee for Baba X and settling her on the chesterfield with the TV on, the two kids went outside and found their mother in the screened-in gazebo at the back of the yard still drinking coffee and trying to read *Cosmopolitan*, turning the pages with fury.

They looked in. She stared back at them, looking as if an insect has landed on her nose. I've been sidelined, she thought. They always sideline me.

Teddy was the first to speak. "We're going out to the airport."

"Does Cosmo girl want to come?" added Marilyn.

What an uncalled-for remark, thought Anna. She gave them the silent treatment, which she always did before screaming at them.

"We won't be long," said Marilyn.

"We'll be back in a few hours," Teddy added.

"There's no traffic at this time."

"We'll be back soon."

They sounded so stupid, talking to the screen of the gazebo.

"Yeah, we'll be back soon."

"Take your time. How about a few years!" Anna slammed down her coffee cup, splashing her forearms.

But that wasn't the right thing to say. So she rephrased it.

"Why bother coming back at all if I have to put up with your pounding me! Look what you made me do. I'm scalded." The back of her throat constricted. And her eyes prickled. She felt the tears were going to flow. What was she going to do with an Arab in the cottage? A pregnant Arab?

"You're not scalded," said Marilyn.

"Yes, I am."

"We're not pounding you," said Teddy softly.

"Yes, you are, you're pounding me."

In her inimitable way she was jostling into the victim slot, really asking Teddy to say he was sorry, so that she could forgive him and make up.

"Do you know what a *neshome* is?"

"Of course," said Teddy, his lips practically pressed to the screen.

Oh no, thought Marilyn, here come the tears.

"Do you know what a *neshome* is?"

"Isn't it Japanese?" said Marilyn.

"It's Yiddish," Anna said, "it's Yiddish for soul."

"Here we go," said Marilyn.

Then Anna started crying, with *cremnys*.

"Ma, don't cry."

"I'm crying with *cremnys*."

Anna either cried with *cremnys* or without.

Teddy knew what his mother was looking for and any other time he would have given in, apologized, but this time he hesitated. Apologize for what? What did he have to feel guilty about? For not advocating the extermination of the Palestinians? For loving one? For procreating? But it pained him to see his mother cry.

Anna expected Teddy to slide the door open and try to make things *iberbetn*. But he hesitated. This she didn't appreciate, but she didn't know where to go from here because she was counting on forgiving him once he gave her an apology. "Calling him an anti-Semite was a stupid mistake, I admit it," she said. But she hadn't meant it. He had trapped her into saying what she didn't want to say, which is what she wanted him to apologize for.

"Ma."

"Stop pounding me."

"Ma."

And now she was really bawling. But she noticed that Teddy didn't flinch, which was unlike him. He could never stand her crying. To hell with him, she thought, to hell with all of them.

"Ma."

"Don't 'Ma' me!"

That hit him like a knuck.

"You always gang up on me, the four of you. You think my *neshome* is a rozhenke. Well it's not. I won't take this crap from you. From all of you."

He usually defended her. He didn't like getting bunched up with the others. But he didn't want to give in. He didn't like being called an anti-Semite by his own mother. He couldn't let her get away with that.

"I don't have to take this," she screamed, got up, and slid the gazebo door off its rails. Teddy caught her in his arms.

"Take what?"

"This pounding."

"We're not pounding you."

"I don't want to talk to you again!" she said straight to his face. "I'm writing you off, you little shit."

This was another mistake, which she corrected right away, shaking free from his grip.

"I don't want to talk to you again if you're going to pound me with your ideology."

"What ideology?" said Marilyn.

"There you go. The two of you, ganging up. Pounding me. You're always pounding me."

He was going to say something to contradict her, but he thought, as always, that his mother was his natural ally, she had always been. He saw that it would be so easy to handle her now, vulnerable as she was, playing her hand so loose. He knew he'd just have to try to hug her again and she would be on his side, accept Aïda, help reorganize the family emotionally. In the end that's what she always did. That's how she let Jack into the family although everyone balked the first time Marilyn brought him home, and how she let him out again, when Marilyn got the separation.

"If she wants to separate, let her separate," Teddy remembered her saying. "He's a nebbish. He's not good enough for her, he never was."

Reconciliation was within Teddy's reach, he knew it, but he resisted. Instead he said the dishonest thing.

"I'm not an anti-Semite," he said, plunging the guilt knife back in. "How could you say that about me?"

He knew she hadn't been thinking when she had said it and that she hadn't meant it. But her having said it had become good ammo. He grappled with his dishonesty here, but he wanted to get back at her, too, for what in particular he didn't really know. But he was enjoying it. For the first time her tears evaporated as soon as they touched his skin.

She again felt the urge to say she hadn't meant it. That she got mixed up, with the heat of the argument. He wasn't an anti-Semite, of course not. She wanted to say she hadn't meant it. It wouldn't be so hard, would it?

"I don't know how you could have said that to me," Teddy added, twisting the knife.

The little shit, Anna thought. The ungrateful cunt, as Sammy had called him. Still pounding.

"Go away from me, I never want to see your face again!" she said. She was going to tell him not to bring home that fat cow here, but she held fire.

Teddy's face turned red.

Anna corrected herself. "I don't want to see your face again this morning." She was giving him an in, the little shit.

"You said 'never.'"

"I meant this morning. It was a figure of speech."

"Like anti-Semite."

"If the shoe fits."

"Well, we're going to the airport."

"Why don't you take your Baba with you? Give me and Sammy a break."

■ ■ ■

They packed their Baba, who liked car rides, into the back seat of Marilyn's BMW, the old woman clutching a melting Revel. Marilyn started the car and a small family of raccoons watched them pull away, rolling over the gravel and light sticky tar, through the beach town and onto the highway to the airport.

The ride across the prairie to the airport was boring and so in the car Teddy and Marilyn inadvertently had the following argument.

Jocularly, Marilyn, even in good humour, began. "Of all the

women in the world, why did you have to fall in love with a Palestinian?"

"Of all the men in the city why did you have to sleep with Max Hershberg?"

"I'll sleep with whomever I want."

"And I'll fall in love with whomever I want. At least I still can." This really stung.

Marilyn was a bit pissed off that Teddy hadn't taken her jibe lightly, as she had meant it. He usually did, but it seems he had changed. And she felt that the stinger, that "at least I can" was uncool and uncalled for. She had been defending him and this was her recompense. Truth to tell, she was envious that he had found someone, a great romantic love, something that had escaped her and which, in spite of her seeming insouciance about romance and sex, had always interested her. Where was her great love? This gnawed at her for thirty miles or so. Envious of Teddy being in love? Maybe she was. The last time she had had sex with someone she liked was months ago.

"So you think I'm just envious," Marilyn said.

"Yes, I do."

"How would you know?"

"I can read your mind."

"I hope you're not psychic too."

"I'm not."

"You know, Teddy, you've got to forget about this Israel-Palestine business. It's got nothing to do with you, and you're not going to convince anybody here, that's for sure."

"I can try."

"You can't reason people out of something that they didn't reason themselves into — Swift, I think."

"I have to try."

"But it's got nothing to do with you."

"It has everything to do with me, with us. It's a moral imperative. We can't let them continue doing what they do in our name."

"It's not in our name. It's in their name."

"You don't understand."

"No, I don't. Tell me what's it got to do with you? You're not Israeli."

"I'm Jewish."

"So what. How can you take a country seriously where they use *matzah* to fan their barbecues. I was there once too, remember? It's a joke."

"You can't take anything serious seriously."

"Look, you're a Diaspora Jew. How many High Anglicans feel guilty about the British in Northern Ireland? Israel means nothing more to me than Serbia or Finland."

"Nothing at all?"

"Nothing. You can hate Sharon all you want, and with reason, but I couldn't care less that he's a Jew. He could be Nestorian for all I care. He's just another murderous head of state bent on stealing other people's land, one more in a long line, so what do I care what his mother's religion was. And why should you feel guilty for what he does just because you were both circumcised in somebody's living room."

"Someone has to care. On TV they don't say the Israeli Army did this or that, they say the Jewish Army, and they don't say Israeli settlements in occupied territory, they say Jewish settlements."

"Not always."

"Always."

"So what's your point?"

"My point. My point. You know what my point is. Someone has to say that not all of us agree with them."

"But most Jews do agree."

"Well, not me. And not you."

"I don't care."

"You always say that. And I can't believe it."

"Believe it. It doesn't faze me. What they do has nothing to do with me. I don't agree with it, I don't condone it, and I can't stop it."

"They stopped apartheid; they freed Nelson Mandela."

"Apartheid was stopped because the Cubans and the Angolans beat the shit out of the South African army at Guaco Ganavale. Stevie Wonder's arrest didn't count for much."

"But it made him feel better."

"That's my point. When the Israeli army is driven out of Jenin, then there will be changes. But your making Sammy and Anna miserable won't do a thing."

"But I am right, aren't I."

"Of course you're right — but what's the point in arguing with them."

"We can't just keep quiet."

"Why not?"

"It's not right."

"Who cares?"

"I care."

"Well, just don't argue with them. They won't change."

"I don't know. I'm just drawn into it. I can't help myself."

"I think you've got other issues to resolve here."

"I hate the way you use that word."

"What word?"

"You know what word."

17

Aïda was two hours clearing customs and when she finally came out of the electric doors she fell into Teddy's arms. She was enormous, Marilyn saw, her belly button had already popped out, looming over the draw strings of her canvas slacks, so that even Teddy found it hard to position himself to embrace her, and, she noticed, was slightly taken aback when he saw her. Marilyn was astonished by her size. Too much strangeness at one time.

Marilyn phoned Anna's cell and told her they were on their way home, just heading out of the airport terminal, crossing over to the car park. She knew Anna worried whenever highway travel was involved, even if it was only an hour's drive, and since they were already so late, she thought Anna would be hysterical by now.

"I was about to call the police," Anna said, transmitting her irritation and hysteria.

"It took her two hours to clear customs."

"You could have phoned. I've been on *shpilkes*."

"We're on our way to the parking lot now. But it's slow going with her and Baba."

"What does she look like?" asked Anna.

"What do you mean? You've seen the pictures." Marilyn was a bit out of breath, pulling one of Aïda's suitcases, wanting to hang up.

Anna didn't answer.

"Oh, I get it," said Marilyn, stopping on the pavement of the steaming parking lot. She waited for Aïda and Teddy to move ahead of her, but they were moving slowly too, stopping every so often to hug and kiss and stroke each other. "She looks like a real Arab. And hugely pregnant. Immensely pregnant. A hugely, immensely gravid Arab woman. I'm not sure whether we shouldn't drive her straight to the maternity ward."

Anna hung up and went back to watching Wolf Blitzer on TV, her heart still pounding but relieved that the phone call from Marilyn hadn't been the highway patrol informing her that they were all dead. There was an interview with a senator from somewhere that she had been trying to watch to distract herself from the car accident fantasy. She could only watch Wolf Blitzer when Marilyn wasn't there, otherwise she'd make fun of her. He's so pathetic, Marilyn would say. How can you believe all that crap he spouts?

I'm watching my program, Anna would reply, and Marilyn would laugh at her.

Sammy remained in bed all day with his sore finger. Anna wondered if he would get up to greet them or if she would have to do it alone.

He wouldn't. His finger was killing him where Baba X hit it with her cane. Maybe he'd lose the nail.

"So you're not getting up."

"No."

"What should I tell them when they arrive?"

"Tell them my finger hurts."

"You tell them."

"I won't. I'm not getting up."

Sammy and Anna heard Marilyn's BMW pull up, crunching the gravel with assurance. Anna parted the curtains and watched. The car doors opened and thudded shut. Anna's heart pounded. Then the trunk popped up and Teddy hauled out Aïda's train of luggage. Anna's heart enlarged to the size of a football. Sammy turned over in bed on his stomach while Anna stood frozen at the window, watching the procession come up the walk. Her eyes flew right to Aïda's belly. It was huge. She never recalled being that big with either Teddy or Marilyn. Then she looked at her face: the girl was a real beauty. And stylish.

Teddy came in first.

"We're back," he shouted with desperate goodwill.

Anna left Sammy in bed and went out to greet them. She welcomed Aïda as if she were royalty, going only on her intuition. When from his room he heard her, Sammy thought all her principle had vanished. Since all the other members of the family were so shitty to her, she was always open, if not to the kindness of strangers, to an alliance with them.

"Let me give you a hug," she said to Aïda, and smothered the girl in warmth, releasing months of anxiety in her tears.

She gave in, Sammy thought. She caved in.

Aïda was moved and almost cried, squeezing Anna's neck, her belly grinding against her midriff.

Teddy went into his father's room alone and reported his return personally.

"Dad, we're back."

"I know that."

"Aren't you getting up? We picked up a pound of corned beef and a fresh rye bread from Abosh's."

"Good for you."

"Are you getting up to have something to eat with us?"

"No, I'm not. And shut the door after you."

After Teddy shut the door, Sammy thought longingly about the corned beef. He could hear them already preparing a delicatessen supper, his favourite. Then came those deep rumblings of appetite. He heard the lid of the pickle jar pop. Then came the hiss of the pickled herring jar. He just knew there was chopped liver too.

The family, that bunch of experts in irritation.

"What's Sammy going to eat?" he heard Baba X say. Yes, he definitely heard her say it.

Everybody ignored her.

Then came the clatter of forks and knives and the fizzing of pop. His stomach grumbled again. He had to fight off his appetite so as not to get up, go out, cave in, like Anna. He thought about what excuses he would present later for staying in bed. Headache. He had a headache. And surely he had developed one, which made him feel better. He was pissed off, and he was right to be, but he also felt embarrassed in front of this Aïda person, whom he still couldn't face.

And it seemed that they were all making friends with her. Yes, that was definitely laughter he heard. Anna was selling out on every front.

I am fucked, he thought. But I have always been fucked, haven't I?

The electric can opener purred. The halvah wasn't safe either.

How he loved halavah, how as a child it tasted the way he imagined silver would taste. They would gobble it all down.

That Aïda had probably never eaten so well, he thought.

He had no idea that Aïda, who as a girl had had many luncheons at Maxim's with her parents, even once with Edward Said, and who, when she had dined on take-out in London with her father, only ate what he would bring home from Selfridges's. But paradoxically Sammy was right: she had in fact never eaten so well as that evening, not because of the spread, but because, in spite of the small revolution going on at the cottage, had never experienced such family feeling, real and potential, which she had discovered, to her delight, was what she had so sorely lacked. Her family was loving, but fragmented, by war, exile and modernity. And she could not, for some reason, ever fully enjoy the fruits of her parents' individualism or her own. What she relished with these people, in spite of their strangeness, or their being Jewish, which she didn't take seriously, as her exposure to the bacillus of religion and her father's atheist inoculation against it had made her immune, and in spite of Teddy's father's opposition — ridiculously masked by his being in bed with a sore finger — was their family consensus. They could never be sundered.

I am Ruth in the alien corn, Aïda thought, but she had a homey feeling. She held Teddy's hand at the table, only releasing it to cut her food, then squeezing it again. Marilyn noticed this, thought about making a smart remark, and decided she would just shut up about it. Aïda's presence disarmed and sedated her. The way Teddy looked at her was a bit much, but she put it down, not to envy, as Teddy thought, but to jealousy. Aïda had absorbed him and she would never recover his complicity.

Baba X would stroke Aïda's straight black hair from time to time, or pat her arm or belly, call her Mrs. Ostrove, which Aïda politely corrected each time — she would keep her maiden name.

Sammy heard the laughter, mostly Marilyn's, and all that female chumminess going on around the food and Aïda's swollen belly. They had sold out, but he never would, he thought. That's what they wanted. All of them. Even that traitorous wife of his. But he wouldn't give in. All these years putting up with her mother and that obnoxious asshole of a brother of hers, and she couldn't back him this one time.

He could hear friendly voices and fluted laughter. There seemed to be more bonhomie than he thought possible. Marilyn's usual bubbly snorts of laughter were now just those soft chortles that were so endearing when she was three. What was so funny all the time with her? You'd watch the news, listen to Bush or who-ever giving a speech, in all seriousness, and she'd giggle, screech, roar, snort, cackle, crack up, laugh her head off. Even during Reagan's funeral. What was always so goddamn funny to her?

It was hot in his room and he was thirsty. And perhaps he was catching a summer cold. They could bring him in a goddamn Coke or something, or an aspirin. Anna could do something, for Chrissakes. There was the pop and fizz of more Coke being opened. Then a definite sawing through of rye bread. A second loaf. How much corned beef had they brought? Then he heard the electric can opener again. Another tin of halvah! Or maybe they had found the herring roe, the herring roe he was saving.

They will rue the day.

He heard Anna talking to Aïda in her friendliest voice, that voice she has for people she meets for the first time. Anna could be such a suck. The woman just got here and already Anna was sucking up to her. He could hear scissors cutting through card-board. No doubt this Aïda person had brought presents and they were opening them.

Women, actually, were experts in betrayal.

Marilyn burst out laughing. The only person not laughing, he noticed, was Baba X, but she's deaf.

"What's Sammy going to eat?" he definitely heard her say.

He heard Baba X say that, again, and it was solace of a sort. It was her raspy, paper-thin ninety-year-old voice, which car-ried all the way to his room, but which those other shits in the kitchen didn't even notice.

He heard the fridge door open and bang shut. It would be the other jar of pickles! That wasn't safe. If there were champagne in the fridge it wouldn't be safe either. Oh, and Marilyn's laugh once or twice again. Probably giggling over getting the jar open. Anna was laughing too when the jar finally popped. How many jars of pickles would resist the onslaught?

It's a world of shifting allegiances.

Then came a collective roar of laughter.

Were they laughing at him? His pout?

During the Six-Day War he remembered how the entire Jewish community had huddled together and worried, how they had done so in their house: they worried, then rejoiced. And now the central committee of the PLO was in his house, eating his corned beef, opening his halvah and pickles. Only Baba X was looking out after him, and he had always been so used to all the women in the house taking care of him, Anna and Marilyn, too. He was their collective son, and he liked that. This tough-guy role had got him nothing, just a sore finger. He wondered again whether he'd lose the nail, which was now slightly blue.

He looked out the window at the grass gently sloping down to the bullrushes and still water, framed at the top by telephone wires. Tiny birds perched on the crushed velvet bullrush cobs, looking at him staring out his window at them. Wild rose hips hung still by the fence. It was so peaceful, the horizon so pink. And him so miserable.

He lay back down again. He wasn't enjoying this.

The hunger rumbled inside his stomach.

But I won't get up, he said to himself. A surge of spite gave him courage again to struggle against the pleasures of the table. During the '48 war he had gone hungry, hadn't he? Well, not really.

He stared up at the idiotic chandelier hanging from the apex of the ceiling. A chandelier in a lake cottage. What had gotten into them?

Why doesn't she bring me in a sandwich and a coke? Or why doesn't Marilyn do something for him? Or Anna's mother. Why don't they listen to her? Would they eat up all the corned beef?

He just didn't matter to them, he thought. He didn't matter to anyone in the world. No one does. The human race is unworthy.

He had loved them all too much. But from now on they'd see. He would lower the temperature to freezing. They would learn.

18

Sammy rolled onto his back when he heard the soft knock. He had been staring down at the broadloom for hours, at that and at his sore finger.

Even though she didn't like his antics, Anna came into the bedroom later that evening with a tray. Actually, Baba X had pestered her so much with her "What's Sammy going to eat" that just to shut her up she loaded the TV table tray with goodies: salami, chopped liver, pickles, pickled herring and Ritz crackers, since the last of the fresh rye bread had already been devoured. She added a can of Coke. All her life she had heard that line from her mother: "What's Sammy going to eat?" When she wanted to go out for tea with her friends in the afternoon, her mother would stop her cold just by saying, "What's Sammy going to eat?" and then she would either have to stay home and prepare a proper supper or go out feeling guilty.

And it still worked. She had been ready to let Sammy go through his tantrum, weather it like a summer storm, but there was her mother, putting her teeth in her glass before going to bed, the last thought in her head, spoken out loud: "What's Sammy going to eat?"

She did feel a bit guilty for how the kids turned out, though. She had filled Teddy's head with do-gooding. The poor always broke her heart. So he got his kindness from her. She was even kind to the Arabs. But that was her goodness again. He got it from her. Maybe she kept Teddy away from his father too much. But Sammy contributed; he didn't make that much of an effort either.

She knocked and pushed open the door with her foot and set the TV table beside the bed.

Sammy looked more irritated than despondent now. Or maybe he was just hungry.

"Are you hungry?"

"No, I'm not hungry," he said, numb with hunger, taking in a hefty whiff of the chopped liver.

This was the silliest thing he'd said all week, he thought.

"Sammy, listen," she said.

She didn't say "Sammy, please listen."

"You've got to eat something."

She touched his hand.

"Watch the finger!"

She pulled her hand away.

"Eat, Sammy."

"I'm not hungry." His tone was more brittle than before, pleading to be coaxed a bit more.

"Just eat anyway."

"There's no rye bread."

"There's crackers. You only eat chopped liver on crackers anyway."

"There's no herring."

"Yes, herring there is. What's that?"

"Where?"

"In front of your nose."

"Oh."

"Oh."

"So, what's it going to be?" Anna said.

"I just wish she'd have the baby already. I'm in *galus*," he said.

"She's a lovely girl," said Anna.

"I don't want to hear it."

"You're going to have to give in."

"I'm not giving in," he said, taking a bite of his pickle.

The juice spurted against his teeth. It was scrumptious. It slid down his *gorgle* and made a definite presence in his stomach. He ogled the chopped liver and corned beef and wondered what to eat first.

"I'm not giving in. If I'm in *galus*, everyone can be in *galus*."

"Nobody's in *galus* but you."

"If that's where you all want me . . ."

He raised the pickled to his mouth.

Anna grabbed his hand holding the pickle. "There are no pickles in *galus*."

The pickle had been really delicious.

"Where's that herring?"

19

The next day Sammy's boredom was verging on fury. It was sultry and he came out of his room in the late morning perspiring slightly. He had half decided overnight to join in daily life, make an effort to be civil. But underneath he felt surly, irritated and constipated. And it was really the boredom that expelled him from his room.

The first thing he saw was Aïda's belly: large and round, truly enormous, and he didn't like it.

He scarcely looked at her face, and did not speak to her. He didn't speak to Teddy either, and kept away from Marilyn. He thought they thought he was acting ridiculous, which hurt, but he couldn't help it. Sometime you get yourself so deep in shit that you can't get out.

Teddy and Aïda had gone to the government pier to buy worms and try and catch some perch. Aïda had never gone fishing before. Neither had Teddy for that matter. Sammy had taught his son to play poker, had explained the difference between Texas Hold 'em and Omaha, pot limit and table stakes, but they had never gone fishing.

Sammy was irritated that they had gone out, as if he was gunning for them and wanted confrontation, which they were avoiding, but he would have been just as irritated had they stayed in. It was a fine balance everyone was managing.

He stared out over the deck, across the mouth of the creek flowing into the lake, then peered out across the lake, over which the sky was mauve and pink with the odd yellow flash. It would rain, it would storm, even. Maybe the summer would be completely fucked weather-wise.

Lounging on the chesterfield, Marilyn, all too comfortably for Sammy in her tight cotton Capri pants and navel-exposing T-shirt, was giggling over a book. Anna was sitting on the other chesterfield, reading a novel, wanting to watch TV news, although she knew Marilyn wouldn't let her turn on the set if she were reading. Marilyn snickered over every word.

Baba X, wedged into the chesterfield beside Marilyn, had on her thick sunglasses and was sucking on a grape Popsicle, which was turning her tongue and lips blue. She was waiting in the living room for her Alex's visit. She had her big brown purse lying flat on her knees, her cane tucked between the arm of the chesterfield and the cushion. Sammy thought she should have had a thermos of coffee with her, for the wait, as usual, would be a long one. Fucking Uncle Alex. Although he hated the idea that the people in the community would see Teddy and Aïda, he was relieved that Teddy and Aïda would be away when Fucking Uncle Alex dropped by to pick up Anna's mother.

Marilyn turned a page and laughed.

What is always so goddamn funny with her? Sammy thought.

"People will see them, you know," he complained, interrupting Marilyn's reading.

"I'm reading."

Sammy let it go, staring out the window onto the creek. The calm water and teeming birdlife was so peaceful, so beautiful, it was a pleasure to look at. The human world was so ugly.

Then he jumped as if he had been shat on by a pigeon when Marilyn burst out laughing.

"What's so funny with you?"

Anna gave her a dirty look too. Baba X stirred a bit, having dozed off.

"It's this book."

Sammy didn't think books could make you laugh.

"What are you reading?"

"A book called *Hadassah Chapters*."

"What's it about?"

"Just stories. Each chapter is named after a Hadassah chapter. Get it."

"That's not funny. It's clever, but it's not funny."

"That's not what made me laugh."

"What's it about?" Since he had decided to be civil, he would show interest.

"It's about this female midget, a real *maven*, in a Hadassah chapter in New York City in the early sixties, who has it off with the Jewish male guest speakers after the meetings, you know, pediatricians, judges, politicians. But the thing is this, right: this Jewish midget makes love to these guys to such satisfaction that their foreskins grow back, and they have to explain this to their wives."

"That's not funny."

"Yes, it is."

"It's sick."

"It's not sick."

"It's a sick story."

"And the first story's even funnier."

"I don't want to hear about it."

"It's called 'Big Nose, Big Hose'. It's about a guy who is granted one wish."

"I don't want to hear it."

"Any wish he wants, the *shofar* has blown the end of Yom Kippur, everyone has left the synagogue. He's alone and is approached by a mysterious beadle."

"Which Beatle?"

"Not Beatle, beadle. The *shames*."

"Oh, the *shames*."

"Where's the *shames*?" asked Baba X.

"Ma, there's no *shames*. It's a story." said Anna.

"What's a story?"

"She's out of the loop."

"Why was the guy at the synagogue on Yom Kippur, after the service? If it's just after Yom Kippur, he'd be so hungry, he would've run home," said Sammy.

"I don't know."

"So what kind of story is that?"

"It's just a story."

"So go on," said Sammy.

"Alright, so this guy is granted one wish. What do you think he wishes for?"

"I don't know. Yom Kippur, right, I'd say world peace."

"Sammy, think. One wish. A man is granted one wish. Story called 'Big Nose, Big Hose.'"

"Oh."

"Right."

"Does he get his wish?"

"Yeah, but the problem is that it's so big, when gets an erection, he faints."

"Why does he faint?"

"Well, you get an erection when blood rushes to the penis, right?"

"Oh, yeah."

"So . . . so much blood has to rush to his enormous penis that it leaves his brain, uh, blood-starved, and he faints."

"And that's funny by you?"

"It's hilarious."

"It's sick. These penis stories."

"It's dick-lit," said Marilyn, finally cracking up.

"What's dick-lit?"

"Never mind. You wouldn't get it."

"Get what? What are you talking about? And what's Hadassah got to do with them?"

"It's not sick. You've just lost your sense of humour."

"No, I haven't."

"Well, what about this one. 'Thracian Hoplite Confects Jarmuschian Gibbet.'"

"There's not one word in that title that I understand."

"You don't know what a hoplite is?"

"No."

"Or where Thrace is?"

"No."

"A gibbet?"

"No."

"And Jim Jarmusch? You don't know who he is?"

"No. Nobody knows those words."

"You've lost more than your sense of humour. You've lost your vocabulary."

"Never had one."

"You're just being cranky. And if you're going to be cranky all the time, you might as well go back to bed."

"I just got up."

Sammy saw the pointlessness of arguing with her and stared out onto the creek again. It was sweltering. The pier far off was warped by the heat, seeming to float in the pearl-grey sky. He thought he heard thunder. His thoughts turned to Teddy and Aïda, out there, being seen by the entire Jewish beach community, as they paraded that enormous belly of hers around, with the *yasel* inside. And after all they had said to people, denying the rumours of the Arab girl. They looked like proper fools.

He sat down at the table in the nook, waiting to be indulged. His stomach rumbled and grumbled.

"Why don't you have some breakfast?" said Anna.

"Finally it dawns on you."

"You can make it yourself."

Sammy stood there, incensed. Nobody moved to make him breakfast. His stomach fizzed and squirted. This he noted right down in his big Book of Life and Death. There would be no breakfast? Alright. So there would be no breakfast.

And this with the coffee percolator only three yards away on the counter. The bagels all cut up beside it, going stale.

"People will see them," he said, his irritation rising, and to think he had got out of bed determined to be civil today.

"So what?" said Marilyn, putting her book down. "Let them see them."

"We can't lock them in," said Anna.

All three thought their truths were self-evident.

Just before they had gone to buy worms, and as Aïda had slipped through the back door, Sammy looked at her belly and thought the baby might be retarded. It was a haunting and nauseating thought that struck deep into the core of soul, close to where his pride was lodged.

What if the baby were retarded?

Uncle Alex would be happy about that; he had been so entirely pissed off when Marilyn graduated from law school, with lauds, the gold medal, the works, while Alex's son dropped out of high school and had to go into Uncle Alex's firm.

Sammy saw he was going to have to make his own breakfast. He went to the kitchen and set up a tray with the coffee pot, a cup and spoon and a plate, which wasn't so difficult. Then from the fridge he took what was left of the chopped liver, the butter and three sliced bagels. He placed the chopped liver and the butter on the tray and took a butter knife out of the drawer. These things were novel, but they were not that hard. He brought the tray to the dining table in the nook and sat down, then realized he had forgotten the sweetener. He felt stupid as he got up again and went to get the sweetener and returned to the table and poured himself the coffee. Perhaps the kid would be retarded like he was.

Down syndrome or retardation of some sort. Could happen. He wondered if the fetus had been tested for these things. It could be blind, their *yasel*. Could you see this blind little retard going into a mosque?

Anna and Marilyn came to join him at the kitchen table and *shnorred* his coffee. Who invited them? Didn't they have enough tormenting him from the living room? As he gnawed on his bagel and butter, and defended his chopped liver from Marilyn who had already expropriated one of his bagels, he realised he just had to get the thought out of his system, so he said to the two of them, "You know, the baby might be born retarded."

"He'd get that from you," Anna said, who had lost all patience with him, and who had bent with the wind already towards Aïda's favour.

Marilyn yelped.

"It seems his auntie has beat the kid to it." Sammy said, glaring at Marilyn.

It might have a club foot. Or a strawberry patch. Or Down's.

"I bet you he'll end up in an enriched program," said Marilyn. "Anyway, you are just being so uncool about this."

"Uncool. Since when have I ever cared about being cool?"

"Never."

"Thank you."

"Just accept it, Dad. You know you will. You go along with everything," said Marilyn, getting her knife into his chopped liver.

"He's an ostrich," Anna said. "No, he's an Ostrove."

"I can't accept this," Sammy said, this time glaring at Anna.

"You've always given in. Admit it," said Marilyn.

"An ostrich," said Anna again.

"Stop calling him an ostrich!"

Anna looked hurt by Marilyn's remark, but tried to keep her lips and chin noble. Sammy was pleased by Marilyn's attack on Anna and thought it had shut her up, but this proved not to be, for Anna turned right back on him.

"Do you want to end up like Sammy Miller? Never seeing your own kid again?" said Anna.

"Did he really offer Richie $200,000 not to get married to a shiksa?" asked Sammy, for whom the gossip about Chickie Miller was a bit vague.

"The girl was on another phone. She heard the whole thing. The whole thing," said Anna, who knew all the gossip. "She was eavesdropping."

"$100,000," said Marilyn, who knew the Miller boy and had heard the story firsthand.

"I didn't think he had that much money," said Anna. "But they always put on airs. The Millers were always running around with the hoi polloi."

"I've got news for you," said Marilyn, 'hoi polloi' doesn't mean the rich; it means the rabble."

Anna hated it when Marilyn corrected her.

Sammy said, "Turned out the kid wasn't worth even that. The ingrate. So his father made one little mistake. They didn't have to rub his face in it all these years."

"One mistake? You call that a mistake? Trying to buy off your own son."

"I do. And Sammy Miller did eventually give in."

"That's my point," said Marilyn, "you will eventually. You're going to have to give in. You know you will. What's with this revenge drama, this Hamlet thing. You should be dressed in black and reading verse."

Revenge drama, Hamlet, where does she get this stuff, Sammy thought. But he had a riposte.

"You talk now as if you didn't want me to give in."

Marilyn saw the logic of that. She wanted him to accept Aïda, but it hurt her somewhere deep inside that he would be made to give in. Go figure.

"Well maybe on some Freudian level I don't."

Anna hacked out a single laugh every time she heard the name Freud, and as always said this: "Freud is just so much talk."

Marilyn screamed. Sammy, befuddled, didn't know what had made her laugh, and neither did Anna.

"Well," Marilyn began, "maybe on some level I don't want you to give in like you always do. All that passivity of yours."

She shouldn't be saying any of this, she thought. Sometimes she regretted having such a big mouth. She thought for a second about rolling it back. Finding an out.

But Sammy saw his in.

"You talk as if you don't want me to accept her," Sammy pounced.

It was too late, she thought. "You're so weak, Dad. You've always been so weak."

Sammy eyed her meanly, the hurt showing on his face, wishing God would intervene.

Suddenly they heard a thunderclap of mosaic dimensions. Baba X canted to the left and opened her mouth in shock. "Tunder," she said, "shut the windows!"

Yeah, fuck it, Marilyn thought. "You've never put your foot down in the past. Never. So why now? You've always let yourself be mollycoddled by these two here."

Marilyn pointed gangsta style at Anna, and then to Baba X over on the chesterfield clutching her big brown purse, her lips bluer than before from the Popsicle, waiting for her son Alex, oblivious to everything but the thunder.

"Here she goes with her two-bit psychology courses," sighed Anna. "They've always run things," she continued. "You're the nebbish."

"Shut your mouth," said Sammy.

"Especially her." Marilyn pointed to Baba X, her fear of thunder contorting her face, folding the Popsicle wrapper obsessively into a tiny bundle on her purse.

Marilyn decided to turn up the shit fan.

"You've always abdicated responsibility. And now you're mounting this pathetic last stand. Wake up and smell the coffee, it's too late."

He hated it when she said "wake up and smell the coffee."

"You know you're going to have to accept it. You always have. Always will."

This was true, he thought. He was dying to give in. If he were only one-tenth as stubborn as Baba X or his wife, he wouldn't want to, but the truth is he wanted to, not because he approved of this Aïda business, but because he hated confrontation.

The thunder rumbled flat across the lake up the creek. It seemed to lap around the cottage and then seep into the ground.

"Shut the windows, it's tundering outside!" urged Baba X, who they were ignoring.

"You accept everything. Take everything. You accepted my marrying Jack, when I know you didn't approve."

Nothing could be truer, he thought. Jack was a nebbish.

"It's true, Jack was a nebbish."

"And you accepted our breakup."

"It's the failure of the sexual revolution," piped in Anna.

"Ma, stay out of this." She pointed a finger at Sammy and continued, "You accepted Teddy dropping out of medicine, although it killed you; you accepted my not having kids, although you know you want grandchildren."

True, true, true.

"And I know you don't like my lifestyle."

Sammy didn't know what a lifestyle was, but he didn't like Marilyn running around, if that's what she meant. And he definitely didn't like people saying in public that she had been buggered and how hot she was and the rest. Who would?

"Even now you just sit there and take it from me. You wanted Teddy to be a doctor, but when he quit you didn't say a word. All these years, all he needed was one word from you. Just one stern word. But now it's too late."

I didn't want to push him. I don't like pushing people. Tell her that, he said to himself, but instead he just said, "Shut up, Marilyn." He just said that.

"Don't say 'shut up'," said Anna.

"Would you let him say what he wants, for fuck's sake."

"I'm defending you!" said Anna.

"Do I need *you* to defend me?" said Marilyn.

That shut Anna up. They always ganged up on her. They would pay.

"You know what? Fuck off, Marilyn," Sammy said.

Marilyn was stunned. "I don't need this, you know, this being here."

"So why don't you just go home. Get in your German car and go home. Go get buggered."

"Sammy!" cried Anna.

That shut her up, Sammy thought.

"Why are you hanging around here?" he asked her.

It was a good question, Marilyn reflected.

"I'm here to help," was all she could say, still stunned.

"You? You're the one who needs help."

"I'm not the one in analysis."

"I'm not in analysis. I just go there. But I don't need a pot of Vaseline on the bed table."

Marilyn was shocked.

The thunder boomed stronger, bringing with it a thick chilly air. Baba X started again. "Shut the window, it's tundering outside!"

Sammy got up and slammed the window. "So now it's not tundering?!" he shouted at her. The reverberation of the slam reached his sore finger and made it throb.

"Don't get on your high horse," said Baba X.

He started to leave the living room, upset with himself for having told Marilyn to fuck off and for the pot-of-Vaseline remark. How could he say such a thing? He rubbed his finger, although it didn't hurt that much, and put on his gnarled old man walk a bit, but not too much.

"He didn't bugger me," shouted Marilyn as he left.

"Of course, those are just rumours!" Why did he keep on. Best not turn around.

Marilyn got up and sat beside Baba X and swaddled her head in the old lady's shift, sticky with Popsicle dripping, feeling a brittle collar bone. Why did I come here? she thought.

"I'm dry," Baba X said.

Marilyn got up and fetched her a candy, then cuddled back up on Baba X's breast.

Anna turned on the TV news channel to get info on the storm. Commercials came on and Marilyn groaned. It's my house, Anna said to herself. If I want to turn on the TV set I can. Why should I let this little shit run the show here?

Baba X sucked the candy a bit, then cracked it with her molars.

"You're just supposed to suck, Baba."

"Sue me."

Baba X sang Marilyn a Yiddish lullaby very softly, still waiting for her Alex to show up.

"The whole family's regressing," Marilyn said wistfully, rocking gently on her grandmother's breast.

Baba X didn't understand what Marilyn meant by "regressing" and sucked on her candy and hummed. For a while the thunder had subsided into a low rumble and there was a certain peace indoors.

Then a blistering ray of lightning waltzed up to the window and looked in, followed almost immediately by a sonic boom. Baba X jumped and Marilyn's head was bumped upright.

"You know, there are more than sixteen million thunderstorms a year," Marilyn said to Anna, her voice carrying above the TV noise. Anna was trying to zap on to a new program about the storm; she was petrified about Teddy and Aïda and the baby being caught in it. She changed channels furiously.

"Why don't you change the channel," said Marilyn.

Anna gave her a dirty look.

Then another tall flash sidled right up to the sliding doors and stood there looking in, followed by a crack of thunder.

"Teddy and Aïda are out there," Anna said in alarm.

"There are more than six thousand lightning flashes per minute in your average thunderstorm. You know what the chances are of getting hit by lightning?"

Then came a tremendous *biff — bam — bang* that smacked the house good. The electricity blew. The TV wound down with a sharp whine and final ping. Marilyn clapped like a seal. Baba X got some leverage from who-knows-where and sat upright in a panic again.

"Where's Teddy and Ida?"

"Aïda, Baba; there's a dieresis."

"Are all the windows shut?!" she strained her voice, banging the broadloom with her cane.

"Baba, you've got brontophobia."

Baba X didn't know what she was talking about. She was in distress. It was her firm, old-country belief that lightning could come into a house through open windows. She had seen it happen. Had smelled burnt flesh.

"Sometimes called ceraunophobia or tonitrophobia."

"Torontophobia?"

"Sort of. Fear of thunder."

"Don't *farmish* her. Why didn't you just say that?" rebuked Anna, bored with Marilyn's archness. She was wishing Marilyn would leave and that Teddy would get back already. She imagined Teddy on the ground, covered by a white sheet, then the funeral, the velvet coffin in the synagogue foyer, the interment, the shiva, even the food in the Tupperware people would bring, repenting their insulting him, her, Marilyn, Sammy, all of them. From the thunder claps she spun an elaborate negative fantasy that made her shiver.

"Shut the windows!" Baba X strained again, trying to shout. "The lightning. The lightning will come in."

Marilyn got up and started pulling down the other sash windows with a thump.

"Anna, what are the chances of getting hit by lightning?"

Anna shot her another dirty look, got up and went over to the big picture window looking for Teddy and Aïda, but mostly for Teddy.

Marilyn answered herself: "One in 700,000. Those are the chances of getting hit by lightning."

"If you go out," said Anna.

"No, if you stay in."

"What's with all the sarcasm?" Anna was getting tired of it and she gave Marilyn another dirty look, then bit down on her cuticles. She was in a panic about Teddy being out there in the storm. Boy, she could really worry. She saw Teddy's coffin again floating over chrome rollers as it was loaded into the hearse, a black Cadillac with brass treble clefs on the side panels.

Suddenly another thick yellow bolt of lightning came up and stood right outside the window there, right in front of her, shimmering and shaking, holding the light for what seemed an hour. Anna took fright, then the lightning vanished with a *kunuck* and some aftercrackle.

"You know, lightning is just a huge electrical spark."

"Shut up already!"

Rain poured down, sweeping in from the lake, up the wide creek bed, landing in giant splashes on the deck board. Suddenly Teddy and Aïda's footsteps banged and stamped outside. You could hear their giggling over the pounding rain. Teddy slid open the patio doors and to Anna's relief they both came in, soaking wet. Drops flew as far as the couch.

"We left the fishing rods."

Both he and Aïda laughed in delight. Such is love, thought Anna. She was thrilled that they made it back safely. She brought Aïda a big fluffy towel and hugged her with it. Teddy gushed.

There was another hammer blow from Thor. Then another, which split a chunky branch off an old elm tree down by the creek.

"Shock and awe out there," said Teddy.

"Shlock and awe in here," said Marilyn.

"You could have been killed," said Anna.

Then for about five minutes down came hail the size of golf-balls, after which the sun came out and the electricity went back on.

■ ■ ■

After he dried off, Teddy left all the women in the living room. Aïda was hitting it off with the three of them again. He walked into his parents' bedroom.

Sammy was annoyed to see him. He didn't want to be confronted, not again. And this was supposed to be his good day. He could go on hating Teddy forever, or all of them for that matter. That's how much spite had been pent up.

Sammy ignored him, concentrating on the Jays game instead.

"He just threw a big hammer. He'll strike him out in four."

Teddy was surprised at how civilly Sammy had said this. Instead of turning off the TVs he sat on the bed and stared at the screen.

"What's a big hammer?"

"Curve ball, with a big sharp break. He'll throw a backdoor curve now."

"How do you know this?"

The pitch looked wide but curved in to cross the corner of the plate. The batter checked his swing and the ump called the strike. The batter stepped away from the plate in embarrassment and tapped his cleats with his bat.

"What's he going to throw now?" asked Teddy.

"O and two. He should make him swing. Something tight inside, across the chest. Fastball. Something intimidating."

The pitch came in straight as an arrow and suddenly dropped before crossing the plate. The batter resisted, checked his swing, his confidence rising as the ump called the ball.

Sammy's face turned sour.

"Stupid pitch?" asked Teddy.

"Stupid pitcher," said Sammy.

"What's he going to throw now?"

"His knuckleball. The guy's a show-off. Too predictable this guy."

"Will the batter swing at it?"

"Not this one. His confidence is up. He knows the pitcher's got a lousy knuckleball. Christ, I know it. He's not a knuckleball pitcher, but he'll have to try it."

The pitch came floating in, no spin, no rotation, like a scudding cloud, then it swooped to the dirt. The ump called another ball.

"That's a knuckleball. Good pitch, wrong batter, wrong time."

"Why's it called a knuckleball?"

"I don't know. You don't use your knuckles. Just the finger tips, or your fingernails."

The fifth pitch came in wide and it was three and two. Sammy was irritated.

"He's going to walk him."

"I thought you were rooting for the Jays."

"I am."

"So why are you mad that he's going to walk him?"

"I'm fair."

Teddy stood up and turned off Sammy's TV.

"Teddy. Don't do that."

Would it be one last shoot-out? Sammy wondered.

"You never said hello properly to Aïda," Teddy said.

"I said hello."

"But not nicely."

"I can't stand looking at her pregnant belly," Sammy said.

"So don't look at it."

"It's hard to ignore. I've never seen anyone so pregnant."

What could Teddy do to turn things around? Why was his father doing this? How long would he let him treat Aïda like this? How long would Aïda take it?

So far Aïda was patient, preoccupied with giving birth, studying the birth books and childcare books. Teddy had discovered she was practical and was enjoying her social elevation to expecting mother, which had earned her everyone's admiration, except Sammy's. Sammy didn't like seeing those books around the house. And then there was the DVD, *Pregnant, and Loving It*, that really made his skin crawl. Marilyn put it on, with no warning, and he had caught sight of a baby's head coming out of a vagina. The voice-over was that of someone describing a Caribbean cruise, to jaunty music: "The shoulders are delivered." Then came another gory scene: "The midwife supports perineum." .

Marilyn saw the distress and disgust crease his face.

"Look," she said. "The first thing that happens to you when you're born, you slide straight into a tub of shit."

He dismissed her with a wave of his hand.

"Look!"

"I don't want to look!"

Teddy knew very well why his father was acting like this. He had marginalized his father from his social environment. He had ruined his social life, which is the only life we really have.

Teddy had come to a decision.

"We're moving out," Teddy said.

"Who said you could move in?" It was a cheap point. "You can't stay here."

"We're going back to Ramallah."

Sammy felt suddenly like vomiting.

"They'll kill you. I know those people. They'll kill you, eventually."

"Why would they kill me? They were very decent to me."

"I'm not talking about them. I'm talking about the Israelis. I know them. I've been there, too. Remember? There's no stopping them."

"Doesn't matter. I can't stay here. Like you say, I'm ruining your life. I'll take my chances there."

Sammy's urge to vomit came back. But then Teddy's maudlin sincerity started to bug him.

"Dad, I've been selfish. I thought you would accept Aïda and the baby. I really felt that. I wasn't thinking. I just fell for her. I couldn't help it. It just happened. But it was selfish of me. I've hurt you guys, and I'm wrong. This is the second, no the third time I've disappointed you. I shouldn't have dropped out of medical school either. You didn't deserve it. You don't deserve it."

This brought a flush of glee to Sammy's cheeks.

He had won. For the first time in his life he was up.

It was like when they expelled the Arabs from a village near Haifa on Sammy's first operation. When the whole village was theirs. An entire empty village. To be peopled by Jews from the camps, or from wherever. The blacksmith's, the bakery, the school, the town hall, all the houses. Everything. Just like that. That was the last victory he could think of. Taking the village had been quick and easy. There were only six rifles for the twenty men or so who were putting up resistance against their well-armed motorized brigade. The Arabs fought first at a road, then down by the sea. They fought to the last bullet. He even saw three men behind a fence sharing one gun. Pathetic. But they had lost four comrades, friends, healthy young men. In revenge the whole population was marched down to the beach, the men separated from the women. Men from the Alexandroni Brigade drove up, said we had to kill all the men. They had done it before, they said. On what orders? Sammy had asked. Unwritten orders, they had said. And they were pissed off about losing those four guys. Why leave these men alive? they asked. When they get the chance they'll be back. Wouldn't you, wouldn't you try to come back, get revenge, if someone stole your house? Your town? The men from the Alexandroni Brigade shot the men that night. The women and children were chased away in the morning like dogs. He wouldn't participate, and was sent to guard the women and children. The other soldiers derided him for being a coward and shamed him thereafter. After that Sammy decided not to live there and he came back home. He never told anybody about it, not even Anna. As far as they knew he had been in Herzliya all the time. No one else had heard of the massacre either, it seems.

Total impunity. To the whole world the Jews were the under-dogs in that war, but it wasn't true. For the first time, we were top dog. He felt an irrepressible urge to tell all this to Teddy. In Israel, his life would have been different. Those bastards from the Alexandroni Brigade — they had ruined it for him.

"Dad?"

"What?"

"Are you paying attention?"

"Yeah, sure."

"Listen, what I wanted to say was that I wasn't thinking. I'm sorry. I'm going back and you'll get your life back."

"Going back?" asked Sammy.

Teddy realized when he said it that he didn't want to go back. Who wants to live under siege? The checkpoints, the army incursions, the gas, the curfews, the boredom of being trapped in one's house in the heat, going days without running water when the Israelis wrench off the mains, the searches, the humiliation, the rubble in the streets, the raw sewage, the mass arrests. And that habit the Israelis had when occupying a town to kill someone right off, no matter who, just to lay down the law. And Sammy was right, too, the Palestinians couldn't win. The Israelis would eventually get rid of them. His child would grow up throwing stones at tanks until one day he would be arrested or exiled or shot. No, he didn't want to go back there, but now he had no choice. He'd said it.

He didn't want to leave home. He had never wanted to leave in the first place. It was a mistake to run away from that rabbi's wife thing. But he had felt ashamed of what he had done. And now he had fucked up again. He wanted to stay here. But now he was stuck. He would have to leave. He had shot his mouth off.

He had discussed this decision earlier with his sister. She had just laughed.

"I wouldn't go back to Jack just to please Dad," Marilyn said.

"I'm ruining their life."

"No, you're not. They can go back to the Sophisticates whenever they want. Nobody really cares. Just a few zealots. Just the big mouths. The rest worry more about their regularity."

"He's grieving for his life."

"It's all an act."

"I've never seen Dad act like this. I've never seen him so down, or so determined."

"He'll get over it."

"They're ostracized. They don't deserve it. They're old."

Marilyn agreed. They were old. And true, they didn't deserve it, but they were the ones who decided to have kids. "No one told him not to pull out," she had said. Although they didn't deserve their misfortune, Teddy couldn't remedy it, only they could, by standing up to the so-called community.

"If they don't get over it, it's not your fault. You owe them nothing."

Teddy stood there by the TV, lost in thought.

"Teddy?"

"What?"

"When are you leaving?" Sammy asked.

"After the baby is born."

"Will there be a *briss*?"

"If it's a boy."

"Then going back there?"

"Back there," Teddy said, in a kind of glum reverie, leaving the room.

Sammy felt the vengeful glee diminish and it made him feel like vomiting again. He wasn't a monster, although he was a coward. Tantura had proved that. Yes, he felt like giving in, which is what he did best. Marilyn was right. They were right in Tantura. He felt an immense sorrow for himself, almost mourning, in the face of the unpreventable. He thought of turning the TV back on, but knew he wouldn't have the patience to watch now.

He stood up and looked outside and saw the creek bed, and how in the wake of the storm the lawn sparkled with raindrops in the sun. He felt trapped. He looked at the little toolshed: it seemed frail, having been buffeted and tossed, and now under a wash of sadness. There was no alternative to Teddy's going back. Or, they could all move away. Perhaps to the coast, but then everything would be lost, and not only the cottage, the creek, their apartment in the city, but a whole way of life — one that no one will remember. He thought of his parents' graves at the Hebrew cemetery being left unattended. But eventually all graves are left unattended. He would be a last Jew. Oh, no man is happy until he's dead.

■ ■ ■

Fucking Uncle Alex did drive up in his black Lexus that afternoon, his louche golf cap tilted back, carrying his obnoxious, dirty poodle, Ming, and shlepping along his wife Dolly. Dolly waddled up the brick path behind him on her hippopotamus calves, ill-dressed for summer in one of her prim blameless blouses with the pie-crust collar and a calf-length skirt that looked more like a rug that had been woven in Isfahan. They knocked but stepped in without waiting for anyone to open the door, dropping the mad Ming on the floor. Ming tilted her head and gave everybody a filthy, poor-relatives stare. Alex, glum and cynical as ever when having to visit his mother and sister, with a Churchill-size cigar sticking out from his babyish jowls, shooed the dog gently aside with his loafer and butted the ash of his cigar in a clean glass ashtray. Aïda was sitting with Teddy watching a Michael Moore DVD and Marilyn was on the other chesterfield with Baba X, reading her book of short stories from Hadassah. Anna was reading her crappy novel in the kitchen nook and Sammy was in his room watching the Jays blow a lead. Everyone but Baba X jumped up in surprise, as though they'd stopped expecting Dolly and Alex to show up.

"Uncle Alex?" went Teddy. "Auntie Dolly?"

"Hi Teddy."

Uncle Alex went over to his mother by the chesterfield and bent over to kiss her.

"Ma, your lips are blue."

"Blue?" asked Baba X.

"Why are her lips blue?" asked Uncle Leo to Marilyn.

"She just had a grape Popsicle."

Uncle Alex pulled himself up and took a long look at Aïda, standing beside Teddy, which Anna caught, while saying hello to his sister.

"How's it going, Anna. Sammy around?"

He cocked a watery eye again at Aïda, then at her belly. Who is this person? He was genuinely shocked. They had been in Palm Springs and obviously hadn't heard the rumours. Teddy started the introductions.

"Uncle Alex, Aunt Dolly, this is Aïda." But for some reason Teddy slurred the dieresis.

"Hello Ida," Uncle Alex said, wondering if he had heard a dieresis. He turned to Dolly and raised an eyebrow.

Aïda stared just a moment too long at Dolly's pie crust collar that hung down almost to the tips of her bust, and then shook their hands. Uncle Alex left a hot moist imprint on hers. Aunt Dolly's hand was icy and limp.

"Are you two married?" asked Uncle Alex bluntly.

There was an uneasy silence.

"Sort of," mumbled Teddy.

"I mean by a minister or something. We were married by a minister," Uncle Alex said, flipping his thumb at Dolly, "the Minister of War."

Teddy had heard the joke before. He felt so awkward that he had to get away immediately. So he asked them if they wanted some coffee.

"Dolly, how about you?"

Dolly made one of her famous moues of distaste and said to him through her slit for a mouth, "Kid, I just took a diuretic." Then she sucked some air through the side of her mouth, which gave her her famous Elvis sneer.

"She just had a diuretic," said Uncle Alex, tacking down Dolly's explanation.

As if I was supposed to know who's had a diuretic of late, said Teddy to himself, moving his eyebrows at Marilyn, who had also gotten to her feet, expectant.

Marilyn stifled a scream, winking back at Teddy. I just had a diuretic. That was a typical Dolly remark, but what could you expect from someone who looked at the world through squinting eyes and spoke through a slit for a mouth? I just had a diuretic. Marilyn didn't know what to do with the laugh. She got up and opened the front door. I just had a diuretic. Now out of earshot she let go a huge bark of laughter.

"I just took a diuretic," she said out loud, and when she regained her composure she went back in and sat beside Baba X.

"Sit," Anna said to Uncle Alex and Aunt Dolly.

"We've been sitting in the car," said Aunt Dolly, who knew that if they sat down now it would take a while to get away. She had already grabbed Baba X's purse and looked poised to hoist the old lady up.

"Alex, how about a scotch or something?" Teddy was still eager to get away from them, even if only to the kitchen, and even if Aïda would be stuck with them.

Marilyn, catching Aunt Dolly's eagerness to pack Baba X off in the Lexus, said, "Aunt Dolly, sit here."

Dolly didn't budge and stood stiffly with Baba X's purse stowed under her arm.

"No more scotch," said Uncle Alex. "No scotch, Teddy, not after the last bypass."

Was that supposed to be my fault too? thought Teddy.

"Would you like a soft drink?" asked Aïda.

"I'd love one."

Uncle Alex looked down into her eyes and finally sat down, just as Baba X had managed to lever herself onto her feet using her cane. Alex lifted the knees of his trousers and sat down on the chesterfield, exposing hairless shins, with blue bulges, see-through socks and tassled loafers. Teddy brought him the ash-tray with his Churchill. Blue ribbons of smoke drifted into Baba X's eyes, but she said nothing, grinning ecstatically about having her children together in the same room.

"Ma," said Uncle Alex, "sit."

"I just got up."

"Sit. Sit."

Dolly gave Alex a look.

"Sit," he commanded. "We're going to have a little visit."

"It's late," said Dolly. But she sat.

Baba X hovered on her swollen feet.

"Ma! Sit. We're not going yet. Did you hear me?"

"I heard you."

"We're going to have a little visit," he said, staring at Aïda.

"I heard you."

Baba X was puzzled and unsettled. Alex never visited, he fetched. Marilyn helped her settle back into the chesterfield, right on top of *Hadassah Chapters*.

"I'm sitting on something."

"You're sitting on my book," said Marilyn, wedging it out from underneath her rump.

Normally, Alex and Dolly would just have whisked Baba X off for her ride, taken her to the tea room at the Pavilion, sitting silently with her while she gnawed on her scone and zooped her tea, Dolly anxiously checking her Rolex, having run out of inane conversation by the time the tea was served, but Uncle Alex was intrigued by the presence of this incredibly pretty, incredibly pregnant young woman. Uncle Alex couldn't stop staring at Aïda. For one thing, it was the bleached gaze of the old philanderer who had always stared at good-looking women. Can I fuck her? he thought. On the other hand, she was obviously middle eastern or Hindu or Mexican or something, and no one had told him about her or the pregnancy. How could he be lacking such information! The misfortune of his sister brought him, as always, immense satisfaction, the same as his misfortune brought her. He remembered the glee he felt when Belle Pearlmutter told them Teddy had dropped out of medicine, just as he remembered the sting of Marilyn's winning the gold medal in law when she graduated. The sibling race to insanity would be played out to the grave. He began to notice Sammy's absence.

Aunt Dolly, sitting stiffly, now resigned to having to visit with these people in their crummy cottage, which wasn't even beachfront property, watched Alex's eyes glowing as he stared at Aïda and for the first time she took Aïda in stock. She's Pakistani, she thought. A pregnant Pakistani. She knew. She knew the races. She was also pleased, because she never could stand Anna or the fact that Sammy had never cheated on her while everyone in the world knew how much Alex had on her.

"Where's Sammy?" Uncle Alex said to Anna, not sure whether he had asked her this already.

"He's lying down. He's not feeling well."

"He has a sore finger," said Marilyn.

"I'll see if he can get up." Anna left the living room and went to coax Sammy to join the living.

Sammy didn't hesitate to answer Anna's call. Years ago, just after finally getting rich, Uncle Alex and Aunt Dolly had delivered the ultimate snub by not inviting Anna and him to their son's bar mitzvah at the Rossmore Country Club, although, of course, they had been invited to the Saturday morning religious ceremony. It irked him plenty that they had overspent on the present and were then so publicly snubbed. Sammy never forgave them for hurting Anna, and vowed revenge, which always came in the form of rubbing Marilyn and Teddy's performance at school into them, since Alex's kids were so borderline. And they always had Marilyn's graduation pictures up everywhere, even in the cottage, the one with her wearing the gold medal for law. And then the Rhodes Scholar photograph. No wonder Alex never stayed to visit; he couldn't stand looking at those photographs.

Against his will, but for a greater, older good, Sammy would have to pretend all was well in the family, which was the best defence against Alex and Dolly. And he would be especially deferential to Aïda.

Anna came back with Sammy and went to the stove to put the kettle on, bumping into Teddy in the kitchen.

Sammy came into the living room and looked at them all smiling like a glee club, except for sourpuss Dolly, and crossed over to the living room. But he would stick to his guns, he would behave.

"Alex, Dolly, what's it gonna be?"

"Hi, Sammy."

Dolly only nodded.

"You've met Teddy's fiancée?" he said, not realizing that the introductions had already been made. He sat down beside her and put his arms around her shoulders with father-in-law warmth. Aïda was puzzled, but not unsettled, and smiled shyly. Sammy noticed the warmth of her smile for the first time, and felt something like a thaw. He caught himself smiling too, like an idiot. Teddy, viewing the whole thing from the kitchen couldn't believe his good luck. Marilyn ogled Alex and Dolly, forever awed by their bad manners as Alex hollered aggressively to Teddy:

"Where's that Coke?"

Teddy had already poured it out and was just about to bring it over to him.

"Do you want some ice?"

"Just bring the Coke. I'll be lucky if I get a glass," he said to Aïda.

"So, Palm Springs. You just got back?" said Sammy.

Alex nodded.

"Palm trees, jacuzzis, eh."

"Jewcuzzis," corrected Uncle Alex.

The two men spoke for a short time about the football game and prospects for the home team. Dolly, with her Elvis sneer, put her two cents in, saying she'd had a lavish lunch with the hotel owner's mother in Palm Springs two weeks ago. Baba X was mildly pleased by everyone's friendliness, but she was easy to please. She didn't like sibling rivalry and had always denied its existence.

But all through the phoney preliminary conversation Uncle Alex was thinking how he could find out who this hot number was and what country she was from. Can I fuck her, he thought, after she has the baby, of course. It was hard for him to curb his enthusiasm. For not only did he want to get her into bed, he was sure that her not being white would have to be bothering Anna. They would have to put her photograph up somewhere, if there was any room left on the walls, covered as they were with family snapshots in tacky frames. They could put her beside the gold-medal winner.

"Where do you live, Ida?" he asked her.

"It's Aïda," said Marilyn.

"I've been living in Ottawa for the past two years," she said, not mentioning her stay in Israel and the Occupied Territories.

This answer didn't mean shit. Anybody can live in Ottawa. But he noticed her accent, which was hard to place.

She's definitely a Pakistani, thought Dolly. She knew accents.

There was an awkward interval. Uncle Alex thought Dolly would help him tease out more information but she just sat there watching and listening to him flirt.

Aunt Dolly didn't help him out because Anna's family really didn't mean *bubkes* to her. She had made that clear the day she decided not to invite them to her son's bar mitzvah. Only a snub would give Anna the message that she was "only family, nothing more" and quite outside their circle. To his credit, Uncle Alex had tried to invite his sister, but he let Dolly prevail, out of guilt for his other misdemeanours. Uncle Alex had, at first, worried that his mother would tell him off for not inviting his sister, but she never did, for which Anna never forgave her. It was true, Baba X never said a word, mostly so as not to cause trouble between Alex and Dolly, whose relationship always seemed rocky at best, but which she tried to conserve, as she didn't believe in "separation or divorce or common-law marriage."

Dolly, her huge haunches now screwed into her sister-in-law's crappy chesterfield, stared at Aïda through her slitted eyes and thought the girl awfully pregnant and for a moment she meant to ask when the baby was due, but thought in the end that it just wasn't worth the bother. Who were these people anyway, to her? She always tired of them so quickly. It was a day she just wanted to get through: get out of this crummy cottage, crummy beach town, where only middle class Jews vacationed, get through the tea at the Pavilion and get home. She was curious about the pregnant girl, and when she was due, true enough, but it was the type of question that she knew her husband couldn't ask, because he thought pregnancy was a big sickening, and the birth itself a lot worse.

"Why Ottawa?" asked Alex, avid and rejuvenated. Instead of shlepping his mother and wife around the beach in the Lexus and getting through the endless tea time at the Pavilion, he was actually talking to a beautiful girl, even if she was pregnant, but beautiful, the first one he had been with in weeks. In Palm Springs even sixty-year-olds were starting to look good.

"Aïda works for the War Crimes Commission in Ottawa," said Marilyn.

"I'm on leave."

"She's a lawyer," added Marilyn, rubbing it in. If there was one thing Alex couldn't stand, it was other people's kids graduating from university, because his kids never did. It was hard for him to admit it, but his kids were such dolts. Why couldn't one of them have graduated from something? He would have paid good money for it. Why is there no God?

Marilyn watched his eyes respond in polite shock as she said "lawyer," saw his irises shooting across and down, raking the brain for a way to deal with the news.

"Did you say lawyer or liar?" quipped Uncle Alex.

"Ha ha ha, Alex," said Marilyn.

Sammy thought there just might be fireworks today. Marilyn could wipe the floor with Alex.

"Where did you go to school?" spat Dolly, because she knew schools.

"In England," said Aïda, baffled a bit by Dolly's stern tone, not knowing that Dolly talked like this to her friends even on their deathbeds.

"Where in England exactly?" went Dolly, for she knew English schools too.

Uncle Alex's heart dropped. Dolly you fool, he thought. Don't go there. Please, if there is a God, not Oxford, not something like that, please God.

Marilyn got ready to answer Dolly's question.

So this is how a dentist must feel right before pulling the molar of someone he can't stand, Sammy thought, watching Marilyn wind up, the delight of revenge in her eyes.

"Cambridge," said Marilyn, watching Alex's eyes for the wince of pain. "She went to Cambridge, Aunt Dolly."

Alex couldn't compete with that.

"And Brown for graduate work, I think."

Aïda blushed, but remained serene.

Sammy was impressed, he hadn't known. Nobody told him anything. Anna, who was listening intently from the kitchen, her hearing aid up high, felt her body sing to her.

Uncle Alex noticed his cigar had gone out. He didn't bother re-lighting it. Now he wanted to know where Aïda was from, looking to Dolly out of the corner of his eye; she stared back with those slitted eyes from the other chesterfield. There was something going on here. Some vital information was lacking. They were keeping something back. But hadn't he already asked where she was from? His senescence was weighing on him. Years ago he would have made monkeys of these people. Fuck Cambridge — fuck Brown. Did I ask her where she was from or where she lived? Fuck. I can't remember. But nowadays where someone is from doesn't mean anything. You could be Bengali and have been born in London or New York or Paris.

Aïda. Teddy didn't say Aïda. He said Ida. But Marilyn said Aïda. There was something there. Why was she called Aïda? And had that amazing colour of hers. And what about those incredible tits. Alex wondered if they were that round when she wasn't pregnant. Could he ask her point blank: what's your ethnic background? Or what's your religion? Or where were your grandparents born? Aïda. Aïda. The name was familiar for some reason. Wasn't there a movie called *Aïda* with Elizabeth Taylor, or a Broadway show? Something like that. What if he asked her her last name? Something was going on here.

The silence was getting too much for Marilyn, who was on the brink of bursting into laughter.

Baba X began poking her cane into the broadloom. Birds twittered outside in the sunshine, bouncing on slender branches, bloated from worms flushed out by the storm.

"Teddy," Sammy said, "could you get me a drink too? Aïda, do you want something?"

Aïda shook her head.

Teddy was pleased by his father's solicitous tone and went back to the fridge.

"I'll have one, too," said Marilyn, to keep herself from squealing. Sammy looked at her, noting that he had not told Teddy to get something for Marilyn. Then he thought about whether he was supposed to still be mad at her.

"Should I take some lunch out?" asked Anna from behind the kitchen counter, still reluctant to join the klatch. But Sammy was with them. He, he of course, had not been directly snubbed by Alex and Dolly all those years ago, so he could entertain them.

"Dolly, can't we offer you anything to drink?" asked Sammy. Marilyn cupped her mouth as if she were about to cough, aware that Sammy had missed Dolly's diuretic remark.

"I just had a diuretic, Sammy, thanks." Christ, thought Dolly, she'd have to explain it to each of them individually. Marilyn clamped her teeth to keep from laughing.

"So," Uncle Alex began, thinking himself sly, swivelling his knees towards Aïda.

"Yes."

"Is it Ida or Aïda?"

"Aïda, actually, but a lot of people call me Ida. I'm not particular. And sometimes it's just simpler."

"But you were born Aïda?"

"Do you think she was born Ida and people started calling her Aïda for short?" quipped Marilyn.

Uncle Alex ignored her.

"Aïda. That's a strange name," said Alex, continuing with his plan to pry open Aïda's third-worldishness.

Aïda wasn't baited. She looked at him serenely, Marilyn observed, because she was serene.

"I mean it's not a common name," said Uncle Alex.

"It's not a concoction, Alex," replied Marilyn.

"It's just strange, that's all. Like something I know, a movie or a musical."

"Or an opera?" said Marilyn.

"Are you sure it wasn't a musical?"

"It was an opera, Uncle Alex. By Verdi."

Sammy felt in his element. Marilyn would wipe the floor with Alex.

"That's it. Don't go to the opera much myself, actually," said Alex.

You've never gone in your life, thought Marilyn. And there is no opera in Palm Springs unless they pipe it onto the golf courses.

"Aïda is the daughter of the pharaoh, isn't she? Some sort of princess?" said Uncle Alex. He had seen the movie or the musical, he thought.

"She's the daughter of the Ethiopian king," said Marilyn. "Amneris is the daughter of the pharaoh." Even Anna, observing, all from the kitchen counter, felt avenged. Marilyn could be really useful sometimes.

"Whatever," said Alex, dissembling with craft. "Takes place in Egypt, doesn't it? Lots of horses or elephants on stage? Did your parents see the opera? Is that how they came up with the name?"

Aïda just smiled and said no.

"Is it an Ethiopian name?"

"It's Arabic," she said and smiled.

So did Alex. Yes! Yes! Like a pole-vaulter landing groin first onto his own pole, that's how hard it hit him. She was a fucking Arab. He looked at Dolly. Dolly knew all along she was either a Pakistani or an Arab. Aïda. Of course. She knew names. Uncle Alex caught Dolly's stony nod and his soul purred. Teddy had knocked up a fucking Arab. This must be killing Anna. He looked over to the kitchen counter where Anna was fiddling with the kettle. Now he understood all the secrecy. He could really have some fun.

"Are your parents from around there?"

"You mean Ethiopia?" asked Marilyn.

"I meant Egypt. Let her answer for herself."

"No," said Aïda.

"Libya?"

"No."

"But from around there, the general vicinity?"

"Not really."

"But they did see Aïda, and enjoyed it thoroughly," said Marilyn.

"So you were named after the princess?"

"Aïda *is* a princess," blurted Marilyn. The whole situation was like *Bewitched*, where a beautiful Samantha with superpowers is forced into the role of the painfully conformist Mrs. Darren Stevens. Marilyn wouldn't tolerate it.

"Her last name's Hawari al-Husseini. She's an al-Husseini, for Chrissakes. One of the noble Palestinian families from before British mandated Palestine. I think they've even got lineage back to the khedive, who incidentally, built the Cairo Opera House, where *Aïda* debuted."

Dolly's complexion turned as green as Alex's cigar, and she turned her head to stare at the wall. Her gaze became more vinegary as on that wall hung a photograph of Marilyn on a dais, receiving her gold medal for law.

And Aïda blushed. Sammy took one look at Alex's face and felt an invader had been repelled. Anna told herself that she had liked Aïda from day one.

Uncle Alex was irked. He sipped his pop inconspicuously. Across the room, Sammy and Anna exchanged a warm smile that carried from the living room to the kitchen. Seeing this, Alex took an impotent puff from his extinguished Churchill. The schmaltziness of their marriage always bugged him. Why's he smiling, that asshole? Christ, fifty years ago Sammy was shooting these people. He even used to tell the story of how they came at him with swords and he just mowed them down. And look at him now, sitting there on his leatherette chesterfield, smiling at this girl who's carrying his grandchild. She's not only an Arab, she's a PLO. A fucking PLO. But he still thought he'd like to fuck her. He wished he could be sharper, wittier, fresher, to deal with this. But that Marilyn always made a monkey out of him. At least he had suspected that something had been going on, but this princess thing trumped him soundly. He looked to Dolly but her stone face and sneer offered little encouragement. As much as he hated the Arabs and the PLOs, like any good Jew, he thought, class and wealth were still what counted in this world, and Anna had trumped him good. His own son had married a hard-drinking loudmouth who he was sure had been a waitress, or even a stripper. He recalled her fingernails bitten down to stumps when she first shook his hand, and the patch of overtanned freckles between her tits, which made her seem older than what she claimed. Nothing had been made clear. She didn't even invite any of her own family to the wedding. And here's Teddy with someone refined.

But then Dolly swivelled her stone face at Teddy and sneered in revenge.

"How's nursing, Teddy?" she spat, coming to Alex's aid, her attack eye gyrating slowly to check Marilyn's expression, then her husband's. Leave it to me, you asshole, her eyes were saying. I know where to punch.

"I left it."

Uncle Alex's brow buckled.

"I'm going to finish med school."

The kettle whistled and Sammy's mouth dropped open. Check and mate.

"Good for you, Teddy," said Uncle Alex. "We'd better be going."

"What about some lunch?"

"We've really got to be going."

Uncle Alex got up and hauled Dolly and Baba X off the chesterfield, leading them and Ming off to his Lexus, leaving his foes behind. They moved slowly to the door, Baba X clutching her big brown purse and poking the broadloom to keep steady. The Ostroves stood up to say good-bye and crowded around the door to wave. Uncle Alex guided his mother along the path feeling bested. The thought that he had a Lexus soothed him a bit, but not much, but then the thought that he had ten million bucks soothed him a lot. Fuck his sister, fuck them all.

As soon as they had left, Anna asked if anyone wanted tea now that the water had boiled.

"I just had a diuretic," screamed Marilyn and banged her fist onto the chesterfield with laughter.

Sammy went out the back door onto the deck. The air was so wonderful it felt like he was being kissed. A sort of platinum gas floated over the creek and the bullrushes. The birds watched him descend the steps onto the sodden lawn and trudge farther down through where the grass was unmowed, into the rushes. Then a weightless feeling bore him almost to the creek's edge, a feeling much like what he used to feel as a child leaving the movie theatre, his eyes blinded, nostrils filled with the smell of popcorn, his heart drenched with the emotion of a pirate cannonade, or Tarzan diving off the top of a waterfall. His animus against everyone had vanished. His eyes prickled and then bubbled up with an enormous tear in each, which then burst simultaneously and streamed into the corners of his mouth. He felt released. Invigorated, he then thought long and deep about lunch.

Outside the apartment block cars were tightly parked, including Alex's Lexus and Oz's Ozmobile, as Marilyn called it. He had driven it himself to the *briss*. He had been back to the hospital several times since his operation and was released yet again only two days ago.

Sammy was grinning madly. He loved a party and was astonished by the big turnout. You just didn't see a *briss* this big anymore. He even counted the people. The caterers had set up a long folding table that was now blanketed with goodies. Platter after platter had been brought out from the kitchen. First came the catered fare: the vrenikes, followed by cheese blintzes, hot fish in a silver warmer, gefilte fish, a kugle, even low-fat garbage too, he noticed. Then the deli items: smoked meat, corned beef, poppy seed bagels, lox, cream cheese, huge pads of butter, sliced koiledge, then the homemade contributions: the rich and extra-rich cheesecakes, tortes and pies. Two big samovars with brass spigots held tea and coffee, and there were silver pitchers of thick yellowy cream and skim milk. There was a healthy mixing of *milkhiks* and *fleyshiks*. What the hell — he had been mixing milk with meat for years, so who cared. After all, the ceremony and operation were going to be performed by a lady *moyel*, the only one they could get under the circumstances, said Marilyn, who had hired her, and with a lesbian "companion", "which makes the *moyel* a lesbian, too," Oz said with a smile. Well, they were just that kind of Jew, and if nobody liked it, they could bugger off.

The two points of light from the silver candlesticks added something, Sammy thought.

He was wearing his shiny silver suit, the one from Marilyn's wedding, which still fit him, so he said. Anna had bought a bottle-green summer suit on sale and was looking like a million bucks. Baba X wore a fire-engine red skirt and a cream blouse with an enormous opal brooch and had tried to get her swollen feet into black pumps, but in the end just wore the pointy leather house slippers Teddy had bought her at a souk in Fez years ago. Before the *briss* she got Teddy into her room and sat him on her bed and gave him a small lecture on parenting. Remember, to have kids you need patience and capital. When Teddy said he was short on the capital, Baba X handed him an envelope with a thousand dollars. Then she shuffled out and sat on the chesterfield. Marilyn, wearing a black A-line skirt and black low-cut top, sat with her while people were arriving, feeling the crinkly skin on her forearms, feeding the information on the new arrivals directly into her ear.

"And there's Uncle Alex and Aunt Dolly."

"Go over and say hello to your uncle."

"You mean my homuncle."

"What?"

A throng of lacquered and perfumed women and droopy-eyed men in suits that were too big for some in the waist and shoulders, and too tight for others in the pant, had configured right from the start by the hot fish. There was an oversized floral arrangement on the coffee table in the living room that blocked the view of the dining table where the *briss* would be performed, behind which sat the squeamish, like Dolly. She was resolute, looking bored and mean in her bronze silk suit, clutching Ming, who had been washed and given what seemed to be a maple rinse and then fluffed up like cotton candy. Bent lily stems and their horns and yellow pistils dipped into her plate, from which she fed Ming morsels of *kishke*. "The girl's from Paris," one of Anna's loyal friends from her mahjongg group said to Dolly, politely striking up conversation. "A real nice girl. They met in Jerusalem."

"She's an Arab," Dolly said, setting things straight, staring with slitted eyes at the woman, "she's an Arab."

That shut her up. Anna, no doubt, had been going around telling people the girl was from Paris. Of all the nerve. She'd give her a Paris, alright. She'd give her a Paris up her ass. She fed Ming another morsel of *kishke*. Up her ass she'd give her Paris.

How could they think of having so many people in this box, Aunt Dolly thought, arms folded, eyes narrowed. The absence of any opportunity for social elevation at the affair had brought Aunt Dolly to the edge of boredom. She was the rich cousin invited to the wedding of a grungy country cousin, and had to think of it in a charitable sense, she told herself, otherwise she'd never get through it. She could hardly wait to get home. There wasn't a single person there who had more personal wealth than them. They were all nobodies, which makes me uncomfortably a nobody myself, she thought.

She noticed Snake, wearing a black fishnet T-shirt standing by the curtains with a glass of their crappy sparkling wine, sneering at her, his forehead acne sparkling. He was listening to a colleague of Marilyn's, a short pudgy woman in a twin set balled over the bust, while staring at Dolly.

"You're just a petty-bourgeois element," Snake said to Marilyn's friend, "you're just a petty-bourgeois element."

"Why do you say that?"

"Feminism is petty-bourgeois. So that makes you a petty-bourgeois element."

The woman blushed and defended herself while Snake kept on sneering at Dolly, only turning his head to come again with his remark: "you're just a petty-bourgeois element."

"This is a really nice affair, Anna. A really nice affair," said Oz's sister to Anna. Oz, too tired to talk, only gave the Oz finger of agreement. And with the same finger flicked cake crumbs from off his sister's silk grosgrain-covered bust.

Sammy appropriated Oz for support, dragging him over to the dining table where the *briss* would be performed. He was nervous about having to hold down the baby's legs. But it seemed Oz needed the support more than Sammy. Since the aneurysm operation Oz was hardly himself, and Sammy had to steady him when a darting maid carrying a tray of potato *knishes* almost knocked him over.

"Well, what's it going to be, Oz?"

"How's it going?" Sammy said.

So how did Sammy feel about a woman performing the *briss?* Oz wondered.

He was worried for the kid's *shmuck*, that's what, he told him.

"In circumcision," Oz said, "there was always the risk of removal of too little, or too much, always the risk of that. I don't know why we do it."

"It's to avoid balanoposthitis — infection of the glans and foreskin," said Marilyn, butting in. "And chancroid is more frequent in the uncircumcised male," she added. "And actually, there's a new thing called a French cut, which is sort of a half-circumcision, not leaving the male so desensitised."

Marilyn had arranged for the *moyel*, the first female *moyel* in the city, who came to the job with excellent qualifications and references. She was also the only *moyel* in the city willing to perform the ceremony. She was the partner of Teddy's ex-girlfriend, but apparently they had all decided to let bygones be bygones. Or as Oz put it, let bygones be bypasses.

"By the way," Marilyn broke in, "did you hear about the *moyel* who lost his job?"

Sammy and Oz looked at her blankly, in all seriousness. "No," they said.

"This is just a joke."

They sighed in relief.

"I'll start again. Did you hear about the *moyel* who lost his job?"

"We said 'no'." .

"You know, the one who missed and got the sack."

Just then a young couple, friends of Marilyn's, came up to say hello. Marilyn introduced them to her father and Oz.

"This is Susie Swarsky and Brian Chomsky."

"Oh, so you're Chomsky," said Sammy.

"What?"

"Marilyn's always going on about a Chomsky."

"You've got the wrong Chomsky."

"Oh."

Uncle Alex, in his three-piece suit, shaved to the eyeballs and looking spruce, was listening in on the conversation and sidled over, a glass of scotch in his hand. Susie and Brian moved on.

Sammy thought for a moment that someone should park Uncle Alex far away from the dining room table, far from the action. He saw Alex knocking the *moyel*'s elbow and the blood spurting up to the ceiling. He shivered for a second. Alex also gave him a slight twinge of guilt, for as Anna's brother he should have been given some sort of honour in the ceremony. Instead, he had assigned the honour to Oz. Uncle Alex had in fact felt a bit snubbed, but also relieved at not having to be front and centre when the foreskin got snipped off. He had had enough at his own son's, when he fainted.

"What's it going to be, Alex?"

"Hi, Sammy, Oz, Marilyn."

Alex looked onto Marilyn's cream and shade décolletage and struggled for something to say.

"What's the baby's name?" he asked.

"Edward," said Sammy.

"Edward?"

"After someone: Edward Said," explained Sammy.

"What did Edward say?" asked Alex.

Marilyn gulped back a laugh, which her father ignored.

"Look, here, it's in the brochure. The baby is named after him, Edward W. Said."

"I've never been to a briss that gave out a brochure," said Oz.

Sammy explained: "In three languages. There's a whole explanation on how they met, even pictures. Here's a picture of him, Edward Said."

"What did he say?" insisted Uncle Alex.

"I don't know what he said," said Sammy. "Look at the brochure! Edward Said!"

"He must've said something," said Oz.

"Not 'said'", went Marilyn, grabbing the brochure. "'Saïd', with a dieresis. Look!"

"Where's the dieresis?" Said her father, grabbing back the brochure. "There's no dieresis. Hah!"

That drew the colour out of Marilyn's face. "I know, I know. But it's understood. You pronounce it as if there were. Everyone knows Edward Sa-id the Conrad scholar. The man who wrote *Orientalism*. He went to school with Omar Sharif."

"Him I know," said Sammy. "But there's no dieresis."

"What's a dieresis?" asked Uncle Alex, but without much interest. He raised his eyes and looked over at Dolly, thinking how he might eject the biddy wedged down tight in the chesterfield next to her. Then he took a look around at a girl in a stiff, white

Jetsons miniskirt talking to Teddy and his friends and thought about creeping over there. But what could he say if he did? He would think of something. There were three or four of those miniskirts around, he reflected. One, a thin girl in zip-up black boots and lobular hooters. Where had she gone to? It was some party, and he had his wife and Ming safely stowed behind that horrible flower arrangement of lilies and roses. No, he wouldn't go sit with his Dolly. He wondered if she had remembered to send a gift, and if maybe she had even sent those horrible flowers. For the time being he would hang out with Sammy and Oz, not knowing anybody else, Anna and Sammy's crowd being so evidently his social inferiors, while working on what to say to Teddy so as to get in with the Jetson skirt group there.

Sammy felt awkward with Alex around and was in a hurry for the ceremony to start. Luckily Oz had started talking about the baseball players' strike.

"Fire them all," Uncle Alex said. "Fire them all. They make too much money."

"No man who has ever worked for another man has ever been paid enough," said Marilyn.

"Who said that?"

"Babe Ruth."

"How do you know all this shit?"

"It's called reading."

"Never had much use for it."

"Evidently."

"And what's with the church music," said Uncle Alex.

"It's Bach," said Marilyn.

"Oh. Bach."

"Were you expecting a march from Aïda?"

Sammy wasn't really paying attention. He was easily distracted now, trying to calm his nerves. He stood there picking off the odd sentence heaved out of the din of the party: "And of course you know Molly," or "He's going back to finish medicine," or "The baby's a *shtick* gold," or "She's had such tsouris from him, but now he's finally settling down," and so on. The woman introducing Molly elbowed the person next to her, dangerously tipping a plate of carefully piled up hors d'œuvres, and said: "Wasn't there a thing between him and a rabbi's wife?" She craned her neck, adjusted the coq feathers on her hat, glanced around to see if anyone was listening: "They almost lost him, you know. But the thing is to keep up the contact, that's the main thing."

He caught a glimpse of Anna, her face glowing with pride, standing with the serving girls by the kitchen door. He had seen in her eye from the word go how she was determined to appropriate Teddy's baby as soon as it was born. He could see Anna's friend Sophie sitting with Baba X, both of them dabbing their eyes, as they reminisced about Sophie's father, *Alav hashalom*. All of Anna's friends looked very much moved, even before the ceremony had begun, and their children or grandchildren were busy bringing them tea and brushing the crumbs off their laps.

"How did they meet?" he heard Sophie ask Baba X, "Teddy and his wife?"

"They met," said Baba X cunningly. "He met her, she met him: they met, the two of them. It was mutual."

"I don't know about you guys," Uncle Alex said, just before the conversation petered out, "but I'm going to squeeze some tit."

Marilyn frowned as Alex pushed off to go over to the group of young people around Teddy, where both the girls in the Jetson skirts were now laughing.

"I knew you could do it," said Uncle Alex. "I knew you'd make monkeys out of them."

"Monkeys out of who?"

"Them." Uncle Alex walked his gaze around the room as he would his dog, sniffing with his eyes any prospects.

Teddy didn't really understand or want Uncle Alex's complicity.

"Them. The Jews."

"Oh."

"Don't play dumb. If it's one thing I can't stand, it's those Jews who think they're more Jewish than other Jews. The ones who gave your father a rough time. I could buy and sell them ten times over. They're the ones to watch. The ones who think they have the franchise. And you fucked them over. You fucked them over."

Odd thing for Uncle Alex to say. Teddy wondered if he detected some admiration in his voice.

"Aren't you going to introduce me?" said Uncle Alex, leaning suavely into the circle with his drinking-hand shoulder, gyrating the glass. Ah, for Uncle Alex life was one big orgone box.

Teddy began the introductions for his uncle, first the blonde in the Jetson skirt.

Over at the table, Sammy felt his head start to ache from the excitement and the smiling. Since the baby had been born he had felt elated and was only worried about one thing: whether the circumcision would go wrong.

"I think something will go wrong," he said to Marilyn and Oz. "As your mother would say, I'm psychic."

"Nothing's going to go wrong," Marilyn said.

"Maybe she has it in for Teddy, this *moyel*."

"She's a professional."

"So was Dr. Mengele. How many of these has she done?"

"I'm not sure."

"Ballpark figure."

"Don't worry. She'll be fine. It can't be that difficult."

"How would you know?"

"I know some anatomy."

"Chrissakes."

Sammy went to the bedroom with Marilyn, Teddy, Anna and Baba X. Aïda was sitting on the bedspread, crying, holding the sleeping *yasel*. Teddy didn't hesitate: he took the baby out of her arms and strode out of the room with his father. Aïda started to sob so badly she couldn't catch her breath. Baba X and Marilyn sandwiched Aïda and held her hands. They didn't want to watch either. Anna, feeling a flush of indecision and envy, looked at the three of them on the bed and the men leaving with the *yasel* and couldn't decide for a moment whether to stay or go. In the end she opted for the ceremony.

Things moved swiftly once Teddy and Sammy entered the living room. The baby was placed on the silver platter on the dining table and heaved out his protest when his buttocks touched the icy metal. The *moyel* already had her instruments out and was saying the Hebrew prayers with such a heavy English accent that Sammy cringed, hoping her surgical skills were better than her Hebrew. He fingered his tie until it was time to hold down the baby's legs. The *moyel* nodded and Sammy stretched out his arms, rotated his wrists, and withdrew them from the air with his sleeves hitched high. Then he clasped the baby's thighs, which were small as drumsticks, and smiled down on him. The baby opened his eyes and looked up suspiciously. The child knew, Sammy thought: he must be exceptional. They would have a special relationship. Death seemed so far away. He cast his eyes to the left, to Oz on one side, looking better than he had seen him in months, and to the right, to Teddy on the other.

Sammy looked up at the *moyel*. She was tall and sleek and black-haired and wearing sparkling eyeglasses as shiny as her instruments. A handsome woman, he thought. When the knife came up the crowd moved in. More prayers were muttered. Oz put the wine-soaked cloth to the baby's lips for him to suckle and two roses bloomed on his cheeks. Edward, son of Theodore. For the first time he noticed how bottle-bottom thick the lenses of her glasses were. Should I watch? Sammy asked himself, still looking up into her face. There was some amen-ing and some more muttering. He saw the little relevant penis rear up, gingerly pinched between the most beautiful fingers he had ever seen. The baby's little fist popped into the air. Then came the burst of light from the scalpel, the crimson splash, and the cry.

One more, Sammy thought. Or one less. Go know.

Acknowledgments

I would like to thank Stan Fogel, Ben Rowden, Paul Peters, and Rolf Maurer and Stefania Alexandru of New Star Books.